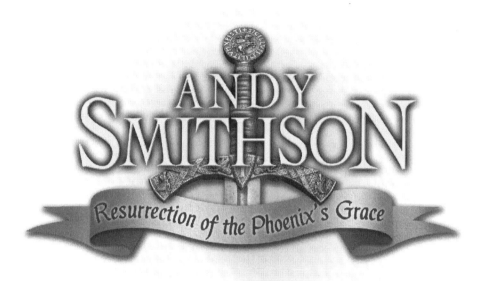

ANDY SMITHSON

Resurrection of the Phoenix's Grace

D1714793

ISBN-13: 978-1511717335
ISBN-10: 1511717335

Createspace Independent Publishing
North Charleston, South Carolina

Dedication

To my wise and skilled mentors who have helped me grow as an author.

Acknowledgments

Thanks to my husband for his support and encouragement, without which my writing journey would lack much of the meaning it holds.

Thanks also to my mentor, Jonathan Lee, from whom I learned many philosophies that changed my life. I have woven these throughout the story line in hopes of helping others experience a more peaceful and satisfying journey through life, as I have.

Thanks also to my editor, Amy Nemecek. I have learned much from her comments and strengthened my writing skills as a result.

I want to also recognize two author groups I'm privileged to be a part of—Dragon Writer's Collective and Emblazoners. I've learned and grown from working with the amazing authors in both. Thank you!

Table of Contents

The Land of Oomaldee

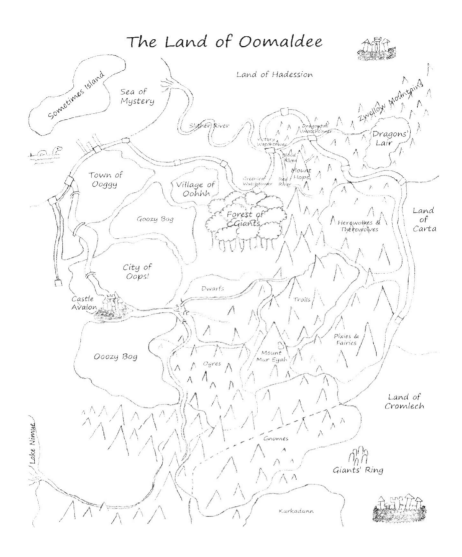

CHAPTER ONE

Let the Games Begin

H ungry flames danced on tippy toes, their prize just beyond the reach of their tongues. Andy twisted his marshmallow a quarter turn, watching it complete its transformation to the perfect poufy shade of tan. Memories of toasting the sweet treats with Alden around a campfire while searching for the dragon lair brought a smile to his face.

"You're quiet tonight," Mom observed.

Andy rotated his marshmallow another quarter turn. The balmy heat of the day had given way to a cooler Friday evening, and Dad had insisted they grill outside tonight. Burgers and corn on the cob had coaxed Madison from her book boyfriend, but with dinner complete, her complaints of mosquitoes allowed her to fall back into the arms of her imaginary love. The discordant sounds of Dad vigorously scrubbing the grill on the deck blended with the choir of crickets and bullfrogs.

"Are you excited to be going to Grandpa Smithson's tomorrow?"

Another quarter turn.

"Looks like your masterpiece is ready."

Andy took two graham crackers and four squares of a chocolate bar and coaxed the oozing glob of roasted perfection off the skewer, then bit into his gooey creation. Despite the tastiness of the treat, he sighed.

"What's wrong, honey?"

"I'd hoped to hear something by now."

"Give them time. It's only been two weeks since you got back. If they send any messages while you're gone, we'll let you know."

Andy forced a smile as he felt his stomach clench.

The night Andy left Oomaldee, Abaddon had been more furious than ever before. His booming threat to kill the one who wielded Methuselah had reverberated off the walls of the dungeon tunnel, forcing Andy to cover his ears.

It was true. Thanks to his blade, Andy had thrice thwarted the dragon's ambition of gaining eternal life.

"I'm worried Abaddon will hurt Father and the others." Andy's shoulders slumped as he exhaled. The nightmare scenarios that had filled his dreams taunted his calm.

Mom reached over and patted his arm. "I know this sounds trite, but things will work themselves out. They always do."

Andy stared into the dying flames for several minutes before breaking the silence. "Mom, can I ask you something?"

"Sure. What is it?"

"What happened with Methuselah? Why did its blade extend for you when it won't for me, at least not here?"

Mom considered the question for a moment. At last she speculated, "I think it might have been a message to remind me that even though I've been in this world for nearly five hundred years, I'm still queen of Oomaldee. Perhaps my work is not yet done."

Queen? Oh yeah, I guess she is.

"What do you mean, your work's not done?"

Mom did not elaborate, so Andy redirected, "If I break the curse…"

Mom held up her hand and shook her head. "Not *if*, Andy, *when*."

"But you'll die!"

Mom glanced quickly at Dad who continued his quest to restore the grill to pristine condition. She reached over and pulled Andy's face toward her, and in little more than a whisper said, "Andy, I've lived over five hundred years. I've experienced more than the average person. I treasure the time I've had. But it is enough."

"That's what the King said too."

Dad approached. "What did the King say?"

Mom cautioned with a look and Andy mumbled, "Oh, nothing."

Dad raised his eyebrows but chose to let it go. "Well then, what say we head inside before the mosquitoes tell their friends there's an all-you-can-eat buffet."

* * * * *

Seven weeks later…

Since Grandpa had retrieved Andy and Madison from the Phoenix airport, the old man had kept them busy at his ranch—inspecting fences on horseback with his three ranch hands, allowing Andy to drive the tractors by himself, corralling cattle, and helping fill the water troughs out in the pastures. While Andy had participated in similar activities on previous visits, the stench of nearly two hundred cattle still proved overwhelming.

I should bottle this and take it back to Oomaldee, he laughed to himself.

For her part, Madison-the-House-Pet made a beeline inside every chance she got. But at least she made herself useful in the kitchen. Grandma Smithson had been an amazing baker and had passed on her skills to her granddaughter. The elder woman had passed away four years ago, and Grandpa kept exclaiming at the tantalizing smells his granddaughter masterfully coaxed throughout the house.

Two weeks earlier, as a special treat, Grandpa had taken them to a shooting range to teach them how to handle a rifle. Andy managed to hit the outer ring of the paper target several times, celebrating with a dance that Grandpa and his sister agreed resembled the flopping of a boneless chicken. Madison, on the other hand, completely missed the targets and came away complaining of a sore shoulder from the gun's kickback. She had sulked back to Grandpa's pickup after two rounds to resume an adventure with another of her book boyfriends.

Despite his tiredness, Andy lay in bed staring at the ceiling. Growing worry over hearing nothing from Oomaldee gusted through his mind yet again, stirring up another tornado of undesirable possibilities. Exhaustion must have finally won, however, for Andy found himself in the lobby of a large office building, a destination he recognized from previous nighttime excursions. As before, it was eerily quiet despite the number of silvery, translucent beings coming and going. An older gentleman dressed in a military-style uniform with translucent sword floated by and stopped at the imposing front desk. A gaunt man wearing a lustrous grayish-white attendant's uniform greeted him. "H-how can I help you, sir?" the spirit stuttered, eyes wide.

"I'm Viceroy Nabulion. I have an appointment with the Committee on Afterlife Affairs. Felius Dudge should be expecting me."

"V-very w-well, sir. P-please have a s-seat over th-there while I c-contact his office." The attendant motioned toward a bench not far off.

In no time, a slight woman in a silvery tailored dress approached, introduced herself, and escorted the general to an elevator. Andy followed unseen.

"Hold on to the railing, please," the uniformed operator bid in a sing-song tone as Andy stepped on.

The elevator rattled to the second floor and stopped to admit another silvery being. After the occupants had rearranged themselves, the doors closed and the car rose one more floor. A jolt and protesting doors announced they had reached their destination. The woman stepped forward and instructed, "Follow me, Viceroy."

Andy followed down a long dark hallway, stopping outside a tall wooden door. The escort rang a bell and led them into a large wood-paneled conference room where a dozen or more spirits sat around a hulking table that dominated the center of the space.

Conversation ceased and a pudgy being at the head of the table turned. "Viceroy Nabulion, I presume? I'm Felius Dudge, Chairman."

The officer nodded, then glancing around added, "Thank you for seeing me."

"Please, have a seat," Chairman Dudge offered, directing the newcomer to a row of chairs lining the front wall of the room. Andy took a seat next to the viceroy as Felius stood and floated to the podium. "I would like to call this meeting to order," he began. "We are here to discuss the viceroy's request for a Stone of Athanasia. Such a request has been granted only once before as part of a beta test—,"

Murmurs rose from those assembled and the chairman waved a hand, adding, "I know it's a highly unusual request, but let's at least hear him out."

"Sir," the chairman invited.

Viceroy Nabulion rose and floated to the podium. He slowly scanned the attendees and the room grew quiet. Several spirits shifted in their seats. "Thank you for this opportunity to come before you on behalf of my son, Naparte Nabulion."

"Excuse me, Viceroy, but why is your son not here representing himself?" one of the committee members interrupted.

"He would have liked to, sir, but he has not yet joined the Afterlife."

Andy had been surveying the room, but the comment grabbed his attention. A chorus of murmurs filled the space.

Who is this guy?

The viceroy raised his hands for silence and continued, "My son has lived for over five hundred years but is not yet ready to join us. He has," the officer cleared his throat, "several matters to attend to before then."

"Didn't we all?" objected another committee member.

More rumblings echoed before Dudge rose and boomed, "Silence! We told this man he could present his case."

"Fine…" someone grumbled. Several others murmured but finally yielded the floor back to their guest.

"My son is the ruler of the kingdom of Hadession."

Abaddon?! He wants a stone of Athanasia? No!

"I heard the ruler of Hadession is a shape shifter. How can he be your son?" another spirit heckled.

"He is," the man asserted. "How he became one is a long story."

"You're asking for a stone of Athanasia. What's he need it for? He should already have eternal life," another spirit chimed in.

Several more committee members lobbed accusations, and Andy could taste blood in the water as the sharks circled for the kill.

But in little more than a whisper, Viceroy Nabulion defended, "It's a matter of honor."

The room instantly quieted.

"Excuse me, but did you say you're making this request as a matter of your son's honor?" Dudge questioned.

Nabulion nodded as he locked eyes with the chairman.

"Please explain."

"I was a citizen of Oomaldee and proudly served King Gerrard I. I advanced in rank to major, which entitled my son to attend the prestigious military school. But despite his exemplary grades, particularly in math and battle strategy, the boys whose fathers outranked me bullied him and treated him as something loathsome. I will not go into the details of their abuse, but you will understand when I say their behavior changed him."

Several spirits around the table nodded.

Uh-oh, Andy thought.

The officer continued, "His teachers, while aware of the brutality, did nothing to address the situation. Rather, they made it clear he needed to become tougher, saying battle did not differentiate except to root out the weak. My son's hatred grew and revenge became his motivator."

Andy glanced around the table. Every committee member sat entranced under the man's spell.

"Thanks to the heir to Oomaldee's throne, my son no longer has the ability to shift to a younger form. His plans for exacting retribution are not yet fulfilled, and he grows weak. As spirits of men and women who lived lives of honor, I ask you to grant my request so he can reclaim his dignity. Thank you."

Viceroy Nabulion turned, glided back to his chair, and sat down.

Andy shot up to object. *You don't know what Abaddon will do to Oomaldee if you give him what he wants! You can't!* His challenge went unheard. Andy bolted to Dudge, but his hands met no resistance as he made to grab the chairman who now reclaimed the podium. *Argh!*

"Thank you, viceroy. If you would kindly adjourn to the anteroom, we will discuss your request."

Andy jiggled his legs as he listened to much heated debate between committee members. At length they called the viceroy back.

Felius Dudge resumed the podium and pronounced, "While we fully support your son's quest to regain his honor, we agree that granting a stone of Athanasia to a member of the Living would establish a precedent we are unprepared to defend going forward. Imagine all the requests…"

"And the chaos…" chimed in another.

Andy heard grumblings and mutterings from others around the table as his dream faded.

The next morning, Andy sat on a hay bale looking out over Grandpa Smithson's ranch through the open doors of the hayloft and wishing for a breeze. It was still early and the heat seemed content to keep his skin moist. It would wait until afternoon to extract rivers of sweat. He watched one of the herds that looked like chocolate-covered ants from this distance as he tried to make sense of the previous night's dream. While he was thankful the committee had declined Abaddon's request, he could not yet deduce the repercussions.

Andy's thoughts returned to Oomaldee and his frustration at the lack of communication grew. Not one word. Each time Andy probed the subject with Mom, she assured him no mail from Mermin or anyone else in Oomaldee had arrived. His stomach rolled.

"Grandpa says you need to hurry up. We're leaving in ten minutes!" Madison screeched from below. Her tone resonated like one of the crows that pestered the cattle.

"Coming…"

A half hour later Grandpa sent up dust clouds as he navigated his well-worn, white pickup across the washboard of a field. He pulled to a stop in an unmarked space between a battered farm truck and a shiny Toyota Corolla. Mushrooms of brilliant color exploded across the expanse—red and green, blue and yellow, orange, purple, and more. Crowds jammed the area behind the ropes to take in the sight. A chorus of *pughh, pughh* sang from burners attached to wicker baskets as pilots levitated their hot air balloons upright.

"Ooh!" Madison squealed. "They're so pretty!"

Andy rolled his eyes. *Amazing, cool, awesome…not pretty.*

Grandpa led them to a uniformed attendant and showed the man three tickets. "Pegasus? That balloon is nine rows up and over three. That way." The attendant pointed and Grandpa nodded.

They made their way between standard multicolored balloons as well as more unusual ones—an inflating saguaro cactus, a blue octopus with legs jutting out above the basket, a giant lightbulb, a flying penguin, and a pair of bumblebees—finally reaching a half-inflated purple Pegasus with wings exploding from the envelope. It reminded Andy of Optimistic.

"This must be us," Grandpa deduced.

"Hello, I'm Thomas Bitmire," announced a younger-looking man as he approached and extended a hand. "And this is my wife Julie. She'll be driving the chase vehicle to pick us up if the wind doesn't work in our favor."

"I'm James Smithson, and this is my granddaughter Madison and my grandson Andy."

"Glad to meet you. You can call me Mr. B."

The pilot checked the progress of the balloon's inflation, remarking, "Great conditions this morning, no measurable ground winds. When it's windy it's easy for the burner to singe the envelope."

Once Pegasus was standing nearly upright, Mr. B. waved them toward the basket. "Let's get you in to weigh her down before she's completely inflated and decides to lift off without us."

Andy shared a grin with Madison and Grandpa as the man steadied their climb into the cramped basket. They wedged themselves between three propane tanks occupying the corners. Mr. B. joined them and jettisoned two of the four ropes holding them in place.

"Just waiting for the signal from the officials," their pilot explained. "They want us all to lift off at the same time. More spectacular that way." He winked at Madison.

A shot rang out in the distance and Mr. B. tossed his rope to the ground. "That's our cue! Unhook that rope and throw it over the side, Andy."

Pegasus began rising in unison with its neighbors, floating between a banana-shaped balloon and one checkered red and orange.

"There's no wind!" Andy realized.

"That's right. You don't feel the wind because we're traveling with it."

"Awesome!" Andy couldn't rein in the smile that radiated across his face.

"Let's see how well we can steer you this morning, my dear," Mr. B. announced to their ride. He reached up and fired the fuel jets, receiving a *pughh, pughh* reply from the burner. The balloon cleared its neighbors and Andy couldn't hold back, "Woot!"

"That's my girl," the pilot encouraged the dirigible.

They left the congested skies of the balloon festival and now drifted over open countryside.

"It's so peaceful," Madison remarked.

"That it is," agreed Mr. B.

"How do you steer it?" Andy queried.

"Watch and learn," Mr. B. replied, smiling.

Pegasus drifted higher and shifted in a new direction.

"Cool!" Andy announced, receiving a smile from Grandpa.

"Wind currents. Winds are layered. Each layer blows in a different direction. I love flights when there are lots of layers. If I want to go toward that rock outcropping this morning," Mr. B pointed at a pair of rust-colored boulders jutting up from the bare soil, "looks like I need to position us a bit lower."

Their pilot pulled on a rope hanging from inside the envelope and released some air. Pegasus complied and drifted downward until they reached the wind current Mr. B had mentioned. Their pilot brought the craft so close to the summit Andy felt like he could reach out and touch it.

"Let's see what going higher yields us in maneuverability, shall we?"

"Excellent!" replied Andy.

They glided over ranches. Grandpa and Madison gazed at the ground far below, clearly delighted. In the stillness, Andy could hear moos emanating from a herd of cattle directly below.

"This is absolutely beautiful!" Madison declared several minutes later.

"Now you know why I love flying Pegasus. I've never forgotten my first flight. I promised myself I'd fly again, and it's become an obsession."

"I can see why," Grandpa agreed.

Nearly two hours into their flight, Mr. B asked, "I'd normally head back about now, but the wind currents are amazing today. Do you mind staying up awhile longer?"

Andy, Madison, and Grandpa grinned, and Mr. B. chuckled, "Looks like I need to do some heavy arm-twisting."

Several minutes later, Andy spotted a black-feathered bird off in the distance and announced, "A crow!"

Everyone looked, but Mr. B. shook his head. "That's not a crow, it's a vulture—crows don't fly this high. Vultures have amazing eyesight. It's probably hunting for breakfast."

Andy examined the bird more closely as they drew near. Still a ways off, he realized, *That vulture's enormous. It's definitely bigger than...* Andy gasped as he locked eyes with the zolt.

"You okay, Andy?" Grandpa asked.

Andy shook his head and dove for the floor, receiving curious looks from his companions.

"What's the matter? Afraid of a bird?" Madison joked. "Well, you don't need to worry, it's leaving."

Andy regained his footing, peered over the basket lip, and watched the bird grow smaller. *It's going for reinforcements!*

"I'd like to head back now, please," Andy requested.

Mr. B and Grandpa threw quizzical glances and Madison shook her head scowling, hands on her hips.

"You're scared of a vulture?" she whined.

Andy refrained from response.

Mr. B raised an eyebrow toward Grandpa. The old man didn't respond, so the pilot concluded, "Very well. Let me contact my wife and have her bring the truck." He picked up his radio handle and hailed.

Several minutes later and close to the ground near their liftoff point, Andy scanned the skies and jiggled his leg.

"What's wrong with you?" Madison probed impatiently.

Andy ignored her, continuing to study the surroundings.

"Okay, bend your knees and prepare for impact," Mr. B. instructed.

Andy gripped the lip of the basket, watching the ground approach. Just before touchdown, he chanced another look to the skies and saw a flock of vultures quickly approaching.

He barely heard the pilot say, "Don't jump out until the envelope is completely down or the basket will bounce and drag us."

Come on, hurry up! Andy's thoughts raced. The festival grounds lay a ways off. He quickly scanned for something to use as a weapon or for a place to hide Grandpa and the others. Nothing.

"Watch your step," Mr. B. finally announced.

"Take cover!" Andy yelled. He flew out of the basket and bolted across the grassy field as a dozen zolt transformed. *If I can just distract the zolt, they'll be safe.*

Andy ran as fast as his legs would carry him. The distance had not seemed that far from the balloon, but as he raced, his lungs started to burn and a stitch stabbed his side. Barreling back onto the festival grounds, he heard a woman scream. The crowd hushed and all eyes turned toward the spectacle.

The enemy took off after Andy at top speed, which thankfully amounted to not more than a fast waddle. Minutes later, Andy chanced a peek over his shoulder and saw he had out distanced them. But as he turned back he barreled straight into a uniformed officer, leveling both of them. Andy hit the ground, sprawling face-first, then scrambled up. But the officer grabbed his ankle and held him tight.

"What's the hurry, son?"

"Let me go!" Andy protested, kicking the official's hand, then looked up. His eyes grew wide.

The officer followed Andy's gaze and instantly understood. The zolt were thirty yards away and closing quickly, swords poised.

The officer bolted upright, grabbed the radio handle from his shoulder, and called for backup, then drew his gun, assuming a ready stance.

Andy did not pause to listen as the officer called after him. He darted into the crowd, hoping to lose his pursuers. He headed for the concession stands and only stopped when the fully mature stitch screamed from his side. Pausing next to a silver trailer selling funnel cakes, he scanned the skies. *Good, no reinforcements yet.* He pulled his cell phone from his pocket and autodialed Madison.

"Where are you? What are you doing?" his sister barked.

Andy spotted three zolt circling.

"I'll meet you at Grandpa's truck!"

"Andy…"

He hung up and ducked under the awning. He ignored Madison's ringtone when it sounded from his pocket as he picked his way among a bevy of concession trailers and oblivious spectators. Rushing into a tent congested with celebrating balloon crews, he didn't pause when an imposing official approached, informing, "I'll need to see some identification, son." Andy raced around the uniformed hippo, bounding through the makeshift kitchen and toppling several cooks who yelled insults at him from their food-covered seats on the ground. He braked long enough to scan the skies once more before bolting for a grove of shade trees standing watch over the endless sea of parked cars.

No cover in the parking lot. Grabbing his phone he hit Madison's number once more.

"What?" Madison fumed.

Breathing heavily, Andy yelled over his sister's protests, "Have Grandpa meet me by the shade trees at the front of the parking lot!"

"Andy…"

"Tell him! Now!" Through the web of branches and leaves, Andy spotted a zolt swooping lower, headed toward him.

"Andy!"

"I'll explain everything! Tell Grandpa!" Andy ended his SOS and scrambled up the lowest branches, trying to make himself invisible. He watched, frozen, as his enemy swept the topmost branches before alighting directly above him. *Please don't see me. Please don't see me.*

Andy dared not fidget. He tried to silence his heavy breathing as his ears tuned in to every creak of the branches and scuffle of the leaves. It felt like an eternity, but the enemy finally lifted off, allowing Andy to exhale.

Several minutes passed before Grandpa's white pickup slowly navigated the ruts. He dropped to the ground and scanned the skies. *Clear for now.* As soon as Grandpa stopped, Andy bolted for the passenger side, ripping the handle of the partially opened door from Madison's hand. He bounded inside and slammed it shut.

"Ouch! Get off me!" Madison yipped.

"Go, Grandpa!" Andy commanded, ducking down.

"Mind explaining yourself?"

"I will once we're on the road," Andy replied from the floor.

Grandpa raised an eyebrow and shook his head, but put the truck in drive.

Headed for the ranch, Andy chanced a glance out the front window as he moved to the middle of the bench seat. *Good, nothing airborne.*

"Well?" Grandpa questioned.

Andy did his best to construct a believable narrative, leaving out the not-so-tiny detail about his pursuers being from another world.

In the end, Grandpa concluded, "I'm not going to pretend I fully understand your story, but I will say this, I think you overreacted. The authorities had things well in hand. You didn't stick around long enough to see them apprehend that gang. And I'm glad they did. They looked vicious...evil even. The TV crews had a field day. I'll bet there's a story on the evening news."

Andy did not respond. His mind was elsewhere, pondering the question that had been running laps around his brain since he first spotted the zolt: *How did they find me?*

Four fifty-five and Grandpa nested himself in his well-worn lounger. Five minutes later and the opening notes of the Phoenix local news heralded this evening's edition of thrills, chills, and ills.

The anchor began, "Back in the fall, residents of a north side apartment complex found mold in their walls…"

Must have been a slow news day, Andy thought.

A story about an underperforming elementary school followed before the anchorman announced, "Maricopa County Sheriff's deputies apprehended twelve illegal aliens at the Phoenix Hot Air Balloon Festival this morning. Our own Tim Bower was on the scene as events unfolded and is here to bring us the latest."

The scene shifted to an older gentleman in a blue plaid shirt standing in front of a mostly empty field that earlier had been populated with all manner of colorful dirigibles. The reporter began his story, quickly shoving the mic in front of Mr. Bitmire and asking his opinion of the strange and unexplained behavior of one of his young passengers.

Andy squirmed as he saw footage of himself dashing toward the food trucks. Thankfully they only captured his back. As the reporter continued, the camera switched to close-ups of the zolt. The commentator followed with several soundbites from an interview with a deputy. "These are not the type of gang members we are used to dealing with. They came heavily armed with medieval broadswords…" The video showed the zolt being disarmed, handcuffed, and put in police cars as the officer continued, "We are asking for help locating the boy. Anyone with knowledge of his whereabouts is encouraged to contact the Sheriff's office."

"What?" Andy exclaimed.

Grandpa looked over at Andy with a grin. "Well, you've made quite a name for yourself. Do we turn you in?"

Mom's ringtone chirped from Andy's pocket.

"Hi, Mom."

"I was surfing the Phoenix local news and just saw the story. What happened?"

Andy quickly summarized and Mom asked him to hand his phone to Grandpa.

"Yes, that's right. That's what he told me too."

The old man's grin faded as he listened and nodded.

"Do you really think that's necessary? Seems like a big fuss…"

More nodding.

"They're scheduled to fly back in two weeks, but…"

Grandpa raised his eyebrows.

"Alright, if you really want…"

Head nodding.

"I understand. I'll make sure they're on the nine o'clock tomorrow morning. Uh-huh. Yes. No, don't worry, Emily. I know. They'll be safe. Uh-huh. Okay…goodbye."

Grandpa handed the phone back to Andy. "You can guess what that was about."

Andy woke early. He yawned and rubbed sleep from his eyes.

Knock, knock. "Come on, sleepyhead. Time to get moving. We need to leave in half an hour if you're going to make that plane," Grandpa announced.

Andy slithered from under the covers and ambled over to the window. Pink and red hues blanketed the sunrise. In the distance he made out the form of a large black bird, circling.

CHAPTER TWO

Hide and Go Seek

A ndy downed his breakfast and dragged his suitcase to the front door, then returned to help Madison with hers to hurry her.

"What's your problem?" she grumbled, not fully awake.

"All set?" Grandpa queried.

Andy studied the skies before opening the door, receiving a raised eyebrow and a shake of Grandpa's head.

"All clear," Andy informed.

"Would you stop!" Madison hissed forty-five minutes into the hour-long ride.

Andy had been glancing out the window like a twitching squirrel since they left the ranch.

"Honestly, I'm with Grandpa. I think you and Mom are overreacting."

Andy chose not to reply as he again surveyed the skies.

Several minutes later, Grandpa followed the signs to their terminal's drop-off lane and Andy exhaled. *Almost there.*

Andy sat crammed in the middle seat next to a guy who should have purchased two tickets. He felt like asking the brute if he wanted to sit in his seat too, but refrained. Madison had demanded the window seat and, considering the situation, he had chosen not to engage in battle.

Now that they had taken off, Andy's brain continued mulling over the question of how the zolt knew to look for him in Phoenix. *I wish I could talk to someone in Oomaldee and see what they know.* Oomaldee. Yes…why had he heard exactly nothing since he left nine weeks ago? He drew his hands over his face and forcefully exhaled, then thrust them forward into the seat in front of him. The occupant was none too happy.

Mr. Seat Hog looked over and ran his eyes up and down Andy's frame before returning his attention to a movie he watched on his computer. Madison ignored him, looking out the window.

I know Father believes things should always be the way they are, but…how did the zolt get into this world? How did they track me? When will they find me again? I don't want my family to get hurt.

Halfway through the flight, Andy got up to stretch his legs. He scanned the heads of passengers on his way to the back of the plane and did a double take when he saw two beady eyes staring at him over a seatback. He felt his heartbeat quicken and instinctively reached for Methuselah without success. *It wouldn't dare attack me up here, would it?* A fellow passenger seeking the lavatory reached him and Andy moved forward. Ten feet away he realized… *Oh, it's just that lady's hat.* He sighed. *I've got to keep it together.*

Forty-five minutes later, Andy spotted Mom waving to him and Madison as they rode the escalator down to baggage claim. Never had he been so glad to see her.

After exchanging hugs, Mom announced, "I just got off the phone with Grandpa. He said several zolt dressed as sheriff's deputies paid him a visit this morning after he got back to the ranch."

Andy's eyes grew wide and Madison stopped fidgeting with her book. She wrinkled her brow as she looked at Mom.

"It's okay. They didn't do anything. They just asked him if he'd seen a boy fitting your description. They claimed they wanted to question you in connection with the incident at the hot air balloon festival. He said it was clear they didn't know you'd left."

"Let's hope it stays that way," Andy replied.

"Grandpa asked me to extend his apology for not treating this more seriously. He didn't realize the threat to you is real."

Andy nodded.

"I don't get it," Madison interjected. "I thought the dweeb was trying to get attention. What would anyone want with him?"

Mom let the name-calling slide, replying, "Let's discuss it on the way home."

*****

A week into the new school year, Andy sat in Mr. Hawkins' social studies class listening to him lecture about life in early America. The man droned on about the settlers' earliest lodgings and the perils they faced. Despite the promise Andy had made to himself to be more diligent with his studies now that he had started middle school, his mind drifted. *I wonder where the zolt are. How can I contact Oomaldee? I've got to find a way.*

He didn't know how long he had zoned, but his thoughts refocused at the teacher standing next to his desk asking, "What say you, Mr. Smithson?" A chorus of laughter told him he had been gone awhile.

"Sorry, Mr. Hawkins. What was the question?" Andy felt his cheeks warming.

"What is John Smith best known for?" the teacher repeated slowly.

"Uh, isn't he the guy who did something with that Indian lady?" Andy stammered, grasping.

The teacher furrowed his brow and met Andy's eyes. "Can you be more specific, Mr. Smithson?"

Andy dropped his eyes to his desk and shook his head.

"For tomorrow, you will all write a five-hundred-word essay on what John Smith is best known for." Groans rippled about the room and his classmates' dirty looks bore into his back. The man cleared his throat, "You will find your homework burden lighter if each of you reads and retains the assigned texts."

"On a different topic..." Mr. Hawkins continued, "since we will be studying American history, both past and present, each week you will read a current news article and prepare a one-page summary. I will select several of you to present your synopsis before the class."

That evening, Andy perused several news websites. One article caught his eye.

ATTEMPTED BREAK-IN AT THE CENTRAL INTELLIGENCE AGENCY

A group of six heavily armed gang members overpowered security guards at the Central Intelligence Agency headquarters in Washington D.C. Monday afternoon. Security cameras reveal the perpetrators carried broadswords and daggers and when requested to remove them for screening, refused, triggering a coordinated attack that killed five guards and left another five wounded.

A spokesman for the CIA indicated the group made its way past the checkpoint and up to the fifth floor to the Information Operations Center. Employees delayed them until additional security arrived and took them into custody.

Anita Boringer interviewed an employee from that department who requested we withhold her identity. "It was frightening. While these guys were relatively short, they had unusually long arms, beaklike noses, and beady eyes. They looked evil. They demanded help locating someone. Obviously we weren't going to assist, but by the way they brandished their weapons it was clear we needed to stall, which we did, until help arrived."

The accused are being held without bail pending a full investigation.

A drawing of the zolt taken into custody followed the article.

Zolt tried to break into the CIA to find me? What, are they crazy?!

"Mom, did you hear about this?"

To say the information upset her would have been an understatement. "It was Phoenix a month ago and now this. Where will they show up next?"

"But why would they have attacked the CIA?"

Mom thought a minute before responding. "I remember when I first came to this world, I didn't understand the meaning behind a lot of things. If you take the name Central Intelligence Agency literally…"

"They probably thought they'd have me in no time."

Mom nodded. "I think it would be a good idea to keep Methuselah in the family room…just in case."

Andy's eyes jetted up and met Mom's.

*****

Still no word from Oomaldee, Andy fumed as he flopped in the bean bag chair in his bedroom two weeks later. Madison had not yet returned from school and he had the house to himself. *After everything I did for Father, for him to treat me this way…* He slammed his fist on the floor.

Just then a thought fluttered by causing him to whisper, "Wait a minute…" He leapt up and ran down the hall.

Andy ran into Madison's violent peach room, landing on all fours in front of her bed's dust ruffle. *If she…* The thought fanned the flames of frustration ever hotter.

He threw up the fabric and scrutinized the neatly arranged containers. *No chest. But she could have hidden it behind…* Andy grabbed the box closest to him, then the next and the next, hoping. He peered under her bed again. *Nothing. Zip. Nada.*

"What do you think you're doing?" Madison's accusation startled him and he glanced up to see steam burst from her ears, the top of her head open, and a whistle extend and blow.

He started a weak explanation, but disappointment overwhelmed and he snapped, "You hid a message from Oomaldee before!" as he raced back to his room.

"You're blaming me for not hearing from that place?" Madison screeched, storming into the hall after him.

Andy knew the incident wasn't over, but he didn't care. He slammed his bedroom door in her face and locked it, then sprawled across his bed. He didn't even try to defend against her pounding and insults. With no response to keep the conflict raging, Madison eventually gave up and retreated back to her cave, no doubt to await Mom's or Dad's arrival home from work.

His conduct earned him the privilege of weeding Mom's flower beds in both the front and back yards on Saturday.

And so at the appointed hour Andy trudged into the garage.

"Be careful not to pull up my flowers as you weed," Mom commanded as he retrieved the requisite tools and ambled to the front yard.

The sun beat down mercilessly, but the rivers of sweat that watered the dry ground combined with the physical exertion provided a constructive outlet to ease some of Andy's frustration.

As he pulled weeds from between the zinnias, the first rational thought in weeks blossomed: *I should try calling Daisy!*

Last year, when the she-dragon had flown him to Oomaldee from the water park in San Antonio, she had told him to call in his thoughts if he ever needed her help.

If there's ever a time I need to hear from you, Daisy, it's now.

Andy stood the trowel up in the dirt, closed his eyes, and concentrated. *Daisy! Daisy? Can you hear me?*

He waited several minutes, but the she-dragon gave no response, so he tried again. *Daisy! Please answer.*

Nothing.

The disappointment he had beaten back all morning threatened to sting once more as he sat back on his haunches. He brought his hand up to wipe more sweat from his brow, and as he did he brushed the pouch hanging from his neck. *The key! It's brought stone statues to life, got us out of the dwarfs' net, and Alden used it to make me wake up after getting hit by that spong. Maybe...*

He pulled the key from its home and, holding it in both hands, repeated his plea aloud. "Daisy! Please answer. Please."

"Daisy, please answer, please..." Andy heard the mocking sentiment from behind him and whirled around. "Daisy, please answer," Madison repeated in an annoyingly high pitch.

"This doesn't concern you," Andy growled.

"Oh Daisy, please answer," she mocked again. "Who's Daisy?"

"The dragon who flew me to Oomaldee last year."

"You're so weird," Madison quipped. "You're calling a dragon? Good luck with that." She raised her brows to exaggerate her point, then turned and walked away, repeating in more dramatic form, "Oh Daisy... Answer me... P-P-Please..."

After Andy heard the back door slam, he threw the gold key as hard as he could across the back yard and yelled at the top of his lungs, "I hate this! I hate Oomaldee! I hate Father! I hate all of it!"

*****

With hope of hearing from Oomaldee exhausted, Andy's mood flagged as October arrived.

"What are you going to dress up as for trick-or-treating, Andy?" Dad asked over dinner.

"I'm not going."

"Really? You always look forward to it and I thought the two of us could go together—make it a guys night. I was thinking of going as Harry Potter, what do you think?"

Andy pushed his green beans across the plate with his fork.

Mom and Dad shared a look.

"You, Harry Potter?" Madison giggled.

"What's wrong with me dressing as Harry Potter?"

"Don't you think you're...a bit old for that, Dad?"

"You're no fun, Maddy. It's Halloween. Besides, you're not even going."

"Now that I'm in high school, I'm too old for that kind of stuff. You should dress up as one of those goons Andy's so nervous about," Madison joked, extending an arm below the table, imitating the overly long stretch of the zolt's appendage.

Andy scowled and Mom corrected, "That's enough, Maddy."

Madison shrugged before asking to be excused.

After dinner, as Andy scanned the news websites for history class, he found an article titled:

GANG HITS CHICAGO MERCANTILE EXCHANGE

The gang of mercenaries that has struck many notable establishments in recent months attacked Chicago's famous Mercantile Exchange this morning wielding broadswords and daggers. The offensive halted trading for over an hour as security guards and police converged to negotiate with gang members who had taken several hostages.

We spoke with an official who indicated the thugs were demanding significant quantities of rope with which to construct an enormous web.

"Somehow, I don't think they understood the Exchange trades commodities but doesn't actually have them on hand," the police chief offered in his briefing. "The gang members were arrested after a brief scuffle and no hostages were harmed."

Despite his mood, Andy couldn't help but laugh. *Sounds like they want to build their own worldwide web.* He showed the article to Mom who responded, "At least they're nowhere near here. Although…it's hard to say where else they might be looking."

Andy felt his stomach clench. *Oomaldee's turned a deaf ear, but these goons are still after me. Perfect. Just perfect.*

*****

December arrived and with it chilly weather that served to further dampen Andy's spirits despite a two-week vacation from school. For her part, Mom embraced the season as she always did and went all out decorating the house as well as having a crew hang festive holiday lights outside.

She insisted the tree be a noble fir, and nothing short in stature; the once-green conifer sparkled and glistened two stories to the top of the round niche the staircase wrapped in the entry, proudly displaying an army of gold and silver ornaments. The lower branches showcased Madison's and Andy's earliest attempts at crafts and an assortment of other keepsakes. The holidays seemed the one time of year Mom's spirits would not be dimmed, and she hummed carols (albeit not always in tune) wherever she went.

Andy sat slumped on the sofa in the family room Saturday morning, staring at the wreath over the fireplace. While he was not into Christmas in the same way as Mom, he enjoyed this time of year. He fondly remembered baking Christmas cookies and trekking out into the woods to cut down the perfect tree with Grandma and Grandpa Smithson.

His thoughts meandered to his best friends, Alden and Hannah. He wished they could be here to share the occasion with him, along with Father, Mermin, Hans, and Marta. *I wonder what they're doing. Do they celebrate Christmas in Oomaldee?* The random thought surprised him. *For all the time I've spent there…I'm the heir, yet how much do I really know about the land?* Andy sighed. *I sure wish they'd write.*

Mom's humming interrupted his contemplations as she descended the stairs. "Want to help make Christmas cookies this morning?"

"I thought you had Madison signed up for that."

"I do, but the more the merrier."

"No thanks."

"Suit yourself. Grandpa Smithson will be arriving tomorrow and I want to make sure we have his favorite goodies."

"May I use the computer?"

"What for? You don't have a current event homework due this week."

"I know, but I want to see…" He did not need to finish his sentence. Mom knew what he was thinking and nodded her approval.

Andy sat down at the desk in the home office and turned on the "kids" computer. He scanned several news websites before he found an article of interest:

NEWS OF THE NEWS

Officials at the historic *Los Angeles Times* today reported its offices were broken into Friday. The thieves appeared to be novices as surveillance cameras revealed the assailants recklessly butchered a door with a broadsword, triggering alarms. The group of twelve made their way to the third floor where security personnel cornered them as they rummaged through files. An eyewitness to the events said, "They kept demanding information on someone by the name of Andy Smithson."

A showdown ensued in which officers fired shots, subduing ten of the suspects. The remaining two charged, and guards fired in self defense. The injured were taken to a nearby hospital for treatment and are in critical condition.

Andy exhaled loudly. *The zolt are after me and no one will talk to me. What did I do wrong? I thought they were my friends.*

*****

Spring rolled around and with it Andy experienced a renewed sense of despair at the steely, cold indifference shown by those in Oomaldee. *It's been ten months and not one word. They could be dead for all I know. And who knows what Abaddon's up to.* He hoped no harm had come to those he loved, but his brain could not reconcile the care and warmth they had shown with the current situation. *Just tell me you hate me, it'd be better than this not knowing!*

He glanced at the end table where Methuselah's hilt rested. *I wish it would work for me when I'm home. I'd sure feel better.* Over the past couple weeks, Andy had become aware that not having the use of his trusted companion had compounded his feelings of helplessness. He and Mom had been at Target shopping for new sneakers when he thought he spotted a zolt stalking them. He had reached for his sword without result. Thankfully the threat had been nothing more than a young child playing with her stuffed animal, but the few seconds he had felt naked without his blade served to intensify his frustration.

What am I going to use to defend myself if the zolt find me? The question plagued his thoughts without resolution, the scenario seeming more and more probable with each news article he read. This afternoon it had been:

LIBRARIES HIT IN COORDINATED ATTACKS

In what appears to be a series of well-coordinated attacks, heavily armed assailants invaded fifty of the largest libraries across the country today.

Sandy Shiffer from the Library of Congress allowed us an exclusive interview. She indicated, "A group of ten odd-looking men with broadswords and daggers forcibly entered the building this morning and demanded help in locating a boy. We informed them we were not equipped to perform such a search, but they proceeded to put a dagger to the throats of three of our staff until we agreed to cooperate." Ms. Shiffer declined to comment on whether the thugs gleaned any information before security officers successfully disarmed and arrested the men.

Other notable libraries included in the attack were the New York Public Library, Cornell and Princeton

University libraries, the Dallas Public Library, and the
library at the University of Texas in Austin.

Andy had reread the article several times as he felt his stomach tie itself in a
hard knot. *They're getting close…*

CHAPTER THREE

The Pizza Guy

With a month remaining until the school year ended, Andy strode into his bedroom after downing a snack, ready to engage the minotaur in an epic battle to end all conflicts. His newest video game, Maze Zing, had grabbed his attention, and he planned to dispense with the well-armed villain before Mom or Dad got home.

As he dumped his backpack on the bed, he noticed a gold envelope on his pillow. A mix of emotions instantly bubbled up as he read the address: Prince Andrew, he whose accusations must cease.

What?! Not one peep out of Oomaldee for months and now…

He opened the flap and slipped out two sheets of parchment. The first read:

> "Thou knowest what thou knows,
> Less so what thou lacks.
> But blind art thou to that which
> Thou knowest not ye lacks."

Andy stopped and reread the paragraph before continuing. "I know what I know…I know some of what I don't know…But I'm blind to what I don't know I lack."

He mulled the last thought over. *I'm blind to what I don't know I lack.* "Well…everybody is." As he said it, a discomforting thought sparked and began growing. He read on:

"Thy fixation on communication,
Causing consternation o'er the duration,
Is thy mind's apparition
lacking sound foundation.

Leap not to accusation,
But instead to admiration.
For love's provocation,
Becomes denial's vindication."

Andy paused, the rebuke causing him to squirm. *I guess I have been accusing everyone of ignoring me. But why didn't they contact me? I have to admit, it doesn't seem like them.*

"Love's provocation becomes denial's vindication." The thought circled and attempted to land. *What if they wanted to contact me but didn't because Alden told them what Abaddon said in the tunnel? Do they know the zolt are after me? Have they been protecting me the whole time?*

Andy felt a riptide suck him below the surface of a love he had longed to believe existed between him and Father and the others, but evidence made it difficult to embrace. *Did Father deny what he wanted for my safety?* The possibility temporarily beat back the frustration that had plagued him.

He turned to the second page and continued reading:

"Dragon scale, venom, and unicorn horn,
Costly ingredients you have borne.
The bonds of your people,
To loose them, you've sworn.

Yet more learning and growing
Embark you upon,
A quest for the noble
Long years have foregone.

A song so pure
Trills listeners to tears.
A sacrifice, a giving,
And new life appears.

Yellow, crimson, orange, or red,
Fire-touched or unscorched, shed.
A quill of this warbler
No creature hath bred."

It's the next clue! But here? That's different.

Andy studied the verses but nothing made much sense other than the part about the quill of a warbler. *It's a bird's feather. But what kind? And there's something about fire. That can't be good. "No creature has bred"—that makes no sense.*

Andy's mind whirled to bring meaning to the puzzle, but as with all the previous clues, simplicity was never part of the answer. One thing he knew, he would be headed back to Oomaldee soon.

That evening, Andy grabbed his flashlight and ventured up to the attic for the first time since his return from Oomaldee. Nearly a year away from the trunk had produced nothing but a layer of dust. He remembered seeing a scroll about Abaddon and briefly regretted wasting the time when he could have been discovering more about his pursuer. There was also a manuscript with the history of Hadession he wanted to digest.

Tossing off what could not be changed, Andy sneezed as he lifted the lid and propped it open. The unsigned note he had disregarded, precipitating a sudden return, sat in the uppermost tray. Next to it were the black leather holster with the purple crest and the small parchment decoder scroll, just the way he had left them. But one more item had been added—the gold key he had thrown in frustration months before. Andy glanced about the attic but all was still. *How?*

Knowing no answer would come, Andy added the token back to his pouch, then pulled the upper tray out of the trunk and set it aside. He searched the fifteen scrolls populating the second level until he located the one titled *History of King Abaddon*.

He unrolled two feet of the parchment and set several of his old Nintendo 64 games across the top to hold it open. *Let's see if my dream was real...*

For the next two weeks, Andy snuck up to the attic every day after school (once Madison was otherwise occupied) and labored over deciphering the scroll. The author confirmed all the viceroy had spoken before the committee, but there was more.

Tonight, Andy finished translating a portion of the scroll and frowned:

> "Rumor of the existence of dark sorcerers in the northern lands has persisted for eons without confirmation, and while I am unable to conclusively prove Naparte encountered these wizards, reports confirm he ventured northward into that region after his graduation."

Dark sorcerers? Andy remembered the chain mail blanket that had trapped Daisy last year and Naria's explanation that its tremendous weight came from evil burned deep into the metal.

Andy continued translating:

> "Not long after Naparte's voyage, word of sightings of a great and terrifying beast began to circulate and quickly spread throughout that region—multiple heads, fire-breathing, enormous wings and tail. The beast swooped low over villages, wreaking havoc, terror, and destruction. It changed the landscape from a land green and lush, to one barren and desolate."

Andy swallowed. *That sure sounds like Abaddon.* His stomach lurched as he remembered his dream of seeing Oomish citizens transformed into zolt—or worse, stiff statues. *Abaddon used a spell…dark magic…to extract energy. What could he have given wizards in exchange for his powers? What would evil sorcerers be after? What is Abaddon capable of?*

*****

With only a week left until the school year ended, Andy lay in bed staring at the ceiling. He had turned his room lights off and now watched the stray rays of headlights passing by on the street. His thoughts turned to Alden and he wondered how his best friend had done in the Tower Chase competition last fall. *I wonder if Oscray season has started?* He smiled as he remembered the amazing cookies Alden's mom, Marta, kept on hand for him and Father. *Yes, Father.* Memories of how special he had felt when he learned he was the King's son and heir to the throne pulled the corners of his mouth upward. But his next thought, *Hannah*, sent a swarm of butterflies flitting about his stomach until dreams overcame them.

Andy found himself standing in an unfamiliar field. Judging by the angle of the sun it was late afternoon. To his left, an army of jagged rock outcroppings burst from the grassy plain at odd angles as if giants had been interrupted in the middle of a game of Twister. A mixture of prairie grass and tufted vegetation filled in the balance of the canvas to Andy's right. Gentle breezes played with the herbage and his nose sniffed out the distinctive smell of herd animals.

Turning around slowly, Andy spotted the source of the odor—a group of a dozen or more pegasi, roaming free. Ignoring his presence, the blue, purple, red, orange, and pink animals continued clipping the succulent greens. From time spent with the cavalry's pegasi, Andy knew these animals, while beautiful, could turn vicious and bite, so he scaled a rock and watched, wondering all the while why his dreams had brought him here.

After quite some time, as his boredom encouraged him to explore, he caught sight of a blond-haired maiden. From this distance it looked like

Hannah, though he could not be sure, and he felt his stomach tense. The girl wore a filthy yellow dress that extended below her knees and a ratty white scarf adorned her locks. She approached the grazing pegasi slowly with outstretched arm and open hand, inviting the creatures to investigate.

What's she doing? Is she crazy?

Fifteen feet away. Ten feet. The animals closest lifted their heads as if warning the maiden to approach no farther. The front-most animal ruffled its green wings to underscore the point.

Andy stood, preparing to charge the pegasus if he needed to. He felt his heartbeat quicken and reached for Methuselah but came up empty as he had all year.

The girl took another step forward and Andy yelled, "Hannah, stop! They're going to hurt you!" Clearly the maiden did not hear his cry, for she advanced several more steps.

Andy's gut would allow him to remain a spectator no longer, and he leapt from the boulder, racing for the foolish girl. He was still a good thirty yards away when the herd attacked, wings unfurled and teeth bared. The sounds sent shivers up and down Andy's back as he rushed to rescue.

"Hannah!" Andy yelled, waking himself. His pajamas and sheets were drenched in sweat.

"Hannah! Hannah!" Madison mocked in a high-pitched squeal downstairs over pancakes the next morning. "I heard you yelling all the way down the hall. Who's Hannah?"

"Don't worry about it," Andy snipped, knowing Madison would never let it go that easily.

"Is she your girlfriend? Like Daisy?" his sister taunted, sensing the tantalizing prize that could be hers if she probed further. When Andy did not respond, she started making obnoxious kissing noises, receiving her reward as his face began to warm.

"She is!" Madison pointed.

"It's not like that!" Andy insisted, despite knowing his adversary had won.

"Madison…" Dad growled, coming around the corner.

"What? Andy's got a girlfriend. Her name's Hannah."

Andy caught Dad glance his way and redirected his eyes to study the granite countertop, which had become fascinating.

* * * * *

The school year ended with a whimper, and tonight the family remembered Andy's thirteenth birthday courtesy of Papa Paul's Pizzeria. While the bigger celebration would happen next weekend at a rock climbing venue, Andy had campaigned for pizza, a forbidden fruit in Mom's book, and won on the condition that someone other than she call and place the order for delivery. Madison had rallied and made the call, insisting Andy would never order what she wanted.

Everyone sat in the family room, stomachs rumbling, waiting for the pizza delivery guy.

"How 'bout we start with cake? I'm starving," Madison suggested.

"Yeah!" Andy echoed as the doorbell rang.

"I'll get it!" Madison exclaimed, jumping up.

No sooner did Andy hear the front door open than Madison screamed and raced back into the family room, drawing everyone to their feet in time to face three zolt brandishing broadswords. Andy saw Mom grab Methuselah's hilt from the end table next to her. The blade extended and she sprang into action, bringing the weapon down on the lead adversary.

Andy ran into the kitchen and grabbed the carving knife and meat cleaver from the rack on the counter. He dashed back into the family room and spotted Madison cowering behind the recliner in the far corner. Dad had vanished, four dead or injured zolt lay bleeding on the carpet, and Mom dueled two more of the enemy. Andy did not have time to question where the additional zolt had come from, for out of the corner of his eye he spotted yet another adversary nearly upon him. He pivoted in place and crossed the blades at eye level as Cadfael had taught him, slowing the sword's downstroke. His instructor's warning rang through his brain: "You never win a dagger fight, you only survive one."

Andy stepped to the side, deflecting the zolt's momentum. With its back now toward him, he brought his top hand down and trapped the attacker's hand behind his knife. The zolt refused to drop its weapon, allowing Andy to push it to the floor with his shoulder. He smashed the blunt handle of the carving knife into the creature's temple and it collapsed. The thud drew a whimper from Madison who still cowered in the corner.

Mom engaged three more zolt and appeared to have them well in hand when Andy spotted Dad standing his ground on the front lawn, attempting to take down two enemies with a garden rake. The rake was not a fair match against broadswords, however, and Andy rushed to help. But as he reached the front steps, five more zolt materialized.

Seeing their prize, the enemy ignored Dad and rushed toward Andy. *We're outnumbered!* As the thought crashed through his mind, he heard Mom yell from behind, "Andy. Closet!"

An ethereal sensation instantly engulfed his body and a black tunnel enveloped him, tightly squeezing every inch of his form. Andy slammed into the wall of a small, dark space and crumpled to the floor, trying to catch his breath. Feeling something sharp digging into his knee, he moved and, thanks to a line of light seeping under the door, identified it as the buckle on one of Mom's boots. *Whoa! How'd she do that?*

"Oh no you don't!" Mom growled on the other side of the door as the knob jiggled roughly.

He righted himself as *swash* and *clang* sounds reverberated outside the closet followed quickly by *flump*, and then something blocked much of the bead of light.

Swash. Clang. Swish.

"Fred, are you okay?"

Swish. Clang. Swash. Flump.

"Fred!"

Mom's voice grew fainter. *She must have gone to fight alongside Dad. I've got to do something!*

Andy turned the door handle and pushed. The door opened no more than an inch, but it was enough for him to see a zolt's head—unconscious. The weight of the enemy's body held him captive. He put his shoulder to the blockade and pushed again, harder, and managed to force it open another inch. All sounds seemed to be coming from the front yard. He peered out but saw no movement, so he wedged his shoulder into the gap and, using the closet wall as a brace, slid the unconscious zolt forward enough to squeeze out of his prison.

Carrying the knives, Andy scanned the family room and found Madison still huddled in the corner behind the recliner. Her face was wet from tears, and the instant she laid saucer-size eyes on him she croaked, "Is it safe to come out?"

Andy glanced about the room to double check before nodding. Madison did not need encouragement. She bolted from her hiding place and up the stairs toward her bedroom. He did not have time to listen for her door to slam, for no sooner had she vanished than another zolt burst through the front door.

The enemy wore deep gashes across its face from which blood flowed freely. As soon as it took a step toward Andy, Mom appeared in the doorway, her hair disheveled and clothes torn but still brandishing Methuselah. The sword was bloodied from combat and red streaks stained much of Mom's attire. Andy could not immediately deduce whether the blood belonged to her or the enemy. Mom took a swipe at the adversary's exposed back and it crumpled to the floor.

"You look awful," Andy commented, glancing at the downed zolt.

"Thanks." Mom smiled, lowering the blade.

But before she could catch her breath, Andy spotted another six enemy materializing on the lawn behind her.

"Mom! Look!"

As she turned, she cried, "Andy. To Oomaldee!"

CHAPTER FOUR
Hope Reborn

A ndy splashed down into a thick ooze of muck. He coughed and
sputtered, then dropped the knives he still clutched and swiped at his
eyes, trying to bring his surroundings into focus.

A forest of old dead trees stretched before him, their roots submerged in
mire. Islands of grass peeked up where sediment had collected. Eddies of mud
swirled around Andy's legs as he righted himself and gazed upward. The
canopy looked to be a tangle of vines supported by skeleton arms. The greenery
vied for sunlight, greedily forbidding most of the sun's rays from reaching the
swamp's floor. It smelled of decay.

What is this place?

He heard a grunt behind him and slowly turned. A hulking, greenish
creature sat in the mire five feet away. Its pumpkin-like head bore oversize
triangular ears, and a pair of canine teeth extended upward nearly two inches
out of its lower jaw. It appeared to be female based upon its long black hair and
the location of the scant attire it wore.

Andy glanced down, hoping to retrieve the kitchen knives, but they had
sunk below the surface of the mud. The creature grunted again and motioned
for him to come closer. When he did not comply, the brute planted a fist in the
muck and pivoted, scooting next to him, coating him with a tidal wave of the
foul-smelling ooze. Before Andy could react, she brought a muscular arm up
and pulled him facedown across her lap.

Though Andy kicked and yelled, the creature kept him down with one
arm and shoveled handfuls of mud onto his hair and shoulders, then proceeded
to smear it around as if giving him a bath. Despite her size, her movements
were surprisingly gentle. After thoroughly coating the back of Andy's head with
mud, she moved a clawed finger over one of his ears and grunted again. Andy
could feel her breath on his neck as she inspected more closely. Another grunt
and more feeling about.

She thinks I'm her kid and she's trying to find my ear!

Andy intensified his squirming as another, higher pitched grunt sounded from behind. The creature turned to look and as she did, he wiggled free of her grasp. He leapt up, distancing himself as quickly as his feet could navigate the swampy muck trying to remove his shoes. He ducked behind a thick trunk and looked back. The creature stood and corralled a miniature version of herself. Her graceless splashdown in the mud sent a myriad of ripples through the bog.

That was close. I wish I had Methuselah. No sooner had he thought it than the hilt splashed at his feet. *That's so cool!*

I know I'm in Oomaldee, but where? Another grunt sounded off to his right, choosing for him the direction his explorations would take. He headed left, sloshing through water and mud while keeping alert for more beasts. He attempted to remove the odoriferous grime with tree leaves, but his efforts proved ineffective. *I feel like I did when I fell in quicksand. At least the mud isn't sanding my skin like then.* Each time he ventured upon a large green brute, he ducked behind a dead tree trunk until it passed or became too engrossed in something else to pay him any notice.

The few rays of sunlight that made it to the ground lengthened and Andy knew he needed to find shelter for the night. But where? And then his stomach started rumbling. *I wonder what those things eat.* Andy could not recall seeing anything edible in his travels. With no other option, he continued on as the sunlight began to fade. Just as dusk settled across the landscape, the trees began to thin and the swamp released him from its soggy grasp.

Mature oaks and chestnut trees stood grouped across the grassy plain before him, and he sighed. *Well, at least there's ground to sleep on.* He scouted out a grove of oak trees that looked promising for camouflage and set about gathering dry leaves to soften his bed. His stomach complained again as he sat down, resting Methuselah next to where he had constructed a makeshift pillow.

As darkness consumed the area, nature began its ritual symphony: branches swaying in time to the gentle breeze formed the melody, while the sounds of crickets chirping and owls hooting provided the harmony. Andy smiled as he peeled drying mud from his ears. Despite the chaos that had brought him here and his ooze-covered condition, all seemed right in the world tonight. *I hope Mom and Dad are okay.* But even as the concern flitted across his mind, having seen Mom skillfully handle Methuselah eased his worry. *When did she learn to fight like that?*

His stomach grumbled once more and he attempted to ignore it. But the harder he tried, the more focused he became. The breeze shifted and his nose picked up faint wisps of something that smelled like Dad grilling. He tried to dismiss the notion. *I'm so hungry, I'm imagining things.* But his rumbling belly compelled him to investigate.

As Andy picked up Methuselah, the blade extended and lit up, illuminating the area. He lifted his nose, located the direction of the tantalizing aroma, and set off with purpose. He had walked a good distance when he spied a campfire in a shelter of trees across the plain. Andy slowed his pace, and Methuselah instinctively dimmed as he approached. His mouth watered with expectation as he drew to within five hundred yards of the camp. Muffled sounds of people talking and laughing echoed in the blackness as he neared the trees.

"Halt right there!"

The command from behind the nearest tree startled Andy, and he berated himself for allowing hunger to trump concerns for safety. He stopped and searched for the source as Methuselah's light extinguished itself.

A sturdy soldier approached, his sword ready for business. "Drop your weapon." On the left arm of his uniform was a crest of two crossed sabers.

Seeing the insignia, Andy sighed with relief, then complied. But as the blade retracted, the man's eyes grew large. The soldier kept his weapon pointed at Andy's heart and hesitantly kicked at Methuselah's hilt, as if expecting it to bite. "Who are you and what are you doing here?" he interrogated, quickly composing himself.

Andy hesitated, pondering how best to respond. The same situation was playing itself out for yet a third time. He smiled as he chose to answer honestly. *Maybe it will turn out differently this time.*

"Something funny?"

"No, officer. Sorry. I'm Prince Andrew, son of King Hercalon V of Oomaldee."

The soldier offered a forced laugh. "Very funny. Now answer the question."

"But I am," Andy insisted.

The man grabbed the front of Andy's soiled T-shirt in his fist and brought him close. "No one insults the royal family, especially the likes of grubby urchins like you," he growled and dragged Andy toward the campsite.

Oh well, I tried.

The soldier strutted to the center of the clearing, proudly displaying his catch as four officers closed in from the periphery. Those seated around the campfire ceased their conversations and stared at the spectacle.

"Andy? Is that you?" Alden queried, staring.

Andy beamed.

"You're back!" Alden rushed to hug him.

Hannah screeched, joyously joining in.

"Andy," Hans chimed in, laughing as he stood and approached.

The soldier's face fell and he released Andy from his iron grip. "But how?" was all he could get out amidst the celebration. He shook his head and wiped his hands together to remove Andy's grime.

"Is my father here?" Andy asked eagerly.

"No. Regent Bellum strongly advised against him joining us based on what happened a year ago," Hans informed.

"Oh. Well, it's still great to see you all!"

With no danger afoot, the soldiers blended back into the foliage.

"What happened to you?" Alden queried, examining his earthy ensemble.

Andy chuckled and recounted his encounter with the muddy mama.

"Those would be ogres," Hans informed. "Lucky for you they don't have very good eyesight. They'll eat humans."

"Oh."

"Well, I just love your attire…so chic," offered Hannah.

Andy laughed, scratching loose more of the drying ooze from his stiff hair.

"We heard the zolt might be after you," Alden chimed in.

Andy frowned. "Speaking of which, why haven't you sent me any letters in the last year?"

Alden and Hannah exchanged glances before Alden said, "The King forbade us."

"What! But why?"

"Look, Andy, I know you're upset," Hannah started, raising her hands.

"Upset?!" Andy exploded. The understatement ignited his temper and, despite the letter, the frustration that had built over the year poured out. "I leave here after hearing Abaddon make a threat on my life. I didn't know if he was going to hurt you guys or not. The zolt came after me. I watched them close in all year. They attacked my family today. My mom sent me here. It would have been nice to know what was going on!"

Hannah cowered and Alden nudged a stray pebble with his foot.

"Are you done?" Alden questioned, sensing the end of the firestorm.

Hans stood watching the exchange, eyebrows furrowed.

Andy nodded and Alden picked up, "Look, I told the King about the threat on your life as soon as you disappeared. He was afraid Abaddon might try something and wanted to let you know, but Mermin was concerned they might somehow trace the appearo beam if we used it. I hated it! You've no idea how many times I wanted to tell you what's been happening." Alden propelled the pebble across the clearing, underscoring his point.

Relief washed over Andy and he let go of his frustration. "Sorry I yelled at you."

Alden nodded. "It's okay. I was as frustrated as you, trust me."

"Would someone mind explaining…" Hans interrupted.

The trio laughed, only now realizing Hans did not know Andy's story.

"Let's eat first," Hannah suggested. "Andy, are you hungry?"

Over a hearty dinner of rabbit stew, Andy filled Hans in on his background. The healer kept shaking his head in disbelief throughout the telling.

"I'd never been able to put all the pieces together, but now it makes sense. Well, at least as much sense as your tale makes," Hans finished with a chuckle. "It's quite extraordinary."

Changing the subject, Andy asked, "By the way, why are you guys here, out in the middle of nowhere?"

"I guess it's my turn to tell a tale," Hans replied.

Andy smiled and settled comfortably against a thick tree trunk near the fire while Alden and Hannah began cleaning up.

"Where to start…" Hans scratched his peppered chin whiskers with a bony hand as he organized his thoughts.

"You know I'm from Cromlech, yes?"

Andy nodded.

"Well, what you may not know is Cromlech, Carta, and Oomaldee formed a troika of cooperation."

"A what?"

"A troika. The three nations pledged to act in cooperation with each other to care for the needs of all."

"When? Recently?"

"Oh no, the agreement happened ages ago. Let me think. It was during the reign of King Savant in Cromlech. I believe it was King Gerrard I on the throne in Oomaldee. I can't remember who ruled Carta at the time." Andy assumed a blank expression and Hans continued, "Cromlech's strength is in the healing arts, both physical and mental. With all its gold and silver mines, Carta's prowess is in wealth management, be it lending or finance. And Oomaldee's advantage is in its technology."

"And?"

"Well, Cromlech agreed to lend healers to the other two nations in exchange for banking support from Carta and technology and innovation from Oomaldee. We healers go in seven-year rotations. I came to Castle Avalon three years ago. Before that I served in the palace of the king of Cromlech, and my assignment before that also brought me to Oomaldee. In all, this is my fifth rotation."

"I had no idea. But what does that have to do with why you're out here?"

Hans smiled. "I received an urgent message from Mermin, courtesy of your friend Daisy off the whisper stream, that Princess Yara is alive." Hans's tone conveyed enthusiasm.

"Who's Princess Yara?"

Beaming, the healer continued, "If the message is true, Princess Yara may well be the queen of Cromlech."

"*May* be queen?"

"Abaddon attacked Cromlech almost three years ago, just after I started my rotation in Oomaldee. He and his army ransacked the castle, killing the royal family. They pillaged the farms where medicinal herbs were grown and decimated the institutions of learning. Anyone who refused to bow their knee and pledge allegiance to Abaddon was killed, or worse." Hans shuddered.

"I'm sorry."

Hans shook his head. "Although risky, I traveled back to see for myself if the reports were true. I nearly got caught, but luck favored me and I escaped notice. Just barely. I searched the castle ruins and came across some survivors who were in hiding. They confirmed my worst fears. I'd watched Princess Yara grow up for the past seven years. She was like a daughter to me." He swiped the back of his hand at the corner of an eye as he continued.

"With heavy heart, I returned to Oomaldee. So you'll understand how, when I heard news that the princess might be alive, I had to investigate." Hans's smile proved contagious, and Andy could not help but mirror his excitement. Alden and Hannah, who had sat down next to Andy after completing their chores, shared the moment.

"Hans was going to go by himself, but we convinced him he needed my super sensitivity," Hannah quipped.

"Yeah, and my awesomeness with the sword," added Alden, smiling.

"How could I resist?" Hans grinned.

"So where are you headed to find her?"

"I'm not exactly sure. The message Daisy replayed was that the princess had run into a herd of wild pegasi that started to attack her but then inexplicably stopped. When she collapsed, the pegasi read her thoughts and put word in the whisper stream that the princess of Cromlech needed help. Daisy heard the message and passed it on to Mermin who passed it on to me."

My dream! As Hans had been speaking, Andy's mind raced. He gasped, drawing curious looks.

"By any chance does Princess Yara have blonde hair?" Andy winced as he asked, and Hans's eyes grew large.

"How did you know?"

"I had a dream." Andy quickly summarized the highlights, or in this case the lowlights. "If the dream revealed what's happening, I think your princess is alive."

"Oh, how I hope you're right," Hans wished aloud.

"So where do we go to find her?" Andy reiterated.

"I thought we'd head toward the palace. Hopefully we'll find her on the way."

"But isn't that like searching for a needle in a haystack?"

Hans, Alden, and Hannah stared back blankly. Finally Alden asked, "Why would a needle be in a haystack?"

Andy chuckled. "It's an expression. It means to look for something that's nearly impossible to find."

"I'm open to other suggestions. Time is of the essence," Hans countered.

"Well, I can describe the landscape from my dream. Maybe that will help narrow things down," Andy offered.

"Yes," Hans agreed.

Andy shared and they planned. Their conversation devolved into catching up on all that had happened during the last year until yawns silenced the reunion. One of the soldiers offered up his bedroll for Andy's use. When Andy resisted, the man assured him there would always be a spare because one officer would be standing watch. Andy relented, and with that resolved, he curled up under the blanket, closed his eyes, and waited for dreams to claim him.

But before Andy navigated to the land of slumber, a voice sounding like Dad growled, "You're back."

Andy opened his eyes and looked around. Seven lumps lay unmoving under blankets around the fire. Snoring sounds sang about the clearing.

Eh-hreehmm, echoed in his thoughts.

Oh, it's you.

"Yes, it's me. I'm rather upset with you."

Andy rolled his eyes, wondering what charges his inneru could possibly level this time.

"Don't mock. The sanitarium just discharged me."

Sanitarium? What's that?

"A sanitarium is an institution for the recovery of health."

What happened?

"Do you remember the anxiety you suffered over whether to give the unicorn horn to the swirling sphere to save your mom, or to keep it and break the curse?"

Andy's mood turned serious. *How could I possibly forget? I was stupid to think I could save her.*

"Did you not hear me cry out? The pain was excruciating. You broke me and then left. I languished in agony for who knows how long until headquarters realized you had left this world again and sent an agent to find me. If not for them, who knows what would have happened to me…or what would have happened to you when you returned."

You've been recovering since I left? That's a whole year! How could your injuries have been that bad?

"Andy, you have no idea the power of your distress. I nearly died. Of course, that's better than some."

What do you mean?

"Some innerus suffer a fate worse than death."

Like?

"It's awful. I hate to think about it."

Oh, come on, what's the big secret?

After a long silence, Andy's inneru reluctantly divulged, "Some innerus are paralyzed, then used as channels through which their human's thoughts are broadcast over the whisper stream. They can't control what they share, let alone help their human modify inappropriate behavior."

How does that happen?

"Dark magic."

Andy's stomach flipped. *Does this have anything to do with Abaddon turning people?*

"I am not privy to the cause. All I know is this fate is happening to more and more innerus and we are powerless to stop it. I'd rather die."

Andy thought for several minutes before reengaging. *I'm sorry I hurt you. I had no idea.*

"You need to learn to listen to me. I only want what's best for you, Andy."

I know. Out of curiosity, what happens if an inneru dies?

"Its human dies too."

CHAPTER FIVE

Tricky Little Devil

"We need to move. Now!" ordered one of the officers, rousing Andy to consciousness. "There's an ogre headed this way."

The group dismantled the campsite and was headed into the foggy sunrise within minutes. Andy, Alden, Hannah, and Hans formed the middle of a wheel formation around which their five military companions walked in silence. Everyone hoped not to hear grunts or other indications of unwanted company. After some time, Andy heard running water and dared to hope for a quick rinse and some breakfast.

As if reading Andy's thoughts, one of the officers announced, "We'll follow the river until we exit ogre territory. It's not safe to stop until then."

Andy nodded even as his stomach objected.

"I've got some jerky," Alden offered. He extricated it from his pack and distributed it among the four of them as they walked.

"What are they eating?" Andy queried, motioning toward their escort as he bit down.

In response, the soldier to Andy's right slipped off his pack and mimicked Alden, distributing jerky to his fellows as they continued walking.

"We didn't introduce you to our guard, did we, Andy?" Hans realized.

Andy shook his head, chewing.

"That's Captain Baldric," Hans said, pointing to the man in the lead. He was of average build with blond hair bound in a ponytail extending well below his shoulders. He sported a green tunic and brown leggings, and a matched sword and dagger hung from either side of a belt that evidenced wear. Hearing his name, the officer turned and nodded.

"That's Sergeant Terric," Hans continued, indicating the soldier to his left, much of whose face was hidden under a full black mustache and beard. A gray tunic and black leggings covered this man's large, muscular frame, and he bore a spiked flail at his waist, the ball swinging with each step of his lumbering gait. *I wouldn't want to bump into him in a dark alley.*

Nodding at the soldier to Andy's right, Hans indicated, "And that's Sergeant Hammond."

Andy recognized him as the officer who insisted he use his bedroll last night. Andy waved and the youngish man responded with a nod and smile. Andy liked him immediately. His eyes were piercing gray and his face was square with a jawline that could chisel granite. Over the back of his brown tunic he carried a bow and quiver with an accompanying sword that extended from his belt.

"And of course you've made the acquaintance of Sergeant Ranulf." Hans grinned as he turned and indicated an officer dressed in a navy tunic who was following the group. The sturdily built man with burnt-orange hair suddenly became fascinated by something on the ground. Andy smiled at the soldier who had mistakenly roughed him up yesterday.

"Rounding out our escort is Sergeant Fulk," added Hans, nodding toward the other soldier at the rear. The man moved his lean, athletic body with confidence, as if daring danger to challenge. The axe and sword hanging at his side told Andy he was more than prepared to handle it.

Andy whispered, "Is it my imagination or are these guys…"

"Better trained," Alden quipped quietly.

"More heavily armed," Hannah added.

"No. It's not your imagination, Andy," interrupted Hans. "The cavalry and army have both enacted more rigorous training standards since last year. No taking chances with anyone's safety these days. The officers who accompanied us last time were not available, so Regent Bellum selected these men."

Andy nodded.

As morning wore on, the fog thinned a bit and Andy glimpsed a golden hue radiating off a tall mountain in the distance to his left. While the fog obscured its summit, Andy speculated he knew its identity.

"Yes, that's Mount Mur Eyah. Pretty isn't it?" Hans read his thoughts.

"The way the sun shines off it makes it look like gold."

"Yes, that it does. We won't be headed near it though. It's not safe."

"What do you mean?"

"Centaurs make their home in and around that mountain. While they're wise, they can also be temperamental and dangerous."

"More dangerous than ogres?"

Hans nodded.

They stopped to rest briefly late in the morning. As Andy sat on a log, he noticed the path ahead rose in elevation, transitioning from the flat, grassy prairie they had been traversing. The trees also became denser. It reminded him of the trolls' territory he had navigated a year ago.

"We're nearly out of the ogres' region. There's a narrow tributary up a ways that will lead us into gnome country," Captain Baldric informed as they resumed their trek. Then, looking squarely at Andy he added, "Prince Andrew, that's where you can have a good long soak."

"THANK YOU!" Andy's enthusiastic response drew chuckles from all.

The sun cast long rays by the time the company scaled the mountain marking the northern boundary of gnome territory. To say the climb up and over the many mountains in their path had been taxing would be a gross understatement. Nearly every muscle in Andy's body ached, so when Captain Baldric commanded they set up camp, Andy did not take another step but plopped down in the path, much to their escorts' amusement.

"Gotta toughen you up," Sergeant Fulk kidded. The man's energy even after the grueling day-long hike revealed the depth of his conditioning, and Andy understood why he exuded such confidence.

Hans, Hannah, and Alden had the dignity to collapse quietly under a copse of nearby trees, but they looked equally spent.

Sergeant Hammond approached Andy several minutes later and inquired, "Interested in that soak the captain promised?"

"Show me the way," Andy replied, rising with a significant smile.

The sergeant led Andy around several thickets and through groupings of mature trees. The sound of gurgling water grew louder with each step. Finally, the officer stopped on the bank of a river that spanned no less than fifteen feet. In front of them flowed a small waterfall, the clear liquid ambling down the terrain and forming a deep pool.

"Perfect," Andy pronounced, receiving a satisfied smile in response.

"I'll stand guard not far away. If you need anything, just holler." With that the soldier disappeared into the trees, leaving Andy to cleaner pursuits.

After glancing about, he peeled every stitch of his muddy clothes off and, filthy apparel in hand, cautiously approached the water, avoiding sharp stones that lined the bank. His toe confirmed that the water, while a tad chilly, was not unpleasant. He laid his clothes on the bank and, after a brief hesitation, added the pouch to the top of the pile before slipping in.

A gratified "*Ahhh*" escaped. *Showers at home don't compare.*

Andy splashed, whooped, and hollered for several minutes. Finally he stopped and focused his attention on removing every speck of foul-smelling goo from his body. He scrubbed until he was satisfied that his cleanliness would pass even Dad's standards. His energy refreshed and his hair smelling better, he dove down one last time, resurfaced, and vigorously shook his head, spraying water everywhere. After wiping his eyes, he headed for the bank to retrieve his clothes for washing. He quickly discovered a small problem, however. As he scanned the shore, he did not see his dirty jeans, soiled T-shirt, muddy socks, brown underwear, caked sneakers, or pouch. Nothing.

Andy scanned the area. *What happened? Am I going crazy?*

With no other choice, he sat back down in the river and yelled, "Sergeant Hammond!"

The officer quickly appeared. "What's wrong?"

"I can't find my clothes."

"Excuse me?"

"I left them on the bank right there, but they're gone!" Andy pointed to a spot five feet away from where his protector stood.

The man's expression turned deadly serious. The soldier scanned the surrounding area, then commanded, "Wait there." He unsheathed his sword and stealthily vanished into the nearby copse of trees. All was eerily quiet for several minutes. Andy's fingers had shriveled and looked like prunes. With no clothes, he did not want to parade on shore, but chills began snaking up his spine and rippling across his back. Dusk threatened to blanket the area.

Several minutes later, as he was on the verge of venturing ashore despite the consequences, Andy heard scuffling from the trees and Sergeant Hammond emerged dragging a creature resembling Merk, the gnome at Castle Avalon. The officer held the man in an iron grip at swordpoint. The roundish being stood no taller than Andy, had a full brown beard, and wore a forest green tunic and gray leggings with their feet cut off, from which extended abnormally hairy pigeon-toed appendages. His head showed signs of balding, and in his chubby hands he carried Andy's still-filthy clothes.

"Let me go!" the little man squirmed.

"Andy, this gnome swiped your clothes…as a joke. What would you like to do with him?"

"A joke?"

The gnome stopped thrashing and replied with big eyes, "I thought it would be funny to see you negotiate the forest in nothing but your…"

"Enough!" commanded the sergeant.

"Well, I'm cold," Andy replied, his teeth chattering.

Sergeant Hammond nodded, then commanded the gnome, "Remove your tunic. Now."

The little man complied with a grin, handing the sergeant his garment, which he then laid on the bank. The two turned, allowing Andy to exit the river and cover himself. *When did this guy last take a bath?* Andy wondered as the stench of the new covering assaulted his nostrils. *Well, at least I'm covered.*

"I think he should wash my clothes," Andy suggested, a chill rocking his body as he put his pouch over his head.

"Very well," Sergeant Hammond agreed.

The gnome plodded knee-deep into the river, stopping near a boulder. He placed Andy's soiled clothes on top, pulled the black T-shirt out, and set to work doing as Andy requested. "Mighty strange clothes you got here."

"Silence," the sergeant ordered, standing with his sword still pointed at the gnome's neck to keep him focused.

The small man diligently scrubbed each article, but every few minutes he paused and looked about.

"What's he keep looking for?" Andy asked himself aloud, absently reaching for Methuselah. The hilt instantly materialized and the blade extended, easing his anxiety only a little.

The gnome gasped at the sight, then smiled and resumed work.

Several minutes later noises sounded behind him. *Crunch. Crack. Thump. Creeeeak.* Andy bolted up and assumed a ready position as his heart began to race. Seconds later a black tunic and gray leggings emerged from the dense trees as Sergeant Terric appeared, spiked flail in hand.

Andy sighed and retracted Methuselah's blade.

The officer lumbered to the riverbank and stated the obvious, "There you are."

No kidding, Sherlock, Andy thought, but held his thoughts in check, instead announcing, "You scared me."

"What happened? When you didn't return, we got worried. I volunteered to scout the area."

The gnome chuckled.

"Back to work," Sergeant Hammond commanded.

"As you wish," the man replied, the corners of his mouth rising.

Sergeant Hammond filled his compatriot in as the gnome finished. They retreated to shore, clean laundry in hand, and the little man slumped on the bank, but not before looking around again.

What IS he looking for?

"I'd like to know how he slipped past me," Sergeant Hammond groused. "I never let my guard down, but I didn't hear a thing. That worries me."

"What'll we do with him?" Sergeant Terric growled.

Wait a minute! Gnomes love practical jokes. The stray thought flitted across Andy's brain. *What would Merk do in a situation like this?*

Ha ha ha ha! Andy forced a laugh he hoped sounded authentic, drawing the others' attention. He doubled over, feigning a belly laugh. Bona fide chuckles quickly overwhelmed Andy and spread to the others, morphing into bursts of laughter from the sergeants. The gnome could control his mischief no longer and he howled, rolling from his back to his side in an unrestrained fit.

"That…that was funny," Andy spit out between snorts.

Stomachs sore, the officers stared at Andy once they recovered. Andy held up a hand. "Our friend has something to tell us."

Puzzled expressions turned to the small man righting himself on the bank and still wearing a broad grin. "I know when I'm bested," he chuckled. "You're smart," he added, nodding at Andy. "Name's Gelon. I'm pleased to make your acquaintance. I spotted you bathing in the stream with your clothes on shore unattended and just couldn't help myself."

Sergeant Hammond opened his mouth and raised a finger.

Gelon looked at the objector. "You didn't stand a chance. We gnomes have doors hidden everywhere—under rocks, in the trunks of trees, in clumps of bushes. When you looked the other way, I popped up five steps away from the pile of clothes and had off with them."

"So why'd you show yourself?" the sergeant demanded.

"There was more fun to be had, of course."

"Yeah, first you made me panic when you stole my clothes, and then you freaked me out when you kept looking around like you were expecting something," Andy added.

"The perfect prank is personalized for each victim," Gelon added, flicking his eyebrows mischievously.

This guy's a master at the art of practical jokes. I can learn a few things. Andy grinned.

Dusk was fading into blackness as the four approached their campsite. *Squish, squirch, squish, squirch,* broadcast Andy's sneakers.

I hope there are no enemies about. They'll hear me for sure.

Andy glimpsed a roaring fire through the trees and smelled delicious aromas. Captain Baldric intercepted the group fifty yards out, but as soon as he realized who they were, he provided an escort the rest of the way before returning to guard duty.

"Oh, Andy! We were worried," Hannah exclaimed upon seeing him.

"We ran into someone I'd like you to meet. This is Gelon. I guess you could call him the welcoming committee."

"I'm glad to see you returned the prince in one piece," Hans joked.

The gnome's eyes grew large and he mumbled something under his breath, but Andy could not make it out.

Hans, Hannah, and Alden gathered around and Andy made introductions. The gnome paused only a second as he caught sight of Alden's neon green hair.

"You hail from Carta?"

"Yes."

"Mighty pleased to meet you! I've always wanted to visit Carta and see the land's gold and silver mines. They're legendary."

Alden smiled.

As they ate, Andy recounted all that happened at the river, receiving a variety of exclamations and laughter. By the time dinner ended, Andy's clothes had dried, thanks to the heat of the fire, and he changed back into what was familiar, although his shoes still announced his every step. The gnome shook his head at seeing Andy's attire but refrained from comment.

"It's not every day I get to play tricks on royalty," Gelon said after putting his tunic back on. "I'd like to give you something to remember me by." He winked as he said it, drawing a round of chuckles. The gnome scrounged in a pouch that hung about his neck, finally extricating an oval-shaped stone. He handed it to Andy who held it up in the firelight. It was highly polished and glowed red.

"It reminds me of the rubies the dwarfs mine," Andy commented. "It's beautiful. Thank you." Andy passed it around for the others to inspect.

"It came from a dwarf mine. I cut and polished it myself."

"Wow, you created this?" Alden remarked, holding the stone up to the firelight once more.

"That I did. We gnomes have a reputation for being the best gem cutters around." Gelon puffed out his chest. "We count dwarfs as our greatest friends and allies, not surprising considering how we depend on each other. I find cutting stones fascinating. One false move and you can turn a precious gem into a worthless paperweight."

"So you finish the stones the dwarfs mine?" Hannah clarified.

"Many of us, yes. Others spend their time caring for the animals of the forest."

Alden's eyes lit up and he questioned, "What do you mean?"

"Back at the beginning of the gnomes, our fathers gave us responsibility to find and care for wounded and dying animals. If we come across an animal caught in a trap, we free it. If we discover a farm animal that has been neglected, or if the farmer is too poor to care for it, we adopt it."

"That's awesome!" Alden exclaimed.

Hans smiled at his enthusiasm and added, "I had no idea. I bet you have many friends among the forest animals."

"True. If a gnome is in trouble, forest creatures always come to help. Makes for a great relationship."

"Do you know Merk?" Hannah questioned, changing the subject.

"Of course! How is he?"

"He is well. He certainly keeps things lively," Hans chuckled. The others shared an understanding laugh.

"So when you're not cutting gems or caring for animals, what do you like to do?" Andy asked.

Gelon smiled. "We love to tell stories."

"Would you tell us one of your favorites?" Alden begged.

Everyone else nodded encouragement.

"Well, if you insist," Gelon relented with a chuckle. "I'll warn you though, you may find it a bit scary." The gnome's eyes twinkled and he winked at Alden who raised an eyebrow.

Despite the presence of Sergeants Terric, Ranulf, Hammond, and Fulk about the campsite, Hannah squirmed and Alden moved his hand to cover hers. Andy watched in his periphery and tried to remain expressionless, though his thoughts were far from that; he felt a fluttering sensation in his stomach. Seated across the fire on a log next to Gelon, Hans let a corner of his mouth rise.

"Long ago, before my fathers and their fathers," Gelon began, "lived the lord of the plains. His white body stood twenty hands high at the shoulder and he had piercing dark blue eyes. He bore the tail of a lion, and a single jet-black corkscrew horn jutted from his forehead. Exceedingly swift and powerful, the beast had no equal and feared neither gnome nor dwarf. It had a taste for blood, and it was so ferocious and territorial that it drove all living beings from its domain…except one."

Andy thought he heard a low guttural rumbling. He peered into the thick forest surrounding them but saw nothing in the dark. Judging from the officers craning their necks about, they heard it too.

The gnome sat forward on the log like a magician casting a spell and waited in silence, drawing everyone's attention back. "The ring dove he did not drive away. *Hooh-hrooo. Hooh-hrooo*, it would coo, enchanting the mighty beast. So entranced was the creature that it lived below the grove of trees the ring dove inhabited, aggressively protecting the bird from all harm."

Andy heard more indistinct rumblings. *That's not the bellicose.* The rolling sounds grew nearer and the officers gripped their weapons. Methuselah appeared in Andy's hand but did not extend.

Again Gelon paused. "Then one day, a gnome on a journey passed nearby and heard the melodic warbles, compelling him to discover their source. Feeling unlike his usual self, he put aside all wariness and made his way through dense undergrowth and over fallen debris. He severed overgrown vines with his bare hands and endured the assault of abundant prickered plants tearing at his clothes, but nothing stopped him. At last he came upon a ring dove laying in the path. A sliver of blood trickled from its back, down its feathers."

Another rumble sounded and Hannah squeaked, "Did you hear that?"

Alden shot a glance at Andy.

"The beast appeared just as the gnome made the discovery, and seeing the injured dove, it charged!"

Andy looked back into the forest. A pair of fast-approaching, dark-blue eyes met his gaze, and chaos erupted.

CHAPTER SIX

In a Fix

Andy leapt to his feet and Methuselah extended. Alden and Hannah quickly fell in with him, preparing to engage. Hearing the commotion as he patrolled, Captain Baldric joined the officers as they raced to defend, arriving just as the giant beast emerged from the forest.

That looks like the thing Abaddon transformed into last time!

The massive beast lowered its black corkscrew horn and charged straight for the defenders. Andy waited until the creature was but three feet away and then swung. The blade passed through the creature, giving no resistance. *What?* From the exclamations of his companions, they experienced a similar result.

The beast circled back, readying a second charge.

And then Andy saw it. Gelon stood at the edge of the clearing, grinning, with Hans at his side looking befuddled. Andy lowered Methuselah.

A cheer went up from the surrounding woods and the giant white adversary evaporated. More than a dozen jovial gnomes streamed into the clearing, clapping and patting each other on the back.

Andy and the others exhaled. "What was that thing?"

"A karkadann," Hans informed, shaking his head.

The laughter of their unexpected company transformed into introductions. "Line up please!" the master prankster yelled above the din. Once the donsy of gnomes had arranged themselves—no small task because they kept joking around and poking each other—Gelon took a deep breath and began rattling off names: "Bixi, Trixie, Jubie, Jinxie, Nibert, Krankle, Tansi, Leib, Girvin, Malin, Loman, Kern, Hewitt, Hampton, Keegan, Gern." Each gnome stepped forward as his name was called, but with so many, Andy smiled politely and hoped no one would quiz him. From a quick check of Hans, Alden, and Hannah, who all wore plastic smiles, Andy speculated they pursued a similar strategy.

"Will you show us how you did that?" Alden begged.

"A magician never tells his secrets," Gelon replied, winking."Well, that was impressive." Alden's eyes danced, and Andy speculated Merk might be on the receiving end of something similar in the not-too-distant future.

"Time for our exit!" Gelon shouted across the crowded campsite.

The gnomes instantly fell silent, formed a circle around their guests, and began humming a slow, solemn melody. After several bars, Gern began harmonizing in a low octave. While the words were in a language Andy had never heard before, they resonated deeply within him—sincerity, fidelity, warmth, brotherhood. These gnomes knew how to have fun, but they also had a much deeper side.

Andy chanced a glance at the company. Hannah held her hands to her cheeks. Alden's head turned slowly, studying each member of the choir. Hans's eyes sparkled in the firelight. The officers were a mix of reactions: they appeared uncertain whether to let their guard down and enjoy themselves or maintain the stoic, protective stance duty demanded.

When the tune ended, Andy exhaled a breath he was unaware he held.

All the gnomes except Gelon bowed, turned, and walked slowly into the forest. "The ballad of blessing," he explained. "Whenever far from home, wherever your travels take you, know you now share a bond with the gnomes who will always extend a hand to help a brother—or sister."

"You're most kind," Hans acknowledged. "The sentiment is mutual."

"As long as you don't play more tricks on us," Hannah commented, her frown sparking a round of chuckles.

"Prince Andrew, that fire ruby will dispel hatred and discord and will preserve its bearer from false friendships. I think you may find good use for it."

Andy raised the stone up to the firelight once more, appreciating its beauty. A question popped into his mind and he opened his mouth to ask, but the gnome cut him off. "Seek not to know but to learn...at least for now."

He sounds like the note in the gold envelope. Speaking of which, we need to discuss the next clue.

"I wish you'd reconsider staying with us for a time, but I understand your need for haste," Gelon was saying as Andy's focus returned. The gnome grasped Hans's hand, then repeated the gesture with Alden and Hannah, and Andy reciprocated when his turn arrived.

"Prosperous travels," the gnome bid as he turned, waved, and vanished into the darkness.

Hannah and Alden yawned, to which Hans replied, "I agree. It's late. Let's all turn in."

While Andy would have liked to discuss the next clue, he knew it would keep. He settled down under a borrowed blanket not far from the fire and dreams soon carried him away.

Remembering the picture Gelon had painted of the wounded ringdove in the path, Andy's brain recalled seeing Imogenia in dove form at that abandoned house, talking with Abaddon who kept shifting his shape. She had been wounded and a trickle of blood dripped from her back, down her pure white feathers.

Now she stood talking with her parents in a stone-walled room. The place looked familiar, like Castle Avalon, though he knew he had never ventured to this particular space within the palace.

"Yes, I'm aware the boy has returned," her father asserted, floating over to join his queen on a couch near the fireplace.

How would they know I'm back?

"I still don't understand why you deceived him the way you did the last time he was here."

"I'd rather not talk about it," Imogenia replied sharply, sitting down on the facing sofa.

"I know, but I think you need to, for your own sake." The king glanced at his wife then back toward their daughter. "Do you remember the concern I expressed when you first mentioned punishing Kaysan?"

Imogenia nodded. "You said hate can change people. You didn't want it to consume me and change me."

"Yes."

Imogenia studied her silvery hands for a time before looking up and replying, "Perhaps my actions were a bit extreme."

"A bit, dear? You mimicked the boy's mother…" the queen chimed in.

Imogenia held up her hands. "Okay, I concede. I acted in a manner unbefitting the dignity of royalty...but I don't want the curse broken."

"I understand, but the daughter I know would never have considered stooping to such treachery. Honey, your hatred has changed you," the king observed.

Andy studied Imogenia, anticipating a fiery reaction. He was surprised when she nodded then added, "I'll admit, what I did has weighed on me. I surprised myself."

"I'm the one you have issue with," the king interjected.

Imogenia raised a silvery eyebrow.

"I'm the one who wants to break the curse…for the sake of my subjects. I stated that at the beginning. The boy is just the messenger. Leave him be."

"But that's just it. I can't leave him alone. If he succeeds, Kaysan's punishment will be over and I'm still not convinced he's truly sorry for killing me."

The three exchanged frowns.

"Then we are at an impasse," the king concluded.

"Imogenia, please consider your father's admonition. I fear for you."

The castle room faded and Andy now found himself crouching at the mouth of a cave. Had he not been kneeling, his head would have hit the ceiling. Night had fallen and the moon peeking between shifting clouds cast slow-moving shadows on the grassy plain before him. Dim firelight danced on the stone wall behind. He reached for Methuselah but discovered his companion absent.

Good thing I'm dreaming.

He crept around the bend and meandered along a corridor between fallen boulders. Rock slabs lay at sharp angles forming a peaked roof through which he could occasionally glimpse moonlight. The firelight grew brighter as he continued, and he finally emerged into a somewhat larger space that permitted him to stand erect. He found a girl with long blonde hair seated cross-legged before the fire. After a time, she stood and retrieved another log for the hungry flames. She wore the same filthy yellow dress he had seen the first time she entered his dreams. Her ratty white headscarf lay neatly folded nearby, next to a stick fashioned into a crude dagger. She sat back down and stared into the flames for several minutes. Just as Andy grew bored, the girl's form began to shake, tiny tremors at first that grew into quaking. She brought an arm up and wiped her eyes.

"Mom. Dad. I miss you so much."

Tears always made Andy feel uneasy, and he scanned the cave for something to comfort the girl, to no avail. After several minutes his dreams finally faded to nothingness and he slumbered.

With Hans feeling time was of the essence, the group set out at dawn in a thicker-than-usual fog. Andy's imagination began running wild. Every creak of the trees, every crunch of rocks underfoot, every whistle or hoot nearby intensified his unease.

Squish, squirch, squirch, squish, sang Andy's sneakers.

Imogenia knows I'm back. Will the bellicose know, too?

Andy fingered the bark and vine holster that Hannah and Alden had woven for Methuselah the night before and that now hung from a belt loop. To lessen some of his uneasiness, Andy recounted his dream about the princess to his companions. Hans welcomed the news and hastened the group's pace.

Mid-morning found the nine scaling yet another tall mountain. Andy held his side trying to staunch a persistent stitch.

"Take deeper breaths," Hans instructed while walking next to Andy, whose nearly dry sneakers were now content to fulfill their duty in silence.

As they crested the summit, Alden called out from behind, "Look."

Everyone paused and Andy eyed a welcome sight. More forested mountains stood as imposing obstacles in their path, but the thick mist ended abruptly in a towering wall. Unencumbered sunshine bathed the sight in clarity, and Andy felt his unease diminish. Smiles broke out on everyone's faces.

"We've reached the border of Oomaldee and Cromlech," Andy deduced, remembering the clear skies he and Alden had experienced when they traveled into Hadession on their way to the dragon's lair.

"That's correct," Hans confirmed.

More trudging up and down mountains consumed the rest of the day, but by late afternoon, as shadows grew long, the last peak rose behind them and rolling hills and grassy plains spread before.

"We'll camp here tonight," Captain Baldric announced. "Before us lies the territory of the karkadann, and I, for one, don't care to meet one of those in the dark."

No one objected.

The first rays of warm sunlight roused Andy the following morning, and in no time the nine had packed up camp. Before they ventured forth the captain warned, "We need to remain silent as we cross the territory of the karkadann lest we provoke them. As our gnome friends so aptly showed us, angering one of these beasts is something to be avoided at all cost."

Andy, Alden, and Hannah shared looks. Hans stood stoically, expressionless. It seemed he already knew.

"Any questions?" When no one had any, the captain finished, "Then let's move out."

Glad my sneakers are dry.

Waist-high tufts of wild grasses sparsely adorned the rolling ground they traversed. Compared to the mountains towering behind, the walk proved easy and they covered the area with haste. They encountered several copses of trees randomly clustering the area. *Hooh-hrooo, hooh-hrooo* sounded from many of these, and the officers pointed and gestured the company around, giving each area a wide berth. Each time Andy squinted, trying to make out any large white beasts that might linger in the surrounding foliage and exhaling when he located none.

By late afternoon, Captain Baldric pointed out the beginning of a series of rock outcroppings jutting up haphazardly in the distance and marking the end of karkadann territory. The group sighed collectively, hurrying their pace to clear the area by nightfall.

As they wound a wide path around one of the final groves of trees, in the open plain rested a ring dove. *Hooh-hrooo. Hooh-hrooo.* From this distance, all could see a reddish-brown substance streaking the bird's limply hanging outstretched wing. Alden crept closer despite cautioning gestures from Sergeants Fulk and Ranulf. Hannah watched, grimacing. Andy scanned the area as his best friend knelt and spoke softly to the creature. Alden stroked the dove, then carefully picked it and approached the group.

"It's injured," Alden whispered. "We need to splint its wing."

Alden knelt and Hans joined him. Then Hans whispered, "I think you can handle this one on your own."

What's that supposed to mean?

Alden removed his backpack and located materials suitable for the task. He cleaned the wound with water from his canteen while Hans tore several strips of material from a spare tunic and handed them to his apprentice.

As treatment proceeded, the officers turned their backs to the medics, their expressions deadly serious. Everyone else scoured the surrounding area, hoping.

Alden carefully wound the material around the dove's wing, then secured it against the bird's body with several more loops, leaving the uninjured wing free.

"Looks good," Hans whispered, receiving a smile from Alden.

Hooh-hrooo. Hooh-hrooo. The ring dove cooed as Alden finished doctoring.

"Okay, put it back," Captain Baldric requested.

"If that bird is to mend, it can't just be left here," Hans cautioned.

"Are you saying we have to bring it with us?" the captain questioned.

Hans and Alden nodded.

Alden picked up the bird and settled it on his shoulder, eliciting more coos.

"This is a bad idea, Alden," Hannah objected, glancing about.

No sooner had the words crossed her lips than the group felt the ground ripple under their feet. Everyone looked quickly about. Another stronger tremor shook the ground seconds later, and the company, eyes wide, drew their weapons and assumed ready positions.

Hooh-hrooo. Hooh-hrooo.

"Shhh…" Alden encouraged his companion.

An even stronger quake rattled everyone.

Andy spotted the great white beast first and pointed. The hulking animal lumbered forward, eyeing its adversary. Fifty yards. Twenty-five yards. Ten yards. It spotted the ring dove and stopped.

Maybe we'll get lucky and it won't attack? Andy hoped.

The karkadann scratched the ground with a front hoof, stirring up dust.

Then again, we may not be that lucky.

It raised its head and bellowed loudly, then lowered its jet-black corkscrew horn and charged.

We're gonna die for that bird!

Seven yards.

Terwit terwoo, oop-oop-oop, sounded from Alden's shoulder. *Terwit terwoo, oop-oop-oop.*

Five yards.

Weapons ready.

Terwit terwoo, oop-oop-oop.

The beast screeched to a halt two yards in front of Alden and snorted.

No one moved.

The karkadann and ring dove glared at each other. Time stopped. No one flinched.

Finally, the white monster shook its head and pawed the ground once before turning and ambling off.

No one so much as shifted until the creature vanished from sight.

Hooh-hrooo. The bird broke the spell, and one and all sighed with relief. Without thinking, Andy grabbed and embraced Hannah who had weathered the storm beside him. Hannah blushed and stepped away, causing Andy to realize what he had done and his cheeks to flush. Hans stepped close and squeezed Andy's arm, providing a welcome escape to the awkwardness as Alden stepped forward, the patient still perched on his shoulder.

"Perhaps you should be a bit more selective in the animals you choose to help," Hannah admonished.

"Are you suggesting we should have left this bird to die?"

Hannah did not respond.

"I'd do the same again," Alden asserted. "I'm not going to stand by and watch an animal suffer when I can do something about it."

Andy wrinkled his brow. *I've never heard Alden so defensive.*

"You put the whole company, not to mention our quest to find Princess Yara, in danger," Hannah huffed as she turned and strode off.

Alden rolled his eyes and sulked off in the opposite direction.

"A lovers' quarrel," quipped Hans, smiling.

Andy was not going to touch that comment, so instead he remarked, "That was close, too close. I agree with Hannah, he acted recklessly." Andy chose not to add "and you encouraged him," although his brain screamed it.

"Seldom do we consider the impact on others of things we are most passionate about. Personally, I'm not surprised Alden acted as he did."

"Really?"

"Over the past year Alden has taken quite an interest in learning how to mend wounded animals. I've been showing him a thing or two."

"Really?"

Hans nodded, adding, "He's got a knack for it, too."

That night, Andy sat down next to Alden on a log near the fire as Hannah took her turn at preparing dinner. Hans put himself to use helping her.

"What happened earlier? Why'd you do that?" Andy queried.

Alden stroked his patient who sat in his lap. "What, save this dove?"

"Yeah."

Alden frowned. "Look, I'm sorry I put us all at risk. I didn't mean to. It's just that when I saw it lying helpless in the road…I couldn't leave it there to die."

Andy did not respond, so Alden continued, "I felt like we stumbled upon this bird for a reason, and I knew I could help it. I won't ignore an animal in pain. It's not right."

Andy heard the passion in his friend's voice. "I knew you cared for animals…"

"I think it all started back when I rescued Optimistic from an early end just because she was born too small."

Andy remembered Alden telling him how the cavalry planned to put her down because she was a runt. His pegasus was certainly no runt any longer.

"Then, when we rescued Daisy, it was so cool when the cavalry and I flew with her to her new home. It felt really good to help her." Alden smiled, remembering.

"I think I'd been pulled back home before then," Andy recalled.

Alden nodded. "Then I had the opportunity to rescue that kappa from the steel trap it got its foot stuck in."

Andy remembered the situation and how he had felt. "I thought the kappas would attack, but you sensed something different." His friend had extricated the creature, and as a reward, the kappas later helped save them from the sea monsters.

"When we removed Jada's and Naria's horns, I felt so helpless. While you steered the troll away from the clearing, Hannah and I headed back to protect them. They were so weak. I'll never forget it." Alden sighed. "After that, I asked Hans to teach me how to mend wounds. He's started showing me some medicines now, too."

Andy smiled. "Well, I think you'll make a good veterinarian."

"A what?"

"A veterinarian."

"What's that?"

"A healer who treats injured animals."

"Oh. Hans just calls me an animal healer."

"Well, then you'll make a good animal healer."

Hooh-hrooo.

The boys laughed and Andy added, "Looks like your patient agrees."

"I think I'll call him Calum."

Andy smiled, but Hannah's frequent glances and glowers had not escaped his notice as they talked.

CHAPTER SEVEN

Hungry Grass

Hannah's pout persisted the next morning, and she walked by herself behind Hans, Andy, Alden, and Calum, refusing to talk about the matter vexing her. Andy had tried engaging her in conversation, but since he had implicated himself around the campfire the previous evening by talking to Alden, he too had earned the silent treatment.

Hannah's mood contrasted sharply from the rest of the company. Between clear skies and no karkadann threats, Sergeant Fulk began whistling. The other officers picked up the tune and added harmony to his melody. Hans, Andy, and Alden smiled, then cracked up when the dove cooed *hooh-hrooo* in time.

"I didn't know your bird had rhythm," Captain Baldric joked.

"And I didn't know you all were so musical," Andy kidded back.

"One of our many hidden talents," Sergeant Hammond jested, bowing.

"We'll have to have you perform at the next dance my father hosts."

Everyone but Hannah laughed.

They stopped for rest and a midday meal several hours later.

We need to discuss the next clue.

But when conversation returned to the joking of the gnomes, the thought evaporated.

The land began to gradually change as they set off. The scattered clumps of waist-high grasses gave way to a more densely populated meadow. From each blade of grass hung spikelets that reminded Andy of wheat except the grains were white.

Several paces into the new growth, Andy began feeling… uncomfortable. Several more steps and his stomach began grumbling.

I just ate, how can I be hungry?

Andy took several more steps and a rapidly growing stomachache made its presence known. Andy reached to massage his belly and looked at his companions. Alden held his stomach and wore a pained expression, and Hans, while still stoic, was grimacing. Andy glanced back at Hannah.

"What are you looking at?" she snapped.

Andy raised an eyebrow as Hans looked back, sharing Andy's surprise.

As Alden turned to see what the problem was, Captain Baldric, who led the company, raised a hand motioning everyone to stop. Hans, Andy, Alden, and Hannah approached while the other officers held their positions, scanning the area. When the four reached the captain, Hannah followed the officer's downward gaze and gasped. A man lay on his back, frozen, with eyes open, grasping his stomach. Captain Baldric felt for a pulse but shook his head a minute later.

"What do you suppose happened?" Alden queried, still holding his stomach.

"No idea," the captain replied, looking for signs of a scuffle.

"Well, we can't just leave him there," Hannah snipped.

"What's wrong with you?" Alden questioned indelicately. "Look, I know you're upset with me about what I did yesterday, but that's no reason to take it out on everyone."

The question jolted Hannah, and a puzzled expression coursed across her face. After a minute of consideration, she finally replied, "I'm sorry. I get crabby when I'm hungry. I know we just ate, but I'm starving."

"Me too!" Andy exclaimed.

"Me three," quipped Alden, frowning and rubbing his stomach.

The other four soldiers made to join the group, but Sergeants Ranulf and Hammond stopped short and called, "Captain, you're going to want to see this."

The captain and the rest of the company approached. Another man lay in a fetal position on his side, eyes wide.

"He's dead," Sergeant Ranulf announced.

"I don't know what happened to these guys, but I've *got* to eat!" Hannah declared. With that, she took two steps and sat. "I could eat a karkadann!" she exclaimed as she opened her pack, grabbed the first edible bits she found, and began gobbling them down.

Hans wrinkled his forehead and rubbed his pepper-stubbled chin.

Andy met Alden's eyes, chuckled, and nodded toward Hannah, unsure what to make of her unusual behavior.

Ummm. Mmmm. Ummm. Hannah murmured as she stuffed her mouth, barely chewing. She gagged, coughed violently, then continued wolfing down food.

"Don't forget to breathe," Andy joked. *This is crazy! What's she doing?*

While Andy felt famished, he held himself in check. A glance at Alden and the others told him they felt more than a little hungry as well.

"Should we all eat?" Andy threw out the question.

The inquiry seemed to provide Hans with the missing piece to his quandary, for his curious expression shifted to deadly seriousness as he matter-of-factly declared, "No. We need to move. Now."

"But what about the dead guys?" Alden questioned.

"Leave them. If we don't move, we'll be like them very soon. I'll explain once we're clear of the hungry grass."

"Hungry grass?" Andy asked.

Hans shook his head and waved vigorously. "Get Hannah. Let's go."

Alden approached and urged, "Come on Hannah, we need to go."

Ummm. Mmmm. Ummm, came her oblivious reply.

"We can't wait!" Hans admonished, his pitch rising.

Sergeant Terric approached, bent and picked Hannah up, tossing her over his beefy shoulder. She did not resist other than to exclaim, "Hey, I need my food!"

"I've got it!" Alden replied, sending Andy a worried look.

In no time Andy had a stitch to accompany his hunger pangs, for the pace Hans set proved to be a vigorous run.

"I need food!" Hannah yelled several times, squirming. Andy saw the sergeant clench his jaw, tighten his grip around Hannah's waist, and assume a laser focus on what lay ahead.

I hate running! I've got to eat! Andy's thoughts ping-ponged as he clutched his side.

"You can do this," Dad's voice sounded in his head. "Hans would not have insisted for no reason."

Andy sucked in a deep breath, the pain in his side sharper than ever. He stared at the passing ground, unable to look around. Step. Step. Step.

I need to eat! I'm going to pass out! Oh, my side kills!

Step. Step. Step. Step.

"Five hundred yards!" Captain Baldric gasped.

"I need food!" Hannah protested somewhere nearby.

Step. Step. Step. Step.

I'm gonna die! I need to eat!

"You can do it!" Andy's inneru encouraged above the din.

"Two hundred yards!"

Step. Step. Step. Step.

Another deep breath. *My side!*

Andy lunged clear of the dense grass, barely missing Alden who sprawled on the ground with Calum standing at attention on his undulating chest. Captain Baldric stood bent over, hands on his knees, panting. Sergeants Ranulf and Hammond paced, hands on hips, sucking air into their hungry lungs. Sergeant Terric crumpled to the ground, setting Hannah down gently, then rolled to his back, eyes closed, chest heaving. Sergeant Fulk stopped, barely winded, and Hans slid off his piggy-back ride.

After Andy's stitch finally let go, he sat up. Hannah sat where the sergeant had dropped her, wiping remnants of food from around her mouth. Her expression revealed confusion.

"Hans, can you please explain what just happened?" Andy requested.

Hans stood and surveyed his audience, then asked, "Anyone starving?"

The sudden absence of hunger pangs dawned on them all.

"But…" Andy began.

Hans raised his hands. "Hungry grass is also known as fairy grass. It is said fairies plant the grass after cursing it. Anyone walking in it is doomed to perpetual and insatiable hunger. I had heard tales of such grass in Cromlech but had never experienced it until now. We were lucky to escape."

The congregation on the ground furrowed their brows and Andy voiced his disbelief. "Hans, that sounds kind of, I don't know…"

"Out there?" Hans finished the sentence.

"Yeah."

"I have to say, I didn't believe it either, until now. When we happened upon the first traveler, I didn't think much of it. But when Hannah started complaining of intense hunger and everyone else echoed her sentiment, it got me thinking. Then, when we came upon the second traveler, I knew we were in trouble. I went with my hunch."

"Well, I'm glad you did," Captain Baldric agreed.

"I'm still not sure I'm right, but I'd rather be safe than sorry."

"Hear, hear," Sergeant Terric echoed.

"So why did Hannah react…like that?" Alden questioned, petting Calum.

Hannah squirmed, studying the ground.

"No need to be ashamed, Hannah," Hans encouraged. "You were actually the key to my figuring it out."

"Me?" she questioned, turning her gaze.

He nodded, then added, "We all know you have a special gift, the ability to sense things more acutely than the rest of us. When you reacted the way you did, it showed me what was in store for all of us if we did not act. So, in a way, you saved everyone's life."

Hannah forced the corners of her mouth to rise.

"Shall we move on now that everyone has recovered?" Captain Baldric interrupted.

As one the company rose and followed the captain, who set a manageable pace. No one uttered a word as they trod four abreast behind him through scattered clumps of waist-high grasses. The other soldiers resumed a protective ring about their charges.

Seeing an opportunity to diffuse some of the tension, Andy shared, "Before I returned, I received a clue about the next ingredient I need to collect."

"What'd it say?" Alden questioned.

"I've read it so many times, I've memorized it. It says,

"A song so pure
Trills listeners to tears.
A sacrifice, a giving,
And new life appears.

Yellow, crimson, orange, or red,

> Fire-touched or unscorched, shed.
> A quill of this warbler
> No creature hath bred."

"I know it's talking about getting a bird's feather, at least part of it is, but what kind? And the bit about a song and new life, I've no idea."

Hooh-hrooo, Alden's passenger contributed.

"Thanks, Calum, but I don't understand bird," Andy joked.

"You may not understand bird, but Calum might just be on to something," Hans interjected.

"What do you mean?" Hannah queried.

"It says the bird in question trills beautifully," Hans iterated. "What birds fit that description?"

Hooh-hrooo, Calum offered, drawing chuckles.

"Yes, ring doves definitely fit that, but they are the wrong color. It mentions yellow, crimson, orange, and red. What do those colors remind you of?"

"A fire?" chimed Alden.

"Yes."

"A bird with a beautiful song that's the color of fire," Hannah summarized, her brow furrowed.

Hans nodded.

"But it says 'no creature hath bred,'" objected Andy. "How would that be possible?"

"I know of only one bird fitting this description," Hans intoned.

"Okay, and…" encouraged Andy.

"Wait! I think I know what it's talking about," Hannah exclaimed, flapping her hands.

Andy and Alden exchanged glances to raised eyebrows.

"A sacrifice, a giving, and new life appears," Hannah reiterated. "It's talking about a phoenix."

Hans nodded. "I think so."

"My Grandpa Smithson lives in a place called Phoenix—Arizona, that is."

The three stared at Andy blankly.

He waved a dismissive hand and added, "Never mind. What's a phoenix?"

"A bird that, when it grows old, burns itself up and is reborn from its ashes. It's said to have a beautiful song, and it's tears are similar to dragons' in their ability to heal," Hannah replied.

"Really?" Andy questioned. "How do you know so much about phoenixes?"

"My parents tell us stories before bed. There's one called 'Flaming Flumage Flaunts Her Fluff.'"

It was Andy, Alden, and Hans's turn to stare.

"It's about this silly bird that's all proud of her plumage, which is unlike any of her friends'—it's red, orange, and yellow. She goes flaunting herself around town making everyone jealous. Then one day, she goes up in flames but miraculously rises from her ashes. Having learned her lesson, she ends up apologizing to the top flum for her behavior."

Andy and Alden cracked up. Hans struggled to keep a respectful expression.

"There's more to the story than that, but those are the highlights. It's supposed to teach kids not to behave that way," Hannah added. "Hey, don't laugh, I didn't make it up."

As Hannah had recounted her tale, Andy's brain raced. Something about the bird tickled his thoughts, but he could not place it.

"Wait a minute!" Andy exclaimed after calm returned. "Wasn't it a phoenix in the legend Jada and Naria told us?"

"I hadn't thought about it being the same bird, but yes," Hannah confirmed.

"Would someone mind filling me in?" Hans requested.

Andy nodded. "I'll do my best. Hopefully I remember most of it. It started a long time ago here in the kingdom of Cromlech. There was this king and his daughter, who he loved a lot. They were the last of their royal line. Something bad happened and his subjects ended up leaving him for a different king. I don't remember all the details."

"Ah, that legend," Hans smiled. "Yes, I know it well. Shall I recount it for you?"

The trio nodded.

"With no one left in his kingdom, the bereft king despaired, and the castle and the kingdom fell into disrepair. The king and his daughter wandered about barefoot, their silk and velvet clothes now patched and faded. One day they came upon the ruins of a grand hall, its beams charred and its stones crumbling. Stopping to investigate, the king spotted something gold glimmering under the debris. With some digging, he unearthed Methuselah."

Andy moved his hand to his blade's holster.

Hans paused. "Yes, the very sword, Andy."

Andy smiled.

"As the king stood marveling at the sword's beauty, a heavy roof beam fell on his daughter, killing her. Beside himself with grief, the king cried out for justice, for no magistrate should suffer the loss of everything—his subjects, his daughter, his kingdom. A unicorn appeared, assuring him he had been granted favor. The unicorn watched as the king prepared a funeral pyre for the princess. When her body had been laid on top, the unicorn offered its horn as a gesture of comfort, which the king accepted. He placed the horn with his daughter's body and lit the fire using Methuselah."

"Jada and Naria said the king also used Methuselah to cut the horn off," Hannah interrupted.

Hans hesitated. "I guess they would know, wouldn't they?"

He continued. "As the flames spread, the king marveled to see a large bird rise up from where his daughter's body had lain. Its feathers were yellow, orange, red, and crimson. The king cried out, "Aray! You have become as your name, a ray of hope, like the sun." It soared up and circled the king, singing a song sweeter than any he'd heard. His heart rejoiced, for he knew his daughter had overcome death itself. The unicorn called her a phoenix, for she had been a maiden of unsurpassed beauty and the bird equaled her former grace."

Hans paused for a moment, "There's only one problem."

"What's that?" Andy queried.

"I've never seen a phoenix in these parts. I've certainly never spotted one."

"Great, so what do we do?" Andy queried.

"Did you know the Giant's Ring was constructed on the spot where legend says that old building and the funeral pyre stood?"

"What's the Giant's Ring?" Alden questioned.

"Only the center of power for Cromlech's healers. We'll be passing near there on our way to the castle. Once we find Princess Yara, we can go see the ring. Perhaps we'll find something of use to your quest."

Andy nodded. *I sure hope so.*

Terwit terwoo, oop-oop-oop. Terwit terwoo, oop-oop-oop.

Everyone's eyes jetted toward the bird, now standing on Alden's shoulder.

Terwit terwoo, oop-oop-oop. Terwit terwoo, oop-oop-oop.

"Zolt!" yelled Andy, spotting several heavily armed vulture-men materializing from behind a large rock outcropping off to their right.

CHAPTER EIGHT
Going Batty

Shiiiiing. Shiiiiing. Shiiiiing. The sound of seven swords being drawn filled the air. All but Sergeant Terric, who started whirling his spiked flail above his head, paired up and braced in ready positions.

"Arrrr!" the zolt yelled in a chorus of high-pitched, nasally cries as they streamed forward, swords raised.

There's got to be at least fifty of them!

Twang. Twang. Twang. Sergeant Hammond got off three arrows in rapid succession, felling as many enemies. *Twang. Twang.*

While the arrows reached their targets with deadly accuracy, the horde continued forward, closing the gap to one hundred yards. *Twang. Twang. Twang.*

Fifty yards to impact. *Twang. Twang. Twang. Twang.*

Twenty yards. Ten.

"Arrrr!" Sergeant Terric matched the bellow as he charged forward. Three zolt met their end as the sturdy man plunged headlong into the fray.

Clang! Thawk. Chiiinggg. Clang. Clack!

The enemy hit the wall of soldiers surrounding their charges, but the zolt numbers instantly overwhelmed the practiced officers and several attackers leaked through the line.

"Cover my back, Hannah!" Andy yelled to his partner as he engaged a particularly muscular adversary.

Clang. Clack! Clang. Swuat.

Out of the corner of his eye, Andy saw one zolt, then a second fall to the ground, Hannah's handiwork. Andy jumped over the bodies, avoiding a downward slash from his foe. No sooner had he done so than the battle slowed for Andy as Methuselah found the opponent's exposed midsection.

Andy whirled about and sliced the next adversary that ran at him, finding purchase between the man's ribs. Pulling Methuselah free, Andy blocked a blow from the next attacker's blade just in time. He parried and thrust, but despite Andy's speed advantage, this zolt would not go quickly.

"Uh!" Hannah yawped nearby.

Focus fixed, Andy blocked another blow as he leapt a fallen zolt. A jab found its mark with his pursuer and the enemy howled as it fell to the ground.

Hannah yelled, "Dirty flea-bitten scum!" as she dealt a quick blow to the neck of her foe.

Andy smiled, then quickly engaged a team of two zolt. His speed proved overwhelming, for as they surrounded him he ducked the pair's first blows, and as they recovered he thrust Methuselah through the belly of one. The second lasted only long enough to clash swords once more before it sprawled to the ground.

Andy turned his head quickly, searching for more attackers, but none immediately appeared. He located Hannah close by where she stood over two more corpses, her jaw set and brow furrowed. Andy scanned the field and saw Alden and Hans best three zolt as they headed down the middle of the fray.

Another beefy zolt charged. Andy waited until the last second and faked right, diverting the enemy away from his partner. In the time it took the bird-man to stop and turn, Andy rounded on his adversary and took a downward slice, ending the contest.

"Take that!" Hannah yelled from behind. Andy turned to discover two more zolt bested, unmoving.

As the enemy's ranks thinned, time resumed its normal pace for Andy, and he watched Sergeant Fulk fell three adversaries while his partner, Captain Baldric, took down another two. From his peripheral vision, Andy spotted burnt-orange hair and turned in time to see Sergeant Ranulf eliminate two more.

A guttural bellow sounded across the field as Sergeant Terric eliminated three more foes with a flick of his flail.

Terwoo woop, oop-oop-oop. Terwoo woop, oop-oop-oop.
Now what?

No sooner had the enemy's ranks expired than reinforcements arrived. But as the next fifty-plus enemies landed and transformed, the ground shook, causing a pause in the fighting.

"There!" Sergeant Ranulf barked, pointing across the open field as the ground trembled again.

A white beast standing twenty hands high at the shoulder with the tail of a lion and a single jet-black corkscrew horn stormed toward the fracas.

Terwoo woop, oop-oop-oop. Terwoo woop, oop-oop-oop.

The zolt took flight en masse as the earth rattled.

"Run for the caves!" Alden yelled, pointing at the rock outcropping from which their foul enemy had emerged.

It took no encouraging. The nine bolted for the safety of the rocks, leaping fallen adversaries in their path. From the pounding beneath his feet, Andy knew their pursuer gained. He chanced a look back and immediately wished he had not.

Crap! It's only ten yards back!

Hannah made it to an opening in the monolith first and scrambled through, followed immediately by Alden and then Hans. Andy panted after coming to an abrupt stop, then watched the captain and sergeants burst through behind him.

Baraag! Baraag! trumpeted the beast.

"Whew, that was close!" Hannah exclaimed.

"I'm guessing that karkadann was trying to protect your ring dove," Hans gasped.

Hooh-hrooo.

Despite the dimness, Andy caught Hannah frown at Alden.

"Well, whatever provoked it, we have a problem," Captain Baldric announced. "Unless we can find another way out, we'll have to wait for our friend to leave."

"Look!" Alden interrupted, pointing to an opening at the back of the cavity.

They meandered single file along a corridor between fallen boulders that looked familiar to Andy, though he couldn't quite place them. Gray rock slabs jutted up at sharp angles to form a peaked roof through which slivers of sunlight penetrated, illuminating floating dust particles. The passage smelled like clay, a bit damp and musty.

After walking for several minutes, sometimes erect and sometimes hunched over, Andy queried, "Where do you suppose this will take us?"

"I'm not sure. I didn't know this tunnel system existed, but it seems like we're headed southeast and in the right direction," Hans replied.

"Well, I'm glad we can walk under cover seeing as the zolt know I'm back," Andy thought aloud.

No one responded.

At least we don't have the bellicose on our trail…yet.

As the sun's rays grew longer and the cave dimmer, recollection that had been tickling Andy's memory finally assembled its pieces. "My dream!"

Alden looked back. "What?"

"Hans, I've seen these tunnels before, in my last dream about Princess Yara. I knew this looked familiar, but I couldn't place it until now. She's somewhere in this tunnel system."

"Oh?"

"I'm sure of it."

Sniff, sniff, sniff. "Do you smell that?" Hannah questioned, scrunching her nose.

"Pee-yew," Alden replied.

"What is it?" Andy followed as Hannah fanned the air in front of her nose. *Skreek.*

"If I didn't know better, I'd say we're approaching a bat roost," Hans surmised.

"A what?" Hannah replied, her voice quaking.

"Hannah doesn't like bats," Alden explained.

"Thanks for letting everyone know," Hannah corrected tersely.

"What?" Alden questioned. "What'd I do wrong? It's true."

Hans and Andy laughed. Sergeant Hammond, who followed close behind, feigned a cough to cover a chuckle.

Skreek. Skreek.

Dim light through the zenith of the tunnel illuminated a sharp bend in the path to the left. Rounding the turn, the stench grew stronger and Andy drew his arm over his nose. *I didn't think I'd ever find something more revolting than cow farts, but this...* He opened his mouth and inhaled, tasting ammonia. *Oh...* The rest of the company assumed a similar pose, and two of the sergeants coughed at the fumes as they stepped forward into the cavernous space. Twilight seeping through a sizeable opening between jutting rocks at the apex revealed a cave that towered a good fifteen feet upward, double that in width and quadruple that in length. Movement on the wall to his left attracted Andy's attention. Closer inspection revealed the source.

Skreek. Skreek. Skreek. Skreek. Skreek. Skreek.

"This place is crawling with bats," Andy whispered.

Hannah cowered, covering her head with her arms.

The ceiling directly above convulsed with life, drawing Andy's attention as his feet slipped in what he prayed was mud. Captain Baldric put a cautioning finger to his lips and shook his head.

Andy nodded his acknowledgment, and as he did, several winged inhabitants took flight, brushing the top of his head. He ducked but Hannah shrieked, coaxing more furry occupants from their upside-down perches.

Another shrill cry escaped Hannah, compelling more bats to flight. She crumpled to the malodorous ground in a protective ball. The rest of the company crouched low against the wall in a rugby-style scrum as a continuous stream of winged bodies crowded the space above. Combined with the tumult of squeaks, the scene unnerved Andy as he felt wings brush his back and neck. The stream seemed endless

Just when he thought it was safe to stand, three more latecomers launched, compelling him downward once more.

Hooh-hrooo, Calum announced minutes later from between his caretaker's hands.

Andy unfolded himself, and Hans and the soldiers gathered, their noses smashed into bent arms. Alden lifted the bird to his shoulder and crouched next to Hannah, attempting to console her.

"It's twilight. Bats leave their roost to hunt," Hans spoke in a muffled tone. "I guess we just happened along at the right time."

"The *right* time?" Hannah objected, holding an arm over her nose. She stood, coughed, and wiped her eyes.

"Perhaps I should say the wrong time," Hans corrected.

"Bats are the only animal I absolutely cannot stand. They're filthy and ugly and disgusting! And just look at my clothes!"

"Let's get out of here," Alden encouraged in a nasal tone.

It took no persuading. Sergeant Fulk led the group along a dim but clear path directly below a fissure in the roof where the rock slabs reached for each other. The bats could not roost in the gap, and the ground below remained clear of droppings. Andy's eyes began to water and, despite covering his mouth, breathing became more difficult as the acrid fumes burned his nasal passages and the back of his throat.

The company quickened their pace in the fading light. Andy extracted Methuselah from his holster and the blade lit up, illuminating the interior. The cave narrowed and resumed a more familiar size as the group distanced themselves from the stench. Several minutes later the tunnel ended, dumping them coughing and wheezing into the open air. Andy and Alden sprawled out in the waist-high grass, sucking in the evening scents. Calum verbalized his displeasure at being unceremoniously ousted from his host's shoulder, then hobbled onto Alden's chest where he immediately sat down. Sergeants Terric and Ranulf chuckled at the sight.

"We need to find a place to camp for the night before we lose the light," Captain Baldric instructed.

"Andy!" Hannah exclaimed, holding her stomach. "I feel evil. And it's approaching fast!"

Andy and Alden scrambled up. The words had barely left Hannah's mouth when Andy caught sight of a black, catlike figure bolting toward them in the twilight.

"Everyone stay clear!" Andy yelled. "I'm the only one who can beat this thing!"

"Never! We're sworn to protect!" Captain Baldric objected, assuming a ready position. The other four officers followed suit, forming a semicircle in front of Andy. Alden, Hans, and Hannah drew their weapons as well.

With no time to explain, Andy took a defensive stance and hoped he could lure the bellicose away using Methuselah's light as bait.

"Here kitty, kitty," Andy taunted, waving the glowing blade. The white mark the creature had left on his arm during a previous altercation glowed in Methuselah's light.

With the defenders' attention focused on the enemy, Andy took several steps, distancing himself from the company. Out of the corner of his eye he thought he saw the silvery image of a lady in a long flowing gown, but he did not have time to confirm before the first cries of pain echoed across the field as two officers fell to the ground, grasping wounded extremities. The beast had cut through the center of the line and now bolted for its target. As it approached, it raised a dagger in its right hand and belted out a loud roar. Andy braced as movement around him slowed. Ten feet away the bellicose opened its mouth wide, exposing large canine teeth as it planted its hind feet and leapt.

The move so surprised Andy that he found himself unprepared as the cat-man barreled into him, bowling him over and knocking Methuselah clear. Searing pain shot across his face and down his arms where the creature touched. His shoulder throbbed, and as he glanced over, he noted a red trail flowing freely down his knife arm where the beast's dagger had found its mark. The creature rounded and approached for a second attack. As it jumped, he rolled to his left.

Methuselah.

The blade instantly appeared in his hand, halting the follow-up rush.

Rrarre! The beast announced its displeasure.

Andy pushed himself up to sitting as the remaining company rushed to defend. They got to within ten feet before the bellicose extended its hand and produced a force field that leveled Alden and Hannah who led the charge. The distraction granted Andy time to wobble to a standing position.

Burning from the beast's touch consumed his senses and he fought to focus. The bellicose assumed a ready stance, its yellow eyes locked on Andy, and the pair began a slow circling dance. The officers, along with Hans, Hannah, and Alden, resumed their assault to identical results. Andy found it increasingly difficult to grip his sword and moved Methuselah to his other hand despite the awkward feeling. He'd never had to fight left-handed before.

He was unsure if he hallucinated or not, but the silvery figure of the lady he had seen earlier floated nearby.

"Imogenia, help me," Andy begged. He thought he saw her grimace, but the ghost took no action to intervene.

Hearing his plea, Alden and Hannah began yelling and making all manner of noise, working to distract the menace. The rest of the company joined in, increasing the tumult.

Rraaarrrr! The bellicose snarled, then lunged.

Andy sidestepped, barely in time, but the creature nicked his hand with its dagger as it flew by, again knocking his blade loose.

"Ahh!" Andy howled.

Methuselah.

With his right arm hanging limply, the sword reappeared in his now-bloody shield hand.

It's toying with me.

Andy struggled to block out the pain, drawing on every ounce of willpower he possessed to lock eyes with his stalker. The beast, dagger poised, resumed the circular ritual. Andy staggered with each step, trying to match his partner in the dance. Growing bolder, the bellicose lowered its dagger as it stalked. That was all Andy needed. Summoning all his remaining reserves, he thrust Methuselah over his head and bolted forward, bringing the blade down.

Andy heard Hannah shriek and Alden cry, "No!"

Rraaarrrr!

He sprawled face-first into the ground. Seconds later, pain shot through his body as the beast clamped its powerful canines into his side and shook. Fog filled Andy's mind, and it barely registered when Alden grabbed Methuselah from his hand.

Yelp! resonated in his ears and rattled about his brain but held no meaning.

The next thing Andy knew, he lay limply on the ground, his appendages jutting out at awkward angles. Figures surrounded him, uttering unintelligible sounds before everything went dark.

Andy woke to sunlight squirming through a crack in the vaulted ceiling above where he lay. Methuselah's hilt rested on the ground near his hand. He inventoried his extremities, side, and shoulder, and was surprised when he felt no pain. His black T-shirt had been replaced with a brown tunic. Movement caught his attention, and he spotted Hans stooped next to the fire, ladling something from the cookpot into a bowl he then handed to Hannah. Sergeants

Fulk and Hammond conversed quietly on the far side of the fire while Alden chatted with Captain Baldric nearby.

Andy sat up and wiped sleep from his eyes, drawing everyone's attention.

"Andy! You're awake!" Hannah exclaimed, rushing over.

The rest quickly followed.

Hooh-hrooo Calum cooed.

"Glad to see you finally decided to come around," the captain kidded.

"Yeah, you've been a real slacker," Sergeant Fulk added.

Hans beamed as he scanned his patient.

"How long have I been asleep?"

"Two days," Alden informed.

"Two days? Are you kidding?"

"Afraid not," Hans informed.

Andy examined both his arms then looked up at Hans. "How?"

"Dragon tears. I threw them in my pack at the last minute, just in case. You never know what you might run into out here," the healer explained. "Healed your wounds right up."

"Well, I'm glad you did!" Andy smiled.

"Unfortunately, it didn't fix the discoloration where that thing touched you," Hans added, frowning.

Andy felt his face. *I wonder what I look like. What will Mom and Dad say?*

"Not to worry, Hammond and I match," encouraged Sergeant Fulk, showing off his arms.

"I'll wear my scars as a badge of honor that I received defending my prince," Sergeant Hammond added.

"Are you hungry?" Hannah questioned.

"Now that you mention it."

Nourishment appeared a minute later, and as Andy bit into some crusty bread, he asked, "What happened?"

"You tried to stab the bellicose, but it sidestepped your attack and you went down," Alden began. "It must have broken concentration on the force field when it sank its teeth into you because the next thing I knew, we got through."

"Yeah, Alden grabbed Methuselah and plunged it into the beast," Hannah interjected, grinning.

Alden caught Hannah's gaze and smiled before adding, "It let out a loud yelp and then made a run for it. I don't expect we'll be seeing it again for quite some time."

Andy finished the last bite of stew but still felt hungry. "Can I have some more?"

Hannah glanced quickly between Alden and Hans, and the soldiers ricocheted the look between them.

"What's wrong?"

Hannah studied the floor as Hans explained, "The bout with the hungry grass drew our provisions down much faster than expected. Between that and an extended stay here, we had to implement rations. Sergeants Ranulf and Terric are out hunting right now, but this area doesn't seem to have much by way of large game, unless you care to down a karkadann."

CHAPTER NINE

Undercover Ops

S ergeants Ranulf and Terric scrambled into camp a long while later carrying long faces.

"Sky's full of zolt. We had to bide our time to get back," informed the orange-haired soldier after catching his breath.

"Hunting's no better," groused Sergeant Terric, holding up three squirrels by their tails.

"Then I suggest we stay put until nightfall. We don't need another encounter with those things," recommended Captain Baldric.

Hans slowly nodded.

Since awakening, Andy had watched Hans pace. *The delays must be killing him.*

"Sky's clear," called Sergeant Hammond several hours later.

Moonlight illuminated the terrain as the nine travelers exited their quarters with still-hungry bellies. The rock outcroppings that had provided camouflage died away and tension grew as they navigated the scattered clumps of grass. The five officers kept glancing upward as they circled their charges.

They had walked for quite some time without incident when Andy's thoughts began to drift. He could not help studying Hannah's golden locks as they shone in the moonlight, and he felt his stomach flutter. He tried to convince himself it was just hunger pangs, but reason refused to accept.

Hooh-hrooo, Calum sounded from Alden's shoulder. Hannah glanced over at the passenger and smiled. Andy could not help but follow suit.

"You said your dream put Princess Yara in a cave that looked like the one we left?" Hans interrupted.

"Oh, yeah…that's right," Andy struggled to reel in his thoughts.

The healer frowned. "I didn't see any sign of her. There's only one other place I know of where rocks jut up like that." Hans said no more as they continued, but his furrowed brow spoke volumes.

The moon had passed its zenith and was halfway toward the horizon when clumps of trees sprang up to add variety to the otherwise spartan terrain. Off in the distance Andy spied the modest beginnings of a monolithic snake slithering across the plain. The breeze carried the scent of a dying fire, and the officers motioned for everyone to gather.

"We should check that out," Captain Baldric asserted. "If the inhabitants are friendly we may have found our next meal. If not, we may have found our next meal." He grinned and the sergeants shared a chuckle.

Sergeant Fulk scouted ahead while the other officers led the group swiftly and silently. They paused under a grove of trees and waited for the fleet-footed man to return. It did not take long.

"It's a zolt camp. Looks like the site's been used for a while based on the stores I spotted. I counted ninety-seven of them. There's only one sentry, but he's alert."

"Did you see a way to help relieve them of some provisions?" Sergeant Terric questioned, smiling.

"It'll be tricky, but if we move now before the moon sets I think we can manage it. There are two stores of food and two weapons caches, one on each side of the camp." The sergeant scratched a crude diagram of the site in the dirt then used four rocks to indicate the rough positions of the targets.

"Well done, sergeant," the captain commended. "I want everyone to pair up—one officer, one civilian per pair. Terric, you go after this weapons cache. Hammond, you go after that one." He pointed to markers on opposite ends of the makeshift map. Again he indicated, "Ranulf, you grab food from this stash, and my partner and I will go after that one." He smiled at Hannah as he said it. "Fulk, I want you to lead us to the camp, then watch all the pairs and make sure no one gets left behind."

"What happens if we're discovered?" Alden questioned, voicing what Andy had also been wondering.

"See those rocks over there?"

He pointed, directing everyone's gaze. Andy saw Hans raise his eyebrows.

"I didn't go in far, but there are more tunnels. If they pursue, it's a good defensive position. Either way, let's plan to meet up there."

Andy felt his heart quicken. He glanced over to see Hannah bite her lip and Alden rub the back of his neck. Calum nestled silently on Alden's shoulder. For his part, Hans looked his usual stoic self, but his repeated calming breaths revealed more.

Captain Baldric unsheathed his sword. "Ready?" Everyone else drew their weapons.

Receiving nods, Sergeant Fulk instructed, "Follow me."

The well-conditioned soldier led them at a brisk pace. The company hunched in single file below the tops of the grass. They navigated around several hulking oak trees, finally stopping behind a boulder.

"The camp's just on the other side," Fulk whispered. "I spotted the sentry over there." He pointed to his right.

Sergeant Hammond pulled an arrow from the quiver slung across his back and nocked it before silently launching from hiding.

Twang.

Andy heard no further sounds. Captain Baldric peered out, then gave a thumbs up. Alden set out after his partner, and Sergeant Fulk used hand signals to direct the paths of the remaining officer-civilian pairs.

Coupled with Sergeant Ranulf, Andy crept stealthily behind the broad-shouldered man. They paused behind a thick tree trunk and the sergeant held up a hand. The man peered around and surveyed the scene.

Once satisfied, he ducked back down and instructed Andy, "The food stores we're after are over there, behind those barrels. Take a look." He indicated with a nod.

Andy made like a gopher and spotted the prize twenty yards away. Next to a disorderly grouping of barrels lay several wild boar carcasses with nine pheasants strung from a line above. He counted eight zolt slumbering only five or six feet away, however, and swallowed hard.

"We won't be greedy. Let's take only the pheasants. It'll be lighter and easier to carry."

Andy nodded.

"When we get there, you cut one end of the line and I'll get the other, then we'll head for the rocks. Got it?"

Andy bobbed his head.

The sergeant ducked from behind the tree and Andy hunched over and followed, holding Methuselah out front. The only sounds to reach his ears were grunts from slumbering zolt. *I hope they stay that way.*

Their path cut through the light smoke wafting on the breeze from the dying embers of the fire. Andy squeezed his eyes to slits and held his breath until they had cleared the haze. They had closed to within three yards of their prize when one of the zolt, who lay too close for comfort, coughed. Sergeant Ranulf froze and crouched low in the grass. Andy did the same. The bird-man hacked several more times before moaning and finally letting out a snore. The sergeant looked back at Andy, then nodded to continue.

They scrambled behind the disarrayed barrels that now formed a protective wall between them and the enemy. Sergeant Ranulf inched forward; Andy copied his movements.

When Andy reached his objective, he poked his head up over the barrels and found the sergeant already holding one end of the line, waiting on him. He chanced a peek around but spotted no threats, so he quickly cut his end. What he had not counted on, however, was the pheasant carcasses hitting the ground with an explosion of noise. He froze, hoping to hear nothing more than snoring. Sergeant Ranulf waved his arms wildly, gesturing to bolt, as nasally craws sounded across the camp.

Firmly grasping his end of the line, the prize dragged behind Andy as he reached the sergeant. Together they dashed from the scene of the crime as more squawks rose in the pre-dawn light. Andy could see Alden and Sergeant Hammond nearly at the rocks, with Hans and Sergeant Terric close behind. *Where's Hannah?*

Minutes later, Andy and Sergeant Ranulf barreled through a three-foot-wide crack between the rocks, still dragging their catch. Andy glanced about, noting the cache of weapons piled on the ground and counting heads. Captain Baldric, Sergeant Fulk, and Hannah were missing. Andy shared a frown with Alden then stuck his head back out the gap.

A significant flock of zolt bore down on Sergeant Fulk, closing quickly. Andy saw the strain on the man's face as he sped for safety.

Sergeant Ranulf, who had watched the scene unfold, yelled, "Prepare to defend!"

Andy ducked back inside, and seconds later Sergeant Fulk barreled through the entrance, collapsing on the floor of the cave where he gasped for air.

Sergeants Ranulf, Hammond, and Terric darted outside.

Shiiiiing. Clang. Clank. Swash. Clang. Clank.

Still breathing hard, Sergeant Fulk rose and, with Andy, Alden, and Hans, headed back outside to bolster their comrades. And just in time.

Clang. Clank. Swash. Clang.

The officers who initiated the defense had felled many of the foe, but more zolt had entered the fray. Sergeant Ranulf was swinging his sword wildly, doing his best to single-handedly repel five bird-men. Andy joined him as an enemy lunged for the sergeant's head. Andy brought Methuselah down, catching the bird-man's exposed torso. The foe dropped. Andy assumed his ready position as another enemy engaged him. He followed the zolt's gaze as it thrust its sword at his left shoulder.

"Shouldn't have done that," Andy admonished as he sidestepped the strike and Methuselah found its target in the enemy's chest.

Two zolt teamed up and attacked Andy from either side. Motion slowed around him and Andy whirled, quickly relieving the pair of their heads. Seconds later, another enemy leapt at Alden who fought a yard away. The foe never knew what happened, for as it jumped, ready to plunge a dagger into Alden's exposed back, Methuselah located its neck.

Anticipating the next attack but experiencing none, Andy and Alden paused to scan the area in the morning light. Carnage littered the field. Sergeant Fulk caught Andy's eye with a thumbs-up as Sergeants Hammond and Terric each felled two remaining enemy. An eerie silence enveloped the scene and Hans, the sword drooping in his hand, wandered over to join the boys. The four officers gathered around.

"Where are Hannah and Captain Baldric?" The question spilled from Alden like floodwaters breaching a dam. His narrowed eyes stared piercingly at Sergeant Fulk.

The officer shook his head as he began, "The zolt grabbed them as they dragged a wild boar clear of the camp. There were too many enemy to defend. Captain motioned for me to alert everyone."

This is all my fault! Andy berated himself. *If I hadn't let the pheasants drop and make all that noise!*

"We've got to rescue them!" Alden demanded, glancing to Andy for support.

"And we will, but not right this minute." Sergeant Fulk raised his hands and lowered his brow, meeting Alden's glare. "The zolt will expect us to do exactly that, and they'll be ready. By my count, there are at least three dozen left in camp, not including reinforcements that may have arrived."

"Besides, if we tried something now, they'd see us coming," Sergeant Hammond pointed out.

"Then what do we do?" Alden hissed.

"Wait until tonight and rescue them under cover of darkness," Sergeant Terric proposed.

"But the zolt could—"

"Other than tying us up and withholding food, the zolt didn't harm anyone last year while you three retrieved the unicorn horns," Hans countered, forcing a smile.

"Let's hope they're as charitable this time," Andy mumbled under his breath. Alden met Andy's eyes as their thoughts aligned.

Before anyone else chimed in, Sergeant Fulk instructed, "Let's head inside, dress everyone's wounds, and eat a decent meal. Then we'll formulate a plan."

Alden clenched his jaw and Andy frowned, but they reluctantly followed the others inside.

With Sergeant Ranulf the only warrior not leaking red, he drew his sword and announced, "I'm going to scout out these caves and make sure we're alone." Sergeant Fulk nodded and the man disappeared down the tunnel. Sunlight snaking through the crack at the zenith lit his way.

"Looks like you're the worst off," Hans assessed, addressing Sergeant Hammond. "Let's tend your wounds first."

Alden set Calum on a rock off to the side, adding, "Looks like he could use a rest."

Hooh-hrooo, Calum cooed, adjusted several feathers, and stuck his head under a wing.

"Looks like he agrees," Hans remarked.

"Might as well pluck the pheasants," Alden announced, then grabbed three of the birds and headed for the exit. Andy followed, offering, "I'll go look for firewood."

"Probably ought to move some of those zolt, lest we attract more attention," Sergeant Terric suggested, following the boys outside.

As the sergeant headed left, Andy caught Alden's eye and gestured to follow him in the opposite direction. Alden nodded.

"This is a bad idea," Andy's inneru cautioned.

Somebody needs to do something!

"You don't know what you're getting into."

Andy ignored it.

Minutes later, while the officer was occupied with removing zolt carcasses, Alden met Andy and they stashed the pheasants at the foot of the jutting bedrock. Andy bobbed a finger to his lips and pointed, then hunched below the tops of the waist-high grass and moved out. Alden trailed close behind.

Halfway across the open field, Andy paused and scanned the skies. *That's good. Maybe they haven't gotten reinforcements yet.* He stopped and sat down, and Alden joined him.

"I think we're far enough away to not be heard."

Alden nodded.

Andy drew a rough map of the enemy camp. "There's a tree over here. Let's approach and assess the situation from there. We'll probably need to split up. I'll plan to distract them. You get Hannah and Captain Baldric."

"You got it," Alden acknowledged.

They broke their powwow and continued on. The path to the zolt camp felt longer this time. Periodically Andy glanced upward. Walking hunched over proved a strain on his back, but his guilt propelled him.

At last, the hulking oak from which he and Sergeant Ranulf had mounted their assault loomed near. The two boys silently drew their swords.

They scurried under the protective arms of the hardwood. Andy peeked his head left and Alden bobbed right, surveying the battlefield. Two zolt, their backs to them, sharpened swords ten feet away, and another two enemy dozen sat scattered about the clearing, cleaning or repairing weapons. Three bird-warriors butchered a wild boar as another supervised. Two more split wood while another prepared broth in a cookpot. Hannah and the captain both sat with hands behind their backs, tied to a thick post on the far side of the camp among a grouping of barrels. Gags constricted their mouths, but Hannah's wide eyes spoke volumes.

They're okay. That's a relief.

The two nearest zolt conversed.

"When are reinforcements gonna get here?" the bald one groused. "You know they'll be back tonight."

"I'm not holding my breath. With Abaddon preoccupied, I'll be surprised if he sends more troops," replied his partner.

Preoccupied?

"You're probably right. At least there's only seven of them since we've got those two, but they fight tough."

"You worried?"

"A little."

"Well, just focus on what'll happen once Abaddon gets eternal life again. He'll be unstoppable and so will we." The zolt chuckled. "I can't wait. Shouldn't be long now."

"If I live that long." The hairless one shook his head.

Andy raised his eyebrows and ducked back behind the tree where Alden's expression mirrored his. Alden furrowed his brow and gestured an unspoken question about what the conversation might mean, to which Andy could only shrug and shake his head.

Alden pointed to his chest and motioned that he would circle around to the other side of the camp, then wait for Andy's signal. Andy nodded his understanding and his friend moved out, disappearing into the tall grass.

But as Andy waited for his partner to reappear, a sharp point jabbed his back.

"Looking for something?" came a nasally question from behind.

CHAPTER TEN

Chain of Command

"As a matter of fact, I am," Andy replied, not missing a beat. "You and your buddies have my friends tied up. I'm giving you only one chance to release them before we—" Andy glanced at the field behind him, hoping to intimidate the zolt as Gelon had the other day.

"Drop your weapon!" the vulture-warrior commanded.

I can't believe I forgot about the sentry. So much for that tactic.

"Okay. Okay," Andy acquiesced, lowering Methuselah.

The zolt kicked the blade clear. "We've got company," he announced as he forced Andy to kneel.

I hope Alden succeeded.

Andy felt coarse rope strangle his wrists before a beefy zolt hauled him up and shoved him forcefully. He staggered and just barely caught himself. The bird-man immediately followed up by planting a foot on his behind, propelling him forward with haste.

The zolt converged in a warbling mass of nasally calls as Andy's captors goaded him across the clearing. Despite the rough handling, he distinctly heard Hannah gasp the instant she saw him.

A third post was quickly erected next to Captain Baldric. Andy's captors released his hands momentarily, but he felt the rough wood bite into his skin as they turned him around and bound him once more. A gag, tied too tightly, quickly followed.

At least Alden's still free, Andy thought as he tested his bonds.

A minute later, Hannah gasped again.

Andy jerked his head up in time to see zolt parading his coconspirator toward them. The captors planted Alden at the opposite end of the row, next to Hannah, initiating a chorus of shouts and jeers.

The blonde-haired maiden refused to give the enemy any measure of satisfaction and sat frozen, her jaw set. The others did the same. With no response, their bird-brained captors quickly grew bored and ambled back to their chores, but periodically they snatched glances and smirked.

The sun rose in the sky and began its descent again. Beads of sweat meandered from Andy's brow into the gag, and he felt his tunic grow moist. A look at his fellow captives told him the others experienced equal discomfort.

With limited ability to communicate, Andy's mind wandered. *What did those guys mean when they said Abaddon would soon regain eternal life?*

Dad's voice sounded in his head, interrupting and accusing, "Quite a bind you've gotten yourself into."

Andy scowled and replied, *Someone had to do something. I couldn't just wait, not knowing if they were okay or not.*

"Have you considered that your impatience will now lead others to wonder the same about you?" his inneru countered.

But Hannah's my friend, and the captain…

"You are heir to the throne, Andy. That makes you different. Your choices are no longer only about you."

Andy remembered Father's counsel about putting the good of the people ahead of his own. He gave a heavy sigh, then tugged at his bonds once more, drawing the captain's attention.

"It doesn't matter if you like it or not; it's the way things are, Andy," his inneru continued admonishing.

That makes me feel—

"Stifled, trapped, repressed, confined, lacking freedom?" the voice continued.

Yeah, Andy grumped.

"And so would the average soul. You must think outside the barrel."

Outside the what? Andy questioned.

"The barrel. It's an expression. It means to consider possibilities that aren't obvious."

Andy laughed, drawing a curious look from Captain Baldric and a sideways glance from Hannah.

Where I'm from we say "think outside the box."

"Well, whether you think outside a barrel or a box, you need to understand that your choices now affect more than just you. Respect that."

Understood, Andy relented, groaning.

"Speaking of thinking outside the barrel, you're in a bit of a bind. Perhaps you should try doing so for yourself."

Andy frowned, then gave his bonds another jerk.

"Like many situations, force won't fix this problem."

Andy scanned the campsite. *They're all preoccupied. None of them are near. But how to cut this rope… Wait! Methuselah.*

The hilt instantly materialized in Andy's hands behind the post. He carefully turned it over it so the pommel now touched the ground. He raised his arms to give the blade clearance, then thought, *I need you to cut my bonds.* Andy felt heat, then smelled smoke. His eyes grew large as he anticipated feeling pain, but none came. Captain Baldric looked over and raised his eyebrows as the odor reached him.

Seconds later, Andy felt his bonds loosen and fall. *You're so awesome, Methuselah!*

"Well done, Prince," Andy's inneru praised. "Now take care of your subjects."

Andy inventoried the captors again. Assured that none looked his direction, he tore off the gag, grabbed his sword hilt, then rolled to his side. He quickly crawled behind the captain and cut his bonds, then did the same for Hannah and Alden. But as they scooted toward cover, their movement drew the attention of one zolt and it sounded the alarm, "The prisoners are escaping!"

Hannah, Alden, and the captain retrieved their weapons from a nearby heap and joined Andy to pair off in ready positions. As the first attacker charged, time slowed for Andy and he whirled around, a tornado of destruction, cutting a swath of carnage through the zolt ranks. Captain Baldric followed, felling enemies who dared assault Andy's back.

A bird-warrior lunged at Andy's right flank as he blew past. The enemy's blade nearly connected, but at the last second Andy felt Methuselah lurch, blocking the foe's further advance. His blade then turned its edge on the assailant, eliminating the threat.

What just happened? Methuselah…

The short lapse in focus brought two more zolt within striking distance. These two he recognized from earlier, when he overheard them discussing Abaddon's condition. They both wore scowls and their piercing black eyes told Andy there would be no mercy if he did not eliminate them. The one to his right raised its sword over its head and charged. The one to his left held its blade at waist height and bolted for him.

The unprotected midsection of the right bird-man proved a temptation Andy could not resist. The enemy neared to within five feet, and Andy started Methuselah in motion. A split second later he connected with the attacker's ribs. The return swing found the other zolt's neck.

Reaching the far side of the clearing, time resumed its normal pace for Andy, and Captain Baldric halted abruptly next to him. They whirled around and surveyed the scene. Alden and Hannah together engaged three foe on the opposing side but quickly bested them.

Zolt corpses littered the campsite. Only two enemies stood in the center, protecting each other's back. The pair took ready positions, waiting.

"If you surrender, we won't kill you," Andy offered.

Their only response was to curl their lips and spit on the ground.

"Okay, don't say we didn't give you a chance."

Andy exchanged glances with Alden and Hannah, then nodded.

"Ready, Captain?" Andy queried his partner.

"Oh yeah."

Andy and the captain took a purposeful step forward, which Alden and Hannah mirrored from their side of the clearing. The zolt turned and began running, transforming, squawking, and screeching as they beat their wings in strong downward flaps. Liftoff never came, however, for just before their feet left the ground, Andy and the sergeant tackled one and Alden and Hannah grabbed the other. It took little effort to finish them off.

Andy had barely breathed a sigh of relief when Captain Baldric holstered his sword and asked, "Where's everyone else?"

"Back at the camp," Alden offered.

"You two came by yourselves?" Hannah clarified.

"Sergeant Fulk told us what happened. He planned to attempt a rescue tonight, once it got dark," Andy explained.

"But we didn't know what they might do to you before then, so we decided to try something ourselves," Alden justified.

"I see," the captain replied.

Hannah volleyed a glance around the circle.

"If any of my men disobeyed the plan of the officer in charge, there would be a stiff penalty." The captain locked eyes with Andy. "As the future king, you must respect the chain of command."

Andy swallowed hard. *Don't be a wimp. Don't look down.*

"You had this coming," Andy's inneru admonished in Dad's voice.

"I don't know whose idea it was, but it was ill-advised."

"Mine," Andy confessed.

Alden shifted and Hannah fidgeted.

Captain Baldric nodded once, frowning.

"The zolt are serious enemies. Abaddon is a worthy adversary. This is no time for childish games."

Andy felt his face warm. "Yes, sir. I'm sorry."

"This is not about being sorry, Prince Andrew. My officers need to see you as a sovereign they respect, a sovereign worthy of giving their lives for."

"Yes, sir," Andy mumbled.

The captain let silence fall for another minute to press his point before surveying the campsite. "We might as well grab a couple of the wild boar. They'll go to waste if we leave them."

Relieved to have something to do, Alden and Hannah jumped enthusiastically to the task. Andy followed, but slowly.

"Don't sulk. Learn from the experience and move on. I didn't say that to embarrass you but to help you rule well when the time comes."

Andy turned to look at the officer, nodded, then increased his pace.

The trek back across the field proved uneventful with no enemy circling the early evening skies. But ten yards from the entrance to camp they discovered it was not the threat from above that should have concerned them.

Terwoo woop, oop-oop-oop. Terwoo woop, oop-oop-oop.

As one, they dropped the boars and drew their weapons, then skulked into the cave. Sergeant Ranulf, who protected the back of the group, whirled around.

"Yikes!" Hannah squealed.

The captain ducked, barely keeping his head. Recognition dawned on the sergeant and he returned his attention to the threat along with everyone else.

The smell of stew over the fire assaulted Andy's senses, drawing a grumble from his stomach, but he ignored it. He stepped around Sergeant Terric, approaching the front.

What's going on? What are those? More gnomes playing tricks? Andy thought as he watched unnatural animated shadows dance across the rough gray walls.

Mwhhhaaa. A high-pitched, drawn-out laugh carried from farther inside the cave.

Fulk signaled his intent to investigate, and Sergeant Hammond followed close at his heels. Ranulf disappeared into the tunnel after them. Seconds later came a wail, then a shriek and a girl's voice demanding, "Let. Me. Go!"

Sergeant Fulk emerged first, his arms wrapped about the shoulders of a violently wriggling, blond-headed being. Sergeant Hammond attempted to hold the girl's writhing midsection, and Ranulf barely managed her thrashing legs and feet.

"Put. Me. Down. Now!"

"Set her down," Captain Baldric directed.

The girl from my dream!

The maiden sprang up and assumed a ready position, fists daring anyone to approach. Even in the dim light, Andy could see the fabric quality of her torn, once-yellow dress was not that of common folk. Dirt dappled the girl's face and strands of her long, matted, golden hair stuck out at odd angles.

She's beautiful. Andy felt his pulse quicken and failed to suppress the smile that burst forth.

"We're not going to harm you, miss," the captain reassured.

"Princess? Is that you?"

Andy looked behind him to see Hans scrutinizing the girl.

The maiden jerked her head back and scanned the group, trying to locate the source of the inquiry.

"Yara!" Hans exclaimed, beaming.

The healer approached and the girl reciprocated, "Hans?"

Hans reached the maiden and engulfed her in a hug. "I can't tell you how happy I am to see you. I thought you were dead."

When the two finally separated, both wore wide grins.

"Everyone, this is Princess Yara. Princess, this is everyone," the healer introduced, adding a gleeful chuckle.

"I'm Andy." His voice came out high-pitched and squeaky, betraying him. He felt his cheeks warm but pressed on, "It's great to meet you." He leaned in and kissed the girl's cheeks, but as he stepped back, a goofy grin embarrassed him further.

Yara giggled, turning the heat up another notch.

Alden stopped next to Andy and imitated the greeting, but when his cheeks grew red, Andy caught sight of Hannah standing sullenly, her arms crossed.

What's her problem?

"Looks like we have two royals to protect now," Sergeant Hammond remarked after introducing himself, drawing a questioning look from the princess. "Andy's the prince of Oomaldee. You two have a lot in common. You should get to know each other."

Princess Yara looked toward Andy, raised her eyebrows, and smiled, causing the color in his cheeks to deepen. Hannah cleared her throat behind him.

Hooh-hrooo. Hooh-hrooo.

Princess Yara followed the sound and tilted her head.

Alden picked up the bird and brought it near. "Princess, I'd like you to meet Calum. He's mending."

The princess smiled and patted the dove, eliciting a satisfied coo.

After all the officers had introduced themselves, Hannah approached wearing a plastic smile.

"Oh, I'm so glad to see there's another girl!" exclaimed Yara and stepped forward to embrace.

She's so...great, Andy's mind gushed.

Hannah's expression remained unchanged as she stiffly reciprocated. "I have a hairbrush if you'd care to use it," she offered, parroting the proper manners drilled into her.

"Oh goodness, I must look a mess. Yes, yes. Thank you!"

Hannah and the princess were gone only a few minutes, but when they returned the sight of Yara's locks was a starter's pistol for Andy's heart.

The princess approached Hans and motioned for him to lean over. She whispered in his ear, causing another smile to explode across his face. "Of course!"

"Let's get the princess something to eat," Hans announced. Not having eaten all afternoon, Andy and Alden's stomachs loudly agreed.

"Looks like we have several hungry mouths to feed!" Sergeant Terric joked, patting Captain Baldric on the shoulder.

"Glad to see you're all back safely," Sergeant Fulk added. The officer whom Andy had ignored shot him a look, bringing him back to the reality of what he had done. His inneru cleared its throat.

"Coming?" the princess queried.

"I'll be right there."

"I've addressed the matter," the captain informed in a low voice, breaking the sergeant's penetrating glare.

Sergeant Fulk nodded once before joining his fellows, who observed the exchange at a short distance.

Andy headed toward chow but kept an eye on the officers. The sergeant joined their circle and briefed them, receiving nods. The listeners returned understanding looks, allowing Andy to exhale.

Ruling will not be easy.

"Well said," his inneru agreed.

Andy's stomach grumbled, bringing his attention back. Hans, Alden, Hannah, and the princess sat perched on large rocks near the fire while consuming aromatic stew. As he approached, Yara caught his eye and smiled. A fluttering sensation he knew was not hunger overwhelmed his belly.

CHAPTER ELEVEN

Princess Yara

An hour later, their stomachs full, everyone sat comfortably around the fire.

"How did you end up here?" Andy questioned the princess.

"Abaddon invaded Cromlech three years ago. He and his minions showed no mercy to my family or my people. They forced me to watch as they executed my father, mother, and brother before my eyes."

Gasps rose from the listeners.

Alden nodded slowly. "He killed my family too. Only my mom and I escaped." He turned his gaze to the ground and Hannah reached over to rest a hand on his arm.

The princess closed her eyes and reciprocated the nod, then wiped away tears and sniffed. "All the servants fled. Abaddon's warriors ransacked the castle, destroying all the art and anything that would remind our people of their past. He declared he was rewriting our history and beginning new traditions. Those who refused to submit he either killed or transformed into hideous birdlike beings. He destroyed our schools and burned the fields where we grew medicinal herbs, nearly eradicating our healing arts."

Everyone sat spellbound.

Hans stared at the ground. Andy thought he saw moisture trickle down the healer's cheek but could not be sure in the firelight.

"How did you survive?" Alden interrupted.

"It hasn't been easy. At times I wished that villain had killed me too, for his actions haunt my dreams." Yara paused as more tears escaped. "I'm sorry. This is the first time I've told anyone."

Hans reached a hand over and squeezed her shoulder. After a minute she continued. "I believe Abaddon intends to demoralize any remaining holdouts among the citizens by murdering me publicly once he regains his strength." Yara exhaled and set her jaw, adding, "It won't work."

"You think he's getting stronger?" Andy questioned, catching Alden's eye.

"Up to a month ago I would have said yes, but now I'm not sure."

"Why? What happened?" Hans questioned.

"They held me captive in the crumbling castle but let me roam where I pleased. Every once in a while they forced me into one of the secret tunnels, as if to hide me, but I never understood from who. Somehow they always knew where I was. At the beginning it was hard because they barely fed me. But then one day, when I was so hungry I thought I'd die, something strange happened.

"One of the guards approached, and in my thoughts I commanded him to bring me a feast. He stopped, looked me over, then disappeared. He returned carrying a tray spilling over with food. I wouldn't call it feast-worthy, but it filled me up nicely. I had no idea what had happened."

Hans lifted his head and the corners of his mouth rose.

"What is it, Hans?" Andy questioned.

"Let's hear the rest of the story before I say anything."

"The next time I was hungry," Yara continued, "I did the same thing, and wouldn't you know, they brought me more food. I started trying it with other things. When I got cold, I had them bring me blankets. When I wanted to wash, I suggested they bring me clean water."

The princess let a devious smile loose before continuing. "And then I suggested they treat me respectfully, and they did. It was amazing. So I tried planting suggestions to release me."

"And?" Andy probed.

"It didn't work. Every time I ventured past the castle gates they came after me."

"But you're here. How'd you escape?" Alden broached.

Yara smiled. "One night, about a month ago, there was a commotion. Lots of yelling and running up and down the halls. I had no idea what was going on. I suggested to a captor that he tell me, but he ignored me. I tried again with the same result. In the morning no one brought me food.

"I decided to attempt an escape. I snuck around the castle that day, gathering provisions. Just before the sun set, I made my way to the castle gate and waited for my chance. When the coast was clear, I dashed over the drawbridge and hid in shrubbery surrounding the base of the walls. Once it was completely dark, I fled. No one pursued.

"Since then, I've lived out here on my own. I've had to fight wild animals, and I was nearly attacked by a herd of wild pegasi. Unfortunately, there's not a lot to eat. The smell of your stew tempted me to investigate. I thought I might frighten you off with a few tricks I picked up from some gnomes that used to visit the castle, before…" She let her words fall.

"I heard about your encounter with the wild pegasi," Hans informed. "That's actually what prompted our expedition to find you."

Yara furrowed her brow in confusion, and Hans related their story. Once he finished, Andy reminded, "Hans, you still haven't told us what you think happened, why Yara was able to get the zolt to do what she suggested."

"Ah, yes. Princess Yara, your mother was a gifted sommeil."

The princess nodded.

"The kingdom of Cromlech is home to healers of the body as well as the mind. Healers of the mind are referred to as sommeils. Any citizen of Cromlech may become a healer of the body after studying at the institutions of learning. A sommeil, however, is born with special abilities that manifest around age ten. They can plant suggestions in another's mind, and their skills have proven effective in curing those who suffer from mental afflictions."

Hannah raised her eyebrows. "So a sommeil can direct people to do whatever they suggest?" she clarified.

"Sommeils attend school to sharpen and control their skills, but there they also to learn a strict code of ethics that prohibits them from misusing their gifts."

"I have the gift of a sommeil?" Yara pondered aloud.

"It would appear so," Hans acknowledged. "You were nine when I left for Oomaldee, too early for it to manifest, but your mother and I talked about the possibility."

The princess grinned, then turned serious. "So what happened that night that suddenly made me unable to plant suggestions in the minds of the guards?"

Hans rubbed his pepper-gray stubbled chin before offering, "That is a good question. I can only speculate, but it's possible something has happened to the Giant's Ring."

"Isn't that the place you said might help Andy with the next clue?" Alden queried, putting the pieces together.

The princess furrowed her eyebrows but remained silent.

"It is," Hans confirmed.

"You said it was the center of Cromlech's healing powers. Why's that?" Hannah questioned.

"Long ago, before the troika was formed, the son of King Gerrard I of Oomaldee contracted devil's fire. Back then they didn't know what caused it, only that half of those afflicted died. The king called on all the healers in the kingdom to help, but the prince's condition worsened. The boy went from suffering convulsions to hallucinations. King Gerrard grew desperate and solicited help from the surrounding lands. And so one day a healer from Cromlech, hearing of the desperate situation, came to offer his help. It wasn't long before the heir recovered.

"The king was so grateful, he commissioned a monument to be built in the land of Cromlech from the golden stones of Mount Mur Eyah. King Savant of Cromlech decided the most appropriate site for the gift would be where the phoenix first rose from the ashes of the princess."

Andy, Alden, and Hannah shared glances.

"At the appointed time, workers brought the chiseled stonework to the site and with great effort raised the mammoth blocks into a circular formation, signifying that the healing gifts of the land would have no end.

"Prior to the ring's construction, healers in Cromlech could treat only the body. Over time and through a series of discoveries, however, a few healers observed they could influence a patient's thoughts, restoring the mind. You can imagine the magnitude of this revelation, which is why they developed a code of ethics."

"We'll have to acquaint you with this code, Princess," Hans added, smiling.

"So what can we do to fix the ring if it's broken?" Alden queried.

"I don't know. I think we should go there and determine if that is indeed the problem. Hopefully the caretakers will be able to tell us what, if anything, happened."

"Caretakers?" Hannah asked.

"Given the ring's importance, there are a host of elders tasked with maintaining and protecting the structure. Perhaps we'll also find out more about Andy's clue."

"Kill two birds with one stone," Andy intoned, nodding.

Alden jerked his head back in horror. "Why would you do that?"

Andy laughed and waved his hand. "It's just an expression. Don't worry, I don't plan on killing any birds."

Hooh-hrooo. Hooh-hrooo.

"You tell him, Calum," Alden added, petting the dove.

Princess Yara quickly brought a hand up, attempting to hide a yawn, but she fooled no one. "Excuse me," she murmured.

The contagion spread to Andy, causing Hans to laugh. "I must agree, time to retire."

Calum's caretaker slid the bird to his shoulder, then stood and offered Hannah a hand up.

A day and a half later found the company crossing more flat grassland under sunny skies. To say Cromlech was devoid of landmarks or natural beauty would have been an understatement. It reminded Andy of the time his family had traversed Texas by car on their way to visit his grandparents—lots of dry and barren terrain without so much as a tree as far as the eye could see.

Andy studied the blue sky yet again. *It's been two days since we saw a zolt. Why is that? What's Abaddon up to?* He ran a hand through his hair and sighed.

"Something wrong?" Yara inquired from his right.

Rather than cause alarm he shook his head, then changed the subject. "I thought you said they grew lots of medicinal herbs here."

"Up north. It's too dry here."

"It's a good thing we found that spring this morning," Hans chimed in ahead of them.

"Yeah, or we'd be mighty thirsty," Alden added from beside the healer.

Hannah glanced back at Andy and Yara but said nothing.

The officers once more surrounded the group as they walked, with Sergeant Hammond in the lead today.

"What's that sound?" Andy asked several minutes later.

The others strained to hear until Yara broke the silence, exclaiming "It's beautiful!"

"Sounds like something dying," Hannah remarked, receiving a frown from the princess.

Alden looked over and said, "Then maybe I can heal it."

Hans brightened. "I believe we've nearly reached the Giant's Ring. The stones make music on the wind."

"You call that music?" Andy groused. At first the wispy notes sounded haunting and vacant, but as the group drew nearer, the hair on the back of his neck rose as higher-pitched moaning tones chimed in.

Not long after, the sun revealed a golden object glistening on the horizon. Several more minutes of walking and Andy could make out a structure rising from the boundary between land and sky.

Stonehenge, but it's gold.

Andy scanned the skies again and exhaled.

Approaching to within a hundred yards, Andy felt dwarfed by the size of the colossal stone giants buttressing substantial cross beams.

Several of the lintels lay broken on the ground while others teetered precariously, as if threatening to dive. In the center of the ring, a grass-covered mound spanned fifteen feet in diameter and rose to eye level with Andy.

"I never thought I'd see anything as remarkable as the unicorns, but this…" Alden voiced his wonder. "How'd they build it?"

Yara pressed a hand to her chest and ran her eyes about the structure.

Hans shook his head, "Still as amazing as the first time I saw it, even though it's broken."

"Wow," Hannah murmured.

The soldiers studied the surroundings. Each walked with a hand twitching on a weapon. Fluttering wings in the center caught Andy's attention. A brightly colored bird about the size of a swan soared and dove about, trumpeting a mournful cry. Dark orange, red, and crimson feathers covered the bird's body while its tail held orange and deep yellow coloring.

"Whoa! Is that a phoenix?" Andy questioned. "Its wingspan must be at least twelve feet!"

"I've never seen one, but it fits the description," Hans replied.

"What's wrong with it?" Hannah queried, noticing the bird's molting plumage and irregular flight pattern.

The phoenix exposed huge, razor-sharp talons as it flew near. *I'm supposed to get a feather from that?* Andy swallowed hard.

The bird soared upward as high as the unbroken lintels but crashed into an invisible barrier and bounced off. Its erratic flapping caught a current a moment later and it resumed circling.

"What just happened?" Yara wondered.

No one had a ready answer, but all watched enthralled for several minutes.

"Everyone behind a stone!" Captain Baldric whispered forcefully, breaking the trance.

Out of the corner of his eye Andy saw two zolt land inside the ring as he ducked behind a mammoth golden rock alongside Hannah, Hans, and Sergeant Hammond. They waited several minutes until the captain gave the all clear.

Andy peeked out from his cover. The phoenix continued its wobbly flight and mournful serenade, but there was no sign of the enemy. "Where'd they go?"

No one answered, but the soldiers drew their weapons. Andy and the others did the same. Sergeant Fulk stepped between two stone giants to investigate but struggled to advance. The officer made a second attempt with the same result.

"Getting weak there, Fulk?" Sergeant Terric joked.

"Be my guest."

The burly black-haired officer moved forward a pace, but like his comrade, his steps halted there. He turned a shoulder toward the barrier and pushed. When that proved fruitless, he backed up and charged, slamming into the blockade and bouncing to the ground.

Fulk grinned, then held out a hand to help him up.

Captain Baldric advanced a step and Andy followed, placing his palms against the invisible wall. It felt smooth yet solid. He pushed, but it didn't budge. The phoenix swooped only feet away and Andy quickly backed up. *That thing's huge!*

"It's trapped," Hannah deduced. "We can't get in and it can't get out. This barrier must cover the top as well as the sides."

Alden tested the invisible wall and declared, "It feels like the force field the bellicose uses. It sure acts like it."

Andy shot his friend a quick glance. "Hannah?"

"I don't sense that thing," she replied, concentrating only a second.

Phew.

With no possibility of entering the ring, the group returned to circumnavigating the structure, testing for an opening between each of the golden stones. They had made it three-quarters of the way around when they paused before a short avenue that jutted out from the circle. Two stone structures, which resembled wishing wells without peaked roofs, guarded either side of the path. Crowning the appendage, another carved stone stood watch. This one measured only half the height of the others.

Andy approached the left well and peered in. Unable to see anything, Methuselah's blade lit and he lowered it in as Alden and Hannah joined him at the edge.

"What's down there?" Hannah questioned.

"It's not far. Bottom looks dry," Alden assessed.

"Looks like a tunnel," Andy surmised as Yara joined.

"I wonder where it goes," the princess pondered.

Terwoo woop, oop-oop-oop. Terwoo woop, oop-oop-oop.

Andy looked up and saw fluttering wings not far away, but they were not those of the phoenix. A dozen zolt had landed and raced toward them.

"Andy! I sense the bellicose!" Hannah exclaimed.

CHAPTER TWELVE

Fides

"Time to see where this tunnel goes!" Andy announced.

It took no convincing. Yara leapt over the side of the well, landing with a thud. She scrambled out of the way as Hannah was right behind her, then Alden followed with Calum held close.

"You're next, Andy!" Captain Baldric insisted as the soldiers surrounded the opening.

With no time to argue, Andy complied, landing hard. Hans came next, then Hammond, Terric, Ranulf, and Baldric.

"They're close! Move!" Sergeant Fulk yelled as he landed, bouncing up and drawing his sword. "Andy, you have the light. Lead the way!"

Shaking off the rough landing, Andy dashed down the earthen passage. The bare dirt walls curved to match the ring above. He raced past a multitude of tunnels jutting off to the right, the rest of the company on his heels. Several minutes later, gasping for air, he turned his head and panted, "Do you hear them coming?"

Before anyone had a chance to reply, three zolt burst from a side tunnel just ahead. With no time to stop, Andy barreled into them, bowling a strike. He and the three bird-pins sprawled on the ground as another ten vulture-warriors emerged from the same tunnel, surrounding the company.

"That's far enough. Drop your weapons," one of the bird-soldiers commanded as he grabbed Hannah and pressed a dagger to her throat.

No one opposed the demand. Two zolt wormed their way among the company, collecting the cache of weapons.

"Now move!" the leader decreed, pointing toward the tunnel with his torch. A vulture-warrior paired off with each captive and escorted them at knifepoint. The warrior paired with Andy held its dagger so close he wondered when he would feel warm liquid trickle down his neck.

Progressing with the grace of three-legged race competitors, they had not gone far when Andy spotted a dim glow ahead. Several more paces and the group was bird-handled into a spartan torchlit cavity. A dozen thick timbers buttressed the space, holding the earthen ceiling aloft. Clattering and clanking shattered the quiet as two zolt dropped the group's weapons near the passageway.

"Very good," a voice cracked from the far side.

A seven-headed dragon slumped on an earthen throne, its wings limp over the arms. Each of its heads was bandaged. *Is that where his ear was when he was a karkadann, before I cut off it?*

Andy recognized the belligerent zolt leader who stood sneering to Abaddon's right. *Dagon.* He also made out Gozler and Maladoca, junior menaces, who stood at Dagon's side along with a dozen other vulture-warriors. To Abaddon's left lingered a shadowy figure clad in black robes, its face concealed. Only dark fingertips protruding from oversize sleeves revealed its identity as human.

A translucent figure floated near a fire burning to the left of the enemy ranks.

Of course. The party wouldn't be complete without Imogenia, Andy thought snidely.

"Watch yourself," his inneru cautioned.

Though unable to turn his head, out of the very corner of his eye Andy spied Hannah biting her lower lip, her eyes wider than he had ever seen.

The dragon nodded two of its heads at the soldier detaining Andy, and it dragged him forward. Andy saw Captain Baldric and Sergeant Terric struggling against their captors.

"If you'd like your prince to die, please continue," Dagon warned.

Movement ceased.

Abaddon cleared his throats, commanding attention once more. "Three times you have impaled me with your weapon, three times impeded my ability to live forever. To say this does not please me…" The dragon paused for effect.

The lady spirit hovered without expression.

Three of Abaddon's heads glanced over. "What? Nothing to add, Imogenia?" they taunted weakly.

The ghost frowned but refrained.

That's interesting.

"And now, little prince, you shall pay," Abaddon added in a whisper.

Dagon took a step toward Andy with his dagger ready for action when Hannah gasped, then yelled, "The bellicose!"

As if directed by a homing beacon, the black panther-man barreled into the room and headed straight for Andy, igniting chaos.

"Stop," Abaddon commanded weakly.

Methuselah.

The sword appeared in Andy's hand and he quickly dispensed with his captor as the beast lurched forward, ignoring its creator's command. Andy turned to face the attack and saw Captain Baldric and his men send their zolt captors slumping to the ground.

"Stop!" the seven-headed dragon repeated with effort, to no effect.

Crackling, followed by a bolt of jagged light, filled the space, causing Andy to jump. Hannah screeched nearby. When the excitement ended, Andy quickly scanned the room. The dark figure lowered his arms, resuming his stoic stance. The bellicose lay unmoving ten feet away.

Is it dead?

"It's not dead, merely incapacitated," Abaddon wheezed in a menacing tone, as if reading Andy's thoughts. "You will not die so quickly, little prince. No, you will experience a slow, agonizing end and feel the pain your blade has inflicted on me."

Dagon and Gozler each took a step toward Andy. As they did, he heard more crackling as bolts of blinding light showered the cave.

"This way!" a deep voice boomed from the chaos.

Unsure, but with no time to spare for convincing, Andy and his companions darted toward the beacon of hope. Everyone stooped and whisked up their weapons before rushing down the tunnel as the ground began to shake. A plume of dust compelled them forward until Andy emerged from the passage, Yara right on his heels. Then came Alden grasping Hannah's hand. Sergeant Hammond appeared next with Hans. The other four officers quickly emerged, coughing and gasping.

A man with long gray hair and dressed in dingy white robes materialized from the haze seconds later. "Quickly!" he commanded.

He can run fast for an old guy, Andy thought as they sprinted past several side tunnels off to their right.

They had gone a good distance when the man abruptly halted. He turned to his left, placed outstretched arms to the wall, and closed his eyes.

What's he doing?

A second later, an opening appeared.

Whoa!

Andy glanced at Yara and Hannah. The princess stood with her mouth gaping, and Hannah exclaimed, "It's a dwarf door!"

Shouts echoed as pounding feet approached.

"This way," the man instructed, directing with an outstretched arm.

With Calum tucked under one arm, Alden bolted through the opening, followed immediately by Hannah, Yara, Andy, and Hans with the officers bringing up the rear. Fulk had barely cleared the opening when two dozen dusty zolt raced by.

"They didn't see the door!" Alden exclaimed, turning to face the man.

"Mount Mur Eyah's goodness."

"What's that supposed to mean?" Yara questioned.

When the gray-haired man offered no explanation, Hannah speculated, "There's a tale of a patrol being chased by savage werewolves on Mount Mur Eyah. Mermin told us about it last year."

Andy and Alden nodded, encouraging Hannah to recount the tale. "With the enemy closing in, they took refuge in a cave and the werewolves mysteriously lost their scent. Apparently the beasts lingered at the entrance for a while, sniffing and clawing, but eventually gave up and the patrol was saved."

"Really?" Yara's voice was skeptical.

As his friend shared the tale, Andy surveyed the small earthen alcove in which they stood. Two torches hung, one on either side of the opening, illuminating a space clearly not designed for a group their size. Everyone stood unmoving, trying not to jostle one another. The man scrutinized each of his charges before finally turning and continuing down the torchlit passageway, albeit at a slower pace. The officers clutched their weapons and looked about.

"Excuse me, but what's your name?" Yara queried up ahead.

Only the scuffling of feet answered. While the passage continued on, their guide took a sharp turn to the right and they emerged into another hollowed out cavity, perhaps half the size of Abaddon's. Similar in construction to that cave, a dozen posts kept the ceiling aloft. Stone benches circled an unlit fire pit that served as the focus of the space. Two tables hugged the earthen walls to one side.

"Allow me to offer you some water to quench your thirst."

Andy stood near the tables. As their host spoke, three canteens appeared, making him jump.

Captain Baldric held up his hands then stepped toward the offering as everyone watched. The robed man, unfazed, waited for the captain to open one, sniff it, and take a sip.

"It's fine," he remarked, smiling.

Their host nodded once, keeping eyes on Captain Baldric, then added, "Perhaps sustenance as well." Platters overflowing with cheeses, dried meats, and fruit filled the tables.

Whoa! This guy's a magician!

The company did not hesitate to accept the man's generosity and eagerly dug in. Andy had not realized how parched and hungry he was. The rest must have felt the same, for full bellies soon produced a satisfied calm among the group. After a while, they all retired to the stone benches, laughing and smiling.

The white-robed man joined the circle. "My name is Fides. I'm a keeper of the ring," he announced, summoning everyone's attention, then igniting the fire with a look. Andy heard a high-pitched yelp and glanced over to see several heads jerk back. A hush fell over the group as blue, green, and violet flames danced about the pit.

"Oooh, it's so pretty," Yara appreciated.

Hooh-hrooo!

Alden laughed at Calum who stood at attention on his shoulder.

"It coordinates with your hair," Hannah joked, nudging Alden.

The Cartesian feigned primping as Hans and the officers chuckled.

"As you have seen, a challenge lies before us," Fides intoned, silencing the merriment. "A moon ago, Abaddon and his dark wizard launched an assault on the ring."

Hans exchanged looks with Yara across the circle.

"Where once fifty served, I alone remain. I have attempted to make repairs, but my efforts have fallen short. I fear the center of Cromlech's healing powers may never be restored." The keeper frowned and shook his head.

"We encountered a barrier around the ring," Hans reported.

Fides nodded. "The dark wizard's doing. He disrupted the lintels, which allowed him to venture into the ring. I and my fellows mounted a defense, but he proved more powerful. He vaporized all but me. Then he erected that force field. Until that is destroyed, the ring cannot be restored."

"How did you manage to escape harm?" Hans queried, brow furrowed.

"Only I had skill enough. The dark wizard possesses the power of the nether regions. Never have I beheld such evil."

A shiver ran down Andy's back. *The blanket of evil that had covered Daisy! Was that this dark wizard's doing?*

"What's Abaddon doing here anyway?" Yara questioned.

"You saw a phoenix caged inside the ring?"

The princess nodded.

"The bird appeared a month ago, shortly before Abaddon arrived."

"It looks injured," Alden chimed in.

Fides nodded. "That is the same phoenix that rose here centuries ago."

"Really?" Hannah marveled, then ping-ponged glances between Andy and Alden.

"It returns each time it regenerates. The beauty of that magnificent bird is what inspires me." The keeper's voice resounded with passion, and Andy could sense the devotion Fides concealed beneath his deadpan exterior. "The phoenix must build a nest of twigs and set it aflame in order to be reborn."

"What happens if it can't get what it needs to build a nest?" Alden hazarded.

The keeper shook his head. "I do not know, son. This is the first time that situation has appeared, but I can speculate."

Alden looked to the man hopefully.

"If it has no nest to fuel its rebirth, I believe it will die."

"No!" the animal healer exclaimed.

"As for your question concerning why Abaddon is here," Fides redirected to Yara, "I cannot answer that."

"I think I can," Andy offered. "When Alden and I went to rescue Hannah and Captain Baldric, we overheard a couple of the zolt talking."

"Yeah," Alden harmonized. "It sounded like Abaddon had found a way to regain eternal life."

Andy nodded, confirming. Then he gasped as pieces of a puzzle arranged themselves in his mind. "You don't think…"

"The two are related?" Fides replied. "I do."

"Wait! Don't phoenix tears heal?" Hannah exploded.

Everyone turned their heads.

"Do you think its tears could cure Abaddon?" Hannah worried.

Hans shrugged and Fides raised an eyebrow.

"If that beast regains endless life…" Andy thought aloud. "We can't let him!"

The officers had been quietly taking in the conversation, but hearing this, Sergeant Terric sat up and bellowed, "What can we do?"

"Find a way to fix the stones!" Yara demanded.

"Now you understand. So much depends on the ring being restored, yet I know of only two possible ways to accomplish this, although only one is remotely realistic."

Questioning gazes focused on the keeper.

"We need to repair the ring by hoisting the lintel stones up and aligning them."

"That's impossible!" Hannah objected.

"Do you know how the builders did it?" Captain Baldric inquired.

"I do. In fact, it's what I've been attempting for the last month, but with Abaddon and his minions running about, I have yet to succeed."

Shoulders slumped.

"There's no other way?" Sergeant Fulk intoned.

"Well…"

As Fides uttered the word, Calum lurched on Alden's shoulder like a bird possessed and let loose with a loud, *Terwit terwoo, oop-oop-oop. Terwit terwoo, oop-oop-oop.*

Everyone grabbed a weapon, whirled around to face the entry, and assumed a ready position. Several tense seconds passed but nothing happened. All strained to hear discordant sounds in the quiet.

Hooh-hrooo, the dove sounded a minute later, nesting again on his host's shoulder as if nothing had happened.

Furrowed brows and frowning faces turned toward Alden who studied the bird. "No idea," Alden dismissed, shaking his head.

The company relaxed and holstered their weapons. Andy retracted his blade and turned back for the benches, but Fides hesitated before approaching, his eyes wide.

"Would you show me your sword?"

"Sure," Andy agreed, handing the hilt to the keeper.

Fides's mouth fell open. He beheld the item in his open hands. "Methuselah," he finally whispered and dropped to his knees.

Everyone paused. Glances ping-ponged around the space.

The man spoke softly as he studied the golden object. "The sword that divides good and evil. This is the very blade whose fire created the phoenix. It has not appeared for generations." He caught Andy's eyes, lifted his palms upward, and murmured, "I am your humble servant."

The memory of Father doing the same when he discovered Methuselah flashed through Andy's mind. He recalled the King's words, *"For the blade to show up now, and to you…I don't know what we're up against."* He remembered fleeing in fear then, but now he took the hilt and helped the keeper stand.

Out of the corner of his eye, Andy caught Yara holding a hand over her mouth. The officers stared as he replied, "Methuselah came to me three years ago."

Fides nodded slowly. It seemed the man knew more than he let on. "I was despairing of finding a way to repair the ring, but this changes everything." A smile burst forth on the keeper's face.

CHAPTER THIRTEEN

The Chosen

"A text from long ago reveals a possibility to fix the ring if we have Methuselah," Fides confided. "But never in my wildest dreams would I have expected the legendary sword to appear at such a time as this."

"Really? There's something written about my sword here, in Cromlech?" The keeper nodded, "Oh yes. More than you know." He then recited:

> "When the heart of the Land
> Bends low, is broken,
> Seekers tested alone
> Are found worthy and Chosen.
> Methuselah's blade,
> Aray the token,
> The Ring to restore,
> Its power unbroken."

As Fides began quoting, Andy jerked back and shot a glance between Alden and Hannah, then mouthed, "It rhymes!"

"What's it mean?" Yara wondered.

"Is the Aray mentioned here the same as the original phoenix?" Hannah questioned.

"What does 'seekers tested' mean?" Alden intoned, creasing his brow. "I'm not sure I like the sound of that."

Fides laughed and held up his hands, pleading for mercy at the onslaught of questions. "One at a time, please. Scholars have studied this passage for centuries and contemplated these same questions."

Everyone ricocheted looks as the keeper continued, "Many an interpretation has been offered and dismissed. While I cannot say with certainty, I will share with you my speculation, which, based upon Methuselah's unexpected arrival, is evolving even now." As he spoke, Fides seated himself on a stone bench and the others followed.

"Now then, the passage speaks to a terrible calamity, one that incapacitates the power of the ring. I think we all agree this is such a time."

Heads nodded around the circle.

"It also makes reference to Methuselah being part of the solution. As I said, I never expected a literal fulfillment. But it also names Aray. And yes, I believe it's referring to the princess who died and was reborn as the phoenix all those years ago, as another component of restoring the ring's power."

"It's hard to believe that's her flying around in the ring above us right now," Yara murmured.

The keeper nodded, a sparkle in his eyes.

"But if Aray is 'the token,' how are we supposed to capture her?" Andy asked.

"I am not sure, but I am confident a way will be provided. You all are proof of that." The man smiled.

"The stones of Mount Mur Eyah," Hannah whispered in awe, drawing a nod from Fides.

"As you pointed out, Alden, the text also speaks to seekers being tested and found worthy. This portion has caused the most controversy over the years. No one has come up with a plausible explanation, at least not one that is agreed upon."

"Then what do we do?" Captain Baldric queried. He rose with his jaw set, one hand resting on the hilt of his blade.

As if in answer to the question, Methuselah's blade extended and lit. Andy nearly dropped the sword, so unexpected was its behavior. The space buzzed with yelps, gasps, and squeals.

"Looks like Methuselah's going to show us," Andy declared. He held up the illuminated blade and, just as it had on previous occasions, it dipped, pointing the way.

In silence, everyone followed out the doorway. The blade directed right when Andy reached the passageway. *We haven't been this way yet.*

Fides and Yara, then Hannah and Alden, followed by Hans and the five soldiers trailed the beacon for several yards until the tunnel abruptly ended in a dirt wall.

"Now what?" Yara questioned.

The officers twitched hands over their weapons and surveyed the situation. Andy stepped aside to allow Fides access. The keeper applied open palms to the barrier as he had before, but nothing happened.

"I believe one of you, as a seeker, will have to do the honors," Fides speculated, stepping back.

Yara took a tentative step forward. "I'll give it a try." She brought her hands up and placed them against the wall. "Please open," she pleaded.

Everyone waited in hushed expectation, but again nothing happened.

"Other suggestions?" Alden invited.

Hannah stepped around Fides and Yara. "Remember how the dwarf door worked?"

"Yeah, we had to believe we could step through," Andy offered, receiving a nod from his friend.

Hannah turned toward the barrier. "Here goes." She raised her chin high and strode toward the wall.

"Where'd she go?" Yara squeaked a second later. Sergeant Fulk bounded forward and the other officers cried out.

Fides smiled broadly and winked at Andy, "A chosen seeker."

"Yara, you try it," Andy encouraged.

The princess raised her brow, then exhaled as she stepped forward once more.

"Believe," Alden coached.

Yara nodded, squeezed her eyes shut, and took a step.

The officers' alarm grew as she too disappeared.

"Hans, you're next," Andy nominated.

The healer smiled, approached the barrier without hesitation, then vanished.

"Alden, after you," Andy joked.

The neon-green-haired boy and white ringdove approached the barrier, but his foot found substance and he slammed into the wall.

"Ow! That hurt."

"Perhaps leave Calum," Andy offered.

Fides reached for the bird, drawing a question from Andy, "Aren't you coming?"

"I'm a keeper, not a chosen seeker. Of this I am sure," he replied as he lifted Calum to his shoulder.

"I don't like this!" Captain Baldric declared. "They're unprotected."

"I believe that is the point," Fides countered, grinning, to which the captain ran a hand through his hair and exhaled forcefully.

"Ready?" Andy asked Alden.

His friend nodded and strode forward without incident.

"Wish us luck," Andy entreated as he took a step, Methuselah forging the way. Fides and the officers faded from sight and his surroundings went dark. He took several more steps and heard Yara worry, "Where's Andy?"

"He'll be here," Alden's voice reassured.

Andy broke through into a dimly lit earthen cavity. It resembled the others the group had encountered, but the ceiling rose twice as high and had no timbers supporting it. Movement drew his gaze to where a host of glowing spheres the size of soccer balls floated as if drawn on a lazy river. Half a dozen steps ascended a circular white stone platform about twelve feet in diameter that rose in the center. A larger glowing sphere hovered above it. A curtain of blackness hid what lay beyond the platform, and a feeling of dread crept into Andy's consciousness. He shuddered before catching Hannah's glance. *She feels it too.*

"What is this place?" Yara quaked.

"Where we will be tested," Hans replied matter-of-factly.

"Now what, Methuselah?" Andy questioned.

The blade directed him toward the platform before retracting.

Andy advanced and the others followed close. As they climbed the steps, the sphere hovering over the center brightened and a table about the size of his parents' dining room table materialized.

Whoa.

Its highly polished surface reflected the ceiling and floating lights. Everyone exchanged glances but remained silent.

Chairs appeared, two on either side and one at the head, drawing a whimper from Yara and widened eyes from Hannah.

"Are we to sit?" Andy threw the question out.

Four pairs of silver goblets materialized before the seat at the head of the table, begging investigation. The five approached, each reaching for a chair. But when Hans, who stood along one side, tried to pull out his chair, it would not move. Andy experienced the same problem at the head of the table.

"I guess I'm supposed to sit there," Hans deduced.

The healer wrung his hands as he and Andy exchanged positions.

Once seated before the drinking vessels, Hans swallowed hard as he reached for the first pair. He drew one then the other under his nose and sniffed, repeating the process twice before looking up. He furrowed his brow and explained, "It seems I'm to identify which cup bears poison within each pair." He held up the goblet on the right of the first pair. "This one is water." Nodding at the other he added, "And this one is hemlock."

"How do you know?" Hannah inquired.

"The smell. It's rather disagreeable."

He set the cup down and exhaled, then glanced around the table. "I've always feared I might accidentally hurt a patient and be unable to save them." He shook his head slowly. "Based upon the fact that there are four pairs of goblets and four of you…"

Everyone inhaled sharply and exchanged looks, reluctant to accept what the healer postulated.

"We trust you, Hans," Hannah interrupted the silence.

The other three looked to the healer and slowly nodded.

"Thank you. While I appreciate the sentiment, I think your confidence in me is greater than mine, at least in the field of poisons. He blew out a series of short breaths. Without warning, the goblet Hans had identified as water began to slide across the table of its own accord.

"What?" Andy stammered.

Hans began rubbing his brow, Yara drew a hand to her chest, and Alden's mouth fell open. Hannah covered her mouth with both hands as the vessel stopped before her.

"I guess we're going to see just how much you trust Hans," Yara observed, receiving a scowl from Hannah.

With shaking hands, the maiden grasped the cup. She glanced around the table, then squeaked, "Okay, here goes." Bringing the goblet to her lips, she took a sip, then closed her eyes for several seconds. She took another drink, then another, finally allowing a smile to crawl across her face. "Hans is right. It's water."

A collective exhale emanated around the table.

"One down, three to go," Hans murmured, drawing everyone's attention back.

The healer pulled the second set before him and took a whiff of the chalice on the left. After sniffing the pair several times, Hans sighed. "I believe there's a trace of belladonna in this one," he declared, giving a half smile.

As before, the goblet identified as non-toxic slid down the table. It stopped in front of Alden this time. The Cartesian reached for it, held it up, and looked back to Hans for reassurance.

The healer nodded. "This one was harder to tell, but I'm nearly certain I'm right."

Alden brought the drink up, then tipped his head back and emptied it, setting it down with a sigh. "Water."

"Halfway there," Andy encouraged, to which Hans nodded.

Hans brought the third set close, then picked up the cup on the right and ran it under his nose. He did the same with the other. After repeating the procedure four times, with the furrow on his brow growing deeper each pass, he scratched his head and pushed back. Several cleansing snorts later he again approached his test. Andy, Yara, and Alden shifted in their seats. Hannah bit her lip.

"I think I detect the slightest semisweet musky odor in this one." Hans held up the left chalice. "I believe it's foxglove."

The other slid over to Yara who scrutinized it with wide eyes. "You're sure?"

"As sure as I'll ever be."

The princess exhaled, staring the vessel down. She extended a shaking hand and grasped it around the stem, then circled the table with pleading eyes.

"You're the only one who can drink it, Princess," Hans affirmed.

"But you weren't sure."

"I'm fairly certain."

"Just drink it," Hannah admonished.

Yara directed a scowl toward her traveling companion, then took a calming breath. She closed her eyes, brought the goblet to her lips, and took a tentative sip. Seconds later she set the vessel down and stared at it.

"Well?" Alden queried.

"If it was poisonous she'd be convulsing," Hans informed.

"You okay, Yara?" Andy asked, a concerned tone coloring his words.

The princess gave a timid nod as she continued staring at the goblet.

"Let's finish this diabolical trial," Hans growled.

Andy followed the healer's every move, a foreboding rumble ricocheting inside his stomach. Hans again sniffed both vessels numerous times, shaking his head and clenching his jaw.

It's taking him longer this time.

"I don't know! I can't tell!" Hans finally exclaimed, bringing a fist down sharply on the table. The healer took several breaths and began rubbing one arm against the other.

The kids all stared. Andy wanted to say something, but what?

"I've failed," Hans moaned. He shook his head. "It's my worst fear come true. I'm supposed to be a healer, yet I have no idea which one will kill."

Andy locked eyes with him. "You're a good healer. Remember when Alden was poisoned by that dart? You figured out the antidote. And you've fixed me up plenty of times."

The healer tilted his head, contemplating. "But what good is it if I poison you, Andy?" Hans gave a heavy sigh.

"Take your best guess."

"That's not good enough! I won't risk killing you!"

"Maybe part of this test is to get beyond your worst fear and believe in yourself."

Hans considered that.

"I trust you, Hans. I know you would never hurt me on purpose. Follow your gut. The ring can't be fixed if you don't choose."

"You're willing to sacrifice yourself?"

"If it means the ring can be fixed so the healers of Cromlech can again do their work, yes."

Hans returned his gaze to the vessels and nodded. Sniffing both once more, he held up the one on the right and declared, "This is the one with poison."

The left goblet slid before Andy. Without hesitating, he grabbed it, brought it to his lips, and downed the contents. Everyone held their breath. Seconds passed, then minutes.

"I feel fine." Andy moved to stand, then crumpled to the floor, eyes wide.

A collective gasp rose and Hans rushed to attend him. The group circled Andy's form, hoping. As the healer knelt and studied his eyes, Andy whispered, "I knew you'd choose right"—and smiled.

Hans jumped and brought a hand to his chest, exhaling loudly.

"You're taking too many lessons from those gnomes," Yara harrumphed.

"Woohoo!" Alden celebrated. He extended a hand and pulled Andy up, giving him a quick squeeze.

Hannah hugged Andy. "I'm so glad you're okay!"

Then Yara moved in and Andy felt his mouth go dry and his pulse quicken as they embraced. Hannah adopted a sullen look.

Hans approached. "Thank you," he murmured. He opened his mouth as if to say more but seemed unable to form the words. He closed his eyes and bowed his head repeating, "Thank you."

Andy stepped forward and enfolded the scruffy man, and Hans reciprocated with a strong embrace. When Andy stepped back, he saw tears streaming down the healer's face.

The floating spheres dimmed and Andy found himself standing alone. *Where'd everyone go?* He tried to stuff down a growing sense of panic, but as the dusk deepened, so did his fear.

"You're afraid," Dad's voice in his head intoned. Never had Andy been more happy to hear his inneru. The creature rummaged loudly through the filing system in his head. "F. F-A. F-E. Here we are…F-E-A-R. Andy, do you remember the lesson about fear from when you had to battle the dragon?"

I don't have to be afraid, I have a choice!

"Well done! And none too soon from the looks of things."

Andy forced air from his lungs and his muscles tightened.

Light breached the curtain of darkness that had shielded the space beyond the platform. The unfolding scene reminded him of the arcade at the carnival he had attended with his family last summer. From three yards away a clown approached wearing bright-red bushy hair, a red polka dot suit, and oversize shoes.

"What are you staring at, loser?" it sneered.

A fat lady with mismatched attire wobbled forward. She made an "L" with her thumb and forefinger and held it to her brow, scowling.

Andy gazed into the dimness and his pulse quickened. Hannah, Alden, and Hans sat high up on narrow boards fifty feet away. Their hands were tied behind their backs and ropes bound their ankles. While Andy did not know how high they perched, a fall would clearly kill them as nothing stood between them and the ground. Three dagger-wielding zolt each occupied a two-foot-square platform no more than a foot away from his friends. The adversaries were clearly enjoying themselves, taunting each victim at knifepoint. A stiff arm displayed a six-inch target above each fiend. *A dunk tank without water! Are you kidding? What sick—*

Before he could complete the thought, Ox materialized nearby and berated, "You're nothing but a spoiled, snot-nosed brat who can't throw worth beans!"

Cadfael joined in, forming a duet, "Think everyone likes you? Ha!"

Lucee harmonized, "Think you're such a brave hotshot, don't ya? Think again."

The insults pierced Andy's mind like flaming arrows. *I knew it! It's been a sham the whole time. They're right! I'm nothing! I'm no prince. I'm a fraud.*

"Andy!" his inneru interjected. "No time! Your friends are in peril!"

But...

"They're lying to you!"

Sir Kay appeared next to Andy on the platform. He lowered his gaze, locking eyes. "You're a sorry excuse for a prince!"

Sir Gawain added, "You do realize the King is just humoring you. You're nothing to him!"

Andy suddenly felt light-headed, and his breathing grew difficult as a host of green spongs appeared at his feet.

Hannah let out a blood-curdling scream.

"Andy! Ignore your fears and doubts. These are your friends! Only you can save them!" his inneru prodded.

Andy squeezed his eyes tight and pressed a hand to either side of his head as his doubts waged war with the voice in his mind.

CHAPTER FOURTEEN

Worthy?

"Arrr!" Alden howled. The desperation in the cry rocked Andy from his inner struggle. He snatched up a spong and hurled it at the target above Alden. Not waiting to see the result, he grabbed another green missile and launched it toward the zolt taunting Hannah. He heard a body hit the ground with a thud as he propelled a third projectile, drawing a dull *thwack* as it connected with its zolt target.

He paused to survey the scene. The zolt bodies had vanished, but so had his friends. *Where'd they go?* Seconds later Father, Mermin, and Marta replaced the first trio. Each struggled to loose their bonds while avoiding contact from the sharp blades that danced precariously in the hands of adversary.

Razen materialized a few feet away from Andy on the steps. "Tsk, tsk, tsk. You're such a disappointment. Just ask your father." He shook his head and wagged a finger to emphasize.

In the distance, Andy saw Father duck, but the enemy's blade found its mark, slashing and drawing blood from his cheek. Like pouring gasoline on a fire, the act ignited Andy's anger. "Oh no you don't!" he bellowed. Ignoring the bird-man, he grabbed a spherical projectile and compelled it to fly.

Marta yelped as a slash of her enemy's blade freed a clump of her bright-purple hair.

"Marta!" Andy shrieked. "Get away from her!" he commanded, grabbing another spong and releasing it with all his might to press the point. Her nemesis blanched and plummeted from its perch seconds later.

Glaucin joined Razen on the step, forming a duet of insults. "You're a reckless one you are, Andy. I'd never trust you to rule my kingdom."

Razen continued, "You're all talk, but no results. At least not that count for anything. You're pathetic!"

Since their appearance, Mermin had chanted spells to fend off his adversary. His strategy appeared to be working, but as soon as Andy saved Father and Marta, Mermin's attacker broke through this defense and sliced the wizard's arm.

"Get away from him!" Andy exploded, letting loose another rocket.

Andy heard a fading cry as the spong propelled Mermin's attacker from its roost. Chest heaving, he collapsed.

"You're putting these people in peril. What kind of ruler will you make?" Glaucin ridiculed.

"The King was better off before you arrived," Razen added.

"You can't listen to them, Andy. Believe in yourself!" his inneru championed.

A high-pitched wail rent the cavern. *Madison!*

Zolt swiped at Mom, Dad, and Madison as he looked up.

"Not! My! Sister!" Andy howled, snatching up another spong. No longer satisfied with hitting the red target, Andy hurled a green cannonball directly at the attacker's head. *Direct hit!* The enemy bobbled for a second before succumbing to gravity's clutches. Madison vanished.

"You're a pathetic excuse for a brother!" Razen continued. "Look at the danger you've placed her in."

Merodach materialized next to Glaucin. "Little thief!" he boomed.

A burly zolt took a swing at Mom. "How dare you!" Andy growled, narrowing his eyes. "She's the queen of Oomaldee!" He launched another spong, knocking the enemy's weapon from its outstretched arm. The attacker turned and grinned at Andy, then proceeded to extract a short knife from his belt. He turned back to Mom and raised the blade above his head.

"No!" Andy screamed at the top of his lungs, unable to quickly reach another projectile.

The enemy leapt from its platform onto Mom, bringing its knife down sharply. Mom shrieked.

"Mom!"

"Emily!" Dad cried, echoing.

Nostrils flaring, Andy scrambled up and reached a spong, then hurled it. The impact rocked the foe and it lost its balance, let out a nasally shriek, and plummeted from its perch in slow motion. Mom lay unmoving, listing precariously on the narrow beam.

The last zolt swung as it lunged at Dad. To this point the man had successfully avoided the blows, but this one landed squarely on his shoulder. "Emily!" he pleaded, the pain of concern seemingly worse than the physical injury. His cry pierced Andy.

Andy launched three spongs in rapid fire as Dad repeated, "Emily…" Dad's attacker succumbed and Dad vanished.

Andy darted toward Mom only to slam into an invisible barrier as he reached the edge of the dais. Bouncing off, he landed hard. He struggled to right himself, then looked on helplessly, tears streaming down his face.

"Worthless!" Glaucin exclaimed.

"What kind of a son are you?" Razen harassed.

"Weak!" Merodach exclaimed.

"Look at that, a crybaby," the bird-man added in a patronizing tone.

"Stop! Please stop…" Andy begged, falling face-first to the floor. "Spare her. Take my life instead!"

As if summoning a magic spell, the words quieted the chaos. Darkness was restored to the theater and Andy collapsed, quaking.

"Andy!" Hans called, rushing toward him from the other side of the platform. Alden, Hannah, and Yara quickly joined, encircling him.

"Are you okay?" Hannah queried.

So sudden and welcome was their reappearance, Andy bounded up and engulfed the four in a group hug.

"We saw the whole thing," Alden informed, shaking his head.

"Is fixing the ring really worth all this?" Hannah queried.

Hans closed his eyes and Yara bit her lower lip, but it was Andy who spoke. "From what Hans and I have been through, it's clear that restoring something as powerful as the ring costs a lot."

The princess nodded as Andy continued, "I get it. If it didn't cost a lot, we wouldn't value it." Andy glanced around the group. "Only you can say if you're willing to be tested."

Alden rocked on his feet, Hannah looked at the floor, and Yara pulled at her ear.

"No one's going to force anyone to do something they don't want to do," Hans encouraged.

Several minutes of silent contemplation passed before Alden stopped his rocking. "I'm willing." He nodded, confirming his choice.

Yara dropped her arms, tightening her hands into fists. "I am too."

Hannah glanced between Alden and Yara. "I'm afraid."

"Me too. But if we can fix the ring, Cromlech's healers can help more people than we know," Alden encouraged.

Hannah nodded but continued to deliberate. At last, she pulled her shoulders back and declared, "I'm willing."

The light immediately dimmed.

"Here we go," Alden observed.

Andy held his breath and clenched his hands into fists.

Hannah yelped, Yara squealed, and Hans shouted, "No!" as a scene illuminated out of the darkness on the far side of the space: Zolt torched a street of wattle and daub homes, screaming children scattered in all directions, mothers shielded babies as they ran, men drew weapons. The enemy cut them down where they stood.

Andy drew Methuselah's hilt but the blade did not extend. He shook it as he dashed forward, but as he reached the edge of the platform he again slammed into the invisible barrier and bounced back. Running next to him with weapon drawn, Alden leapt from the platform and raced into the fray. "Dad!" he screamed.

Seconds later, a man and the two children who clutched him fell to a blade.

"No!" Alden cried out.

"Alden!" a purple-haired woman yelled.

"Mom!" Alden returned, bolting after. But before he reached her, dark shadows flew overhead. Talons found flesh and lifted a shrieking Marta skyward. The enemy taunted, dangling her just beyond reach. Alden raced after, casting insults with each stride.

Andy beat his fists against the barrier while Hannah and Yara huddled together, tears streaming down their faces. Hans watched unwillingly, a hand covering his mouth.

Alden reached his mom and grabbed at a foot just to have the zolt jerk her upward. The scene repeated itself time and again.

"Mom!"

Other zolt joined in the taunting and began dive-bombing Alden as he raced after his mother. With no small advantage, the enemy soon grew bored and began tossing Marta between them, receiving a shriek from their toy as a reward.

Andy had no idea how long the torment went on, but he watched Alden's steps falter. He stumbled but refused to fall, then swatted a diving zolt with his blade.

How long? Andy pounded at the restraining field with all his might to the same result. "Argh!"

Eventually Alden stumbled and fell. He lay on the ground, his chest heaving, sobbing as Marta's silhouette grew smaller. "No!"

Several minutes passed before Alden finally sat up. He wiped dirty streaks from his face and looked about. At last his nostrils flared and a smile erupted.

What?

Andy stopped pounding on the barrier, the girls raised their eyebrows, and Hans tilted his head as Alden bounded up and shouted, "This isn't real! This is a test!"

The scene of devastation instantly vanished, and a minute later Alden mounted the steps of the platform. Andy mauled him the instant he broke through the restraint.

"Well done, Alden!" Hans patted him on the back.

"Is that what it was like when your dad…?" Hannah queried in a hushed tone.

Alden nodded.

"How'd you figure it out?" Yara questioned.

"I couldn't keep chasing. While I was catching my breath, I thought about how unfair it was, losing my father and my brother and sister twice, and now my mom too—"

Before Alden could finish the thought, a dozen or more furry winged creatures buzzed the group. Hannah screamed and took off running.

An oversize bat swooped down. The creature had a flat monkey-like face, pointy ears, and a wingspan of at least ten feet. It held its mouth open, revealing two-inch-long serrated teeth and filling the space with high-pitched squeals.

"It's Olitiau, the granddaddy of all bats!" Hans shouted.

The others rushed to protect Hannah but were once more confined to the platform by the invisible barrier.

"Argh!" Alden yelled, pummeling the blockade with the butt of his sword.

Hannah tripped and planted her face in the dirt floor as the monster swooped low. Once it had passed, she jumped up and unsheathed her sword, then with shaking arms assumed a ready position. A cloud of smaller bats locked on and dipped down. She narrowed her eyes and set her jaw, swinging as the pests came within reach. Dismembered bat bodies quickly littered the floor. A second and third wave assaulted to the same end.

"Go Hannah!" the onlookers cheered.

The monster bat approached once more. It bellowed an ear-splitting screech as it dove, and Hannah froze. Seconds later, it grazed her with a claw as if readying to open her up like prey. She dropped her weapon and clutched her face, trying to staunch a stream of red.

"Look out!" Yara cautioned at the top of her lungs, jumping and waving.

Hannah dropped to the ground, barely avoiding the enemy's outstretched claws as it swooped low. It let out a high-pitched shriek, frustrated at the miss.

"It's not real!" Alden coached.

Still holding her face, Hannah hastily grabbed her blade, then stumbled up and assumed a one-handed ready position.

"It's not real!" Alden shouted again.

The monster approached and Hannah took a swing when it came within striking range. But the effort unbalanced her. She took an unsteady step into a flapping wing and fell to the ground as the adversary circled.

"Hannah!" Alden cried.

Tiring, she directed her gaze toward her name.

"The bat's not real!" Alden tried again.

"The bat's not real," she repeated as if in a trance.

Furry wings neared.

"Move! It's coming!" Yara shrieked.

"Hannah, you can do this," Hans coaxed, struggling to sound calm.

Ten yards and closing.

"This is a test! None of this is real!" Andy called.

Five yards.

"Hannah," Alden begged.

Two yards.

Hannah closed her eyes and gasped, "The bat's not real!"

Like suddenly waking from a nightmare, the monster vanished and the area went dark as it had after the previous tests. Hannah gasped, then felt her face. Not so much as a scratch. She rose and meandered toward her compatriots in a daze, slowly mounting the steps.

The instant she cleared the barrier, Alden engulfed her in his arms. "I was so scared for you."

Hannah buried her head in his shoulder and sobbed as the others looked on.

"These tests are inhumane," Hans complained. Andy looked downward and nodded slowly.

"That leaves me," Yara grimaced.

As if flipping a switch, the words compelled a spotlight to illuminate a throne. The royal seat, made of highly polished white marble, was inlaid with rubies, sapphires, and emeralds. The overstuffed crimson seat cushion was velvet, and intricate carvings accented the seatback.

"That throne's beautiful," Yara marveled.

I wonder why Father doesn't have a throne. The random thought flitted about Andy's brain but disappeared as quickly as it had come.

A second spotlight revealed a chaise that glittered gold.

Is that stone from Mount Mur Eyah?

Lavish purple silk pillows lined the seat and back, and ornate scrollwork added a sophisticated touch to the length.

"Oooh," Yara whispered.

A third light illuminated a roughly hewn wood table. Five warped planks formed the uneven rectangular top. A brown burlap skirt was gathered around the front and sides, blocking any view of what was underneath.

Interesting…

Yara studied the three objects.

After several minutes, Andy broke the silence as he questioned softly, "What's she supposed to do?"

"Pick one," Hans speculated from the opposite end of the semicircle he and the others formed behind the princess.

That's it? After what we've all been through?

Hannah shot Alden a glance as Yara descended the steps.

"What kind of a test is that?" Hannah whispered once she was out of earshot.

"She must choose her future," Hans speculated. "If I'm not mistaken, the throne represents power—with power comes great responsibility. A queen will be tested throughout her reign, both by the people she seeks to help as well as by the lust for increasing influence and control. While I don't sense she craves power, it will still entice."

Andy shifted as he listened. Hannah met his eyes with an empathetic look.

"I believe the chaise represents comfort and pleasure. While that choice might seem easy, if you consider it fully, I think not. At some point, pursuing nothing but one's own enjoyment would become meaningless and leave you feeling empty. If you woke up each day with only entertainment before you but with no ambition to help others or make a difference…"

Hannah and Alden nodded.

"Responsibility, diligence, and dignity are the keys to success in life." Father's philosophy jogged through Andy's mind. *You couldn't have any of them if you just sought pleasure, which means you couldn't be truly successful,* Andy reasoned.

"Well done," his inneru encouraged.

The princess stood only a few feet from the three objects, considering.

"But what about the table?" Hannah queried.

"I believe it represents humility and sacrifice. While it is not the obvious choice, it may well be the one that leads to the brightest future."

"How so?" Alden interjected.

"When you are humble and sacrifice yourself for the sake of others, my personal experience is that innumerable rewards appear that are more satisfying than pleasure or power. However, with sacrifice comes great pain—sometimes physical, sometimes emotional." The healer gave a half smile and fell silent.

"You think she gets all that?" Hannah asked.

Hans considered for a moment before responding, "Her parents made plain these three paths to their children. I would overhear them from time to time. Though Yara was young, she would have learned."

"At first I couldn't believe how simple her test seemed, but after listening to you, I can see it's not easy," Andy shared. "I would have chosen the throne."

"I would have chosen comfort," Alden added.

"Yeah, me too," Hannah echoed.

"What would you have picked, Hans?" Andy questioned.

The healer slowly shook his head, staring at the floor. "I'd like to say I would have chosen sacrifice, but I don't know if I have that much courage."

Andy felt his stomach roll as Hannah brought a hand to her chest. Alden swallowed hard and glanced between his companions.

Yara now stood staring at the wood table. At length, Andy saw her back straighten as she took a deep breath. She nodded once, then took an unhurried step forward. Five steps brought her within reach of the wooden platform. She climbed atop and lay down, closing her eyes. The throne, chaise, and spotlights disappeared.

Footlights illuminated a path to the wooden table from where they watched, and Hans stepped forward. Andy thought he saw more tears on the healer's face.

What's gonna happen to her?

The four descended the steps and silently approached. As they stepped into the circle of light, a dozen unlit torches appeared, surrounding them. Hans made his way around the table and the others positioned themselves equidistant around the princess.

Once in position, Andy saw Hans glance below the table. His shoulders sagged and he closed his eyes as more tears fell to his tunic.

At length, he stooped and pulled out a unicorn horn.

"Yara," he whispered and handed it her.

The healer stooped again, this time bringing up a pitcher.

Jada and Naria's tale of the funeral pyre from which the phoenix emerged now filled Andy's thoughts. Judging by the size of Alden and Hannah's eyes, they also were remembering the story.

Air, water, earth, and fire—the elements to make something eternal!

"Andy, I think you're supposed to light the torches with your blade," Hans requested weakly as he poured the contents of the pitcher around and over the princess.

Andy glanced between his companions. Hannah covered her eyes. Alden held his cheek in his hand.

Andy extracted his sword from the makeshift holster and the blade extended. His hands trembled as he approached the first torch.

Aray

Lifting the tip of Methuselah's blade near the first wick, a flame emerged. Andy walked unenthusiastically toward the second lamp and repeated the movements. He exhaled, trying to calm himself.

After lighting the eleventh lamp, he paused and scanned his companions' faces. All wore wrinkled brows. Tears continued dripping down Hans's face. Yara remained prone with her eyes closed. The unicorn horn she held rose and fell evenly, unhurried, to her rhythmic breathing.

I couldn't do it.

Hans bowed his head as Andy reached the last torch, lifted the blade, and lit the final wick. As if on cue, Andy felt the ground begin to shake and he heard rumblings from above as dirt began sifting down from the ceiling. The four shot looks between each other.

"It's going to cave in!" Andy cried.

Hans nodded, then reached to help Yara up. "Come!" he coaxed.

"But I thought…" Yara stammered, still clutching the horn.

"Come on!" Hannah yelled as part of the ceiling gave way.

The five bounded toward the raised platform. They were only two yards away when the large floating sphere that had illuminated the space burst and zigzagged like a balloon rapidly losing air. The smaller floating spheres began bumping into each other and clumping. The group skirted the stage as more chunks of dirt gave way from the ceiling.

"This way!" Andy yelled, leading the group by Methuselah's light.

The undulating ground made it difficult to run, but within several minutes they plunged into the darkness that separated the place of testing from the tunnel. Andy hoped the rest of their company waited for them.

Andy barely realized when they had reached the earthen wall. So sudden was their arrival that the five of them nearly leveled Sergeant Hammond, who stood with his back toward their exit. Fides stood with his hands raised. Brilliant beams of light extended from each of his palms, bracing the quaking ceiling.

"Good! You're back!" Sergeant Hammond exclaimed, thrusting Calum at Alden.

Terwit terwoo, oop-oop-oop, the bird scolded at the rough treatment.

"Sergeant Fulk, lead the way! I'll bring up the rear. Move out!" Captain Baldric shouted.

Fulk bolted down the tunnel and everyone did their best to keep up. Fides ran in the middle of the pack, his arms still upraised and radiating energy. Loud scraping sounds filled the passage as the ground continued convulsing, and Andy felt like he was inside the sorting machine of one of his games back home. He barely stayed upright as he pitched and slammed into the side of the tunnel when the ground gave a particularly violent jolt. They had just turned left into the main passageway when the shaking suddenly stopped.

"Keep going! The ceiling's going to collapse!" the captain commanded, breathless.

Yara, still clutching the unicorn horn, charged behind Sergeant Fulk, followed immediately by Hannah and then Alden. Andy chanced a backward glance at Hans. Sergeant Ranulf buoyed the healer with an arm around his back.

Andy spotted daylight streaming through a thick haze not far ahead. *That's got to be the exit!*

Sergeant Fulk and Yara had stopped in the beam of light and stood staring up, their chests heaving. "How do we get out?" the princess panted as the company screeched to a halt.

Seconds later, everyone heard an ear-splitting bellow, "Nooo!"

"What was that?" Hannah queried.

"I don't know, but it doesn't sound happy," Alden assessed.

Everyone looked upward, but their concerns about frightening bellows were quickly overwhelmed as a **melody of idyllic notes drew near.**

Hooh-hrooo. Hooh-hrooo, Calum replied.

Andy looked up to see the silhouette of a large bird perching on the side of the well above them. "The phoenix!"

The bird dove through the opening, scattering the group as it came to stand next to Sergeant Terric. The sergeant drew back, eyes wide. The phoenix glanced about with deep-set black eyes that shone with unmistakable intelligence.

Whoa! Andy remembered Mom measuring him at four foot nine just days ago. This bird towered above him by nearly half a foot. *It's as tall as Madison!*

The bird lifted its long slender beak and peered at the company until at last it seemed satisfied. Andy and the others heard a girl's voice in their heads saying, "My name is Aray. Thank you for restoring the ring."

Unaccustomed to hearing voices, the five officers drew hands up to their heads and glanced about.

"My name's Andy." He introduced everyone then asked, "What do you mean we restored the ring?"

"The shaking and rumbling you felt were the stones moving back into place and repairing themselves. My time of new birth has come. Because of what you did, I am now free to build a nest so I can be reborn. Had you failed, I would have perished, for I did not have the materials necessary to build a pyre."

"Someone said you're the princess who died and came back to life out of the fire," Yara stammered.

The phoenix tittered before responding. "That's right."

A second outraged exclamation filtered through the hole.

"That would be Abaddon. He's none too happy the ring has been restored," Aray explained.

Andy looked the bird up and down and noticed gray pinfeathers peeking out from beneath patchy, tattered plumage. Several pinions wafted to the floor. *It's in bad shape.* Knowing he needed a phoenix feather for the next ingredient, Andy thought, *The clue didn't say what condition the feather has to be in.* He stooped down and retrieved a stray plume and added it to Methuselah's holster.

"Now then, you all need to find safety and I have a nest to build," echoed in everyone's minds. "These tunnels are not safe, for your adversary prowls about. With the ring's power restored, the mound near the center will conceal and protect you. I will deliver you two at a time if you'll just grab hold of my tail."

"Really? Are you sure?" Alden questioned, his brow furrowed.

The phoenix let loose another giggle, adding, "Of course."

"Ranulf and Hammond, you go first and scout it out," Captain Baldric commanded. "Andy, you and Yara go next. I'll come last." No one dissented, so the first recruits stepped forward and grabbed hold. The phoenix leapt on her substantial taloned feet, and with one mighty and perfectly timed flap of her wings, she hauled the two soldiers through the hole.

Andy could not help laughing at the officers' white knuckles and tightly squeezed eyes as they disappeared.

In no time Aray returned. "Prince. Princess," the bird invited.

Yara stowed the unicorn horn with her sword, then she and Andy grabbed Aray's tail tightly and the phoenix launched. The sudden acceleration tested Andy's grip, but he managed to hold on. Emerging from the hole, the grassy field stretched before them. The bird increased altitude and Andy chanced a look around. Between his taut arms, he saw their long shadows sway on the ground below, then noticed the lintels now formed a perfect circle. He and Yara shared a grin.

Halfway to their destination, Andy spotted a flock of five zolt bearing down.

"Aray!" he beckoned.

"I see them. Don't worry. You'll be safe," came the phoenix's reassurance.

Her wings fully extended, the large bird swooped low on a collision course with the earthen mound in the center of the ring.

"Aray!" Yara shrieked.

Had Andy not had a similar experience atop Daisy last year, he too would have panicked. Instead, he smiled and overheard giggles as they burst through the mound.

"Ahh!" the princess screamed.

The phoenix quickly halted and gently set her passengers down.

"Wha—?" Yara faltered.

Andy could only chuckle.

"You knew!" Yara accused.

Grinning, Andy replied, "A friend of mine pulled the same trick on me a year ago."

Sergeant Hammond drew a finger to his lips and pointed to the zolt that now prowled around the circumference of the mound.

Whoa! The mound looked nothing like Andy expected. He imagined they were caterpillars gazing out at the world from inside a giant, lidded glass jar.

The four grabbed their weapons and assumed ready positions. The phoenix strutted toward the side, climbed the six sunken steps that ringed the space, then ruffled her bedraggled plumage and let out a warbling squawk next to one of the enemy.

"Stop!" Yara hissed.

The zolt had no reaction except to gaze about stupidly. It took several strides up the mound as it continued its search. The four watched the soles of their enemy's boots as it scaled the invisible barrier, then got more than they bargained for when it reached the apex under which they all stood.

"Really?" Yara cried, drawing a hand over her eyes and turning away from the sight.

"They can't see or hear us! Excellent!" Andy yipped.

"Quite right," came a higher-pitched voice in everyone's head. "As long as you remain inside this mound, you'll be safe." Several minutes later the phoenix glanced about. "It seems our pursuers have given up."

Andy caught the last glimpse of a beady-eyed head disappear down the twin of the well where the rest of the company waited.

Oh boy...

"I'll go retrieve the others posthaste," the phoenix announced, and with a flap of her mighty wings she soared out of the mound.

Hannah and Alden, with Calum perched on his shoulder, arrived next, followed by Hans and Fides. Sergeants Fulk and Terric suffered a bumpy landing thanks to their uneven weight distribution, but neither was seriously hurt.

As the company awaited Captain Baldric's arrival, Alden meandered about the space, studying its structure. He stopped short next to Andy and pointed. "It's gone!"

Andy followed his friend's finger. "Awesome!" Andy rejoiced, rubbing his arm where the bellicose had whitened his skin a year before. He moved toward the invisible wall for more light. No trace of discoloration remained.

"Your face is fixed too!" Alden exclaimed.

"Wha—?" Sergeant Fulk scrutinized where the same beast had left its mark on him just days before.

"Mine's gone too!" Sergeant Hammond announced, grinning.

"It must have happened when the ring was restored," Yara surmised. "It's the center of healing for Cromlech after all." She lifted her chin high, drawing a chuckle from Hans.

Moments later Aray swooped in with Captain Baldric as another dozen zolt landed.

Alden charged the invisible barrier, put his thumbs in his ears, and stuck out his tongue. "Neener, neener!" he taunted the bird-warrior standing no more than a foot beyond.

"Would you stop," Hannah admonished.

"What?" Alden retorted, turning back to the group with mischief in his eyes.

No sooner had he said it than Hannah drew her thumbs to her armpits, hunched forward, bent her knees, and began jerking her head back and forth. She took a stride forward, and Alden shot Andy a quizzical look. Conversations ceased as everyone stared. She ruffled her bent arms as if they were wings and took another step.

"Hannah?" Alden queried.

She did not respond but bobbed her head, taking another step. "Bwak. Bwak. Cluck. Cluck. Bwak," she added. Hannah took several more strutting strides, then ruffled her bent arms again.

"What are you doing?" Alden pleaded. "Look, I'm sorry I teased that zolt." Everyone looked on helplessly.

A minute later Hans growled, "Yara?"

The blond-haired royal could no longer control the snicker that begged to be free. Yara covered her mouth with both hands and convulsed in laughter. "I'm—I'm sorry…"

The healer frowned at the princess. "This is why we have rules of ethics that all sommeils must abide by."

Hannah stood with her hands on her hips, glaring.

"Look, I'm sorry," the princess tried weakly. "When I saw Andy and the sergeants' skin restored, I had to see if my powers had returned."

"It seems they have," Hannah harrumphed.

Yara glanced over to Andy. He suddenly felt his face warm while the corners of his mouth began to rise.

"Stay away from me and my friends," Hannah snarled, then turned and walked away. Alden followed without a word.

From the officers' expressions it was clear they did not know what to make of it.

"Well, on that note, I have a nest to build," Aray announced, defusing the tension. The phoenix took several strides toward the barrier and launched, soaring clear of the hideaway. Andy watched as she flew a dozen loops above and around the ring before disappearing into the dusky sky.

"Is anyone hungry?" Fides probed.

When several of the company answered affirmatively, the keeper waved his hands and made a fire appear in the center of the space. Stone benches quickly surrounded it. A few more hand movements produced a table to his right filled with tasty offerings.

"You've *got* to show us how you do that!" Andy exclaimed, receiving a chorus of chuckles from his friends.

After everyone had eaten their fill, a contented hush fell over the company as they gazed into the dancing flames.

"I have to ask," Fides broke the quiet. "What happened during your testing? After waiting so many years for the fulfillment of the ancient text, you'll understand my curiosity." The keeper and the officers turned their gazes toward the five seekers and leaned in.

None of them offered a quick reply, only stared at the floor. At length, Hans broached, "It was one of the most painful experiences of my life." He went on to detail each test, concluding, "We must have passed, for the ring has been restored."

"I don't understand why I didn't have to die," Yara murmured.

Hans could only shake his head.

"Perhaps I can help with that," the keeper offered. "The ancient text said, 'Aray the token.' As princess of Cromlech, you are a direct descendant of the king whose daughter became the phoenix. As such, I believe you serve as a token. The original unicorn horn was present, as was Methuselah. When you found that pitcher of water, that completed the four elementals needed to create eternal life. As the blade lit the torches, it effectively reignited the funeral pyre. No life was required, for the sacrifice had already been made once for all time."

The thought of how close they had come to losing Yara made the group fall silent. Her willingness to sacrifice herself for her country's good awed them and cast a trance across the group.

Yawns erupted before long, announcing the conclusion of the gathering. Silence reigned as everyone reached for their bedrolls. With Aray having proven the ring's protection, Captain Baldric decided to dispense with the watch for one night as a gift to his men. But it meant they were now one bedroll short. Fides compensated, producing two bedrolls, one for himself and the other for Andy.

"Thanks!" As Andy sat down on his blanket, Fides leaned over and whispered, "New phoenix feathers hold the most power."

"Excuse me?"

"For your quest. You want a feather from the phoenix just after she is reborn. That one in your holster is old and devoid of the strength you will need for the task set before you. Wait for her to offer you one."

Andy's jaw dropped.

The keeper gave a quick wink, then lay down, drew up a blanket, and closed his eyes.

Despite his weariness, Andy's brain kept sleep at bay for some time.

Bright sunshine streaming through the clear walls of their hideaway woke Andy the next morning. He brushed sleep from his eyes and sat up. Everyone but he and Yara gathered around the fire eating a breakfast of bread, cheese, and fresh fruit.

"Good morning, sunshine," Hans greeted.

Hooh-hrooo. Hooh-hrooo.

"Good morning to you too, Calum," Andy answered in a monotone.

He staggered over and plopped down between the healer and Alden. Hannah handed Andy a chunk of warm bread, and he inhaled the tantalizing aroma before taking a huge bite. *Ohhh...that's so good!* The smell combined with the nourishment brought Andy fully awake and he joked, "Your mom's got stiff competition, Alden."

A shadow passed by the window in his periphery, and he turned to see Aray shuttle a hefty branch to a tall pile of brush. She carefully wove the addition into the rounded structure.

"She's been at it since I woke," Captain Baldric informed.

"Judging by the size of that stack, she's been working all night," Fulk added. The pile of wood came to at least four feet high and looked to measure double that in width.

"That's amazing!" Yara interjected, finger-combing her hair as she joined them.

"Have some breakfast, princess," Fides invited. "I dare say it won't be long now." His comment hushed all conversations.

Hannah shared glances with Andy and Alden but said nothing.

"This is a good thing. She will emerge strong and new in three days. We should celebrate," the keeper added.

Hannah refused to look at Yara, and Andy raised an eyebrow, noting the slight.

Turning his attention back to breakfast, he devoured a block of cheese and a good number of moonberries. Andy had just popped the last bite of bread into his mouth when the ground began to rumble.

CHAPTER SIXTEEN

Marionettes

"What's happening?" Hannah cried, clutching her seat.

Jagged white streams of light shot toward five of the lintels.

"Look!" Alden pointed to a dark figure standing near one of the giant stone columns, arms extended.

"The dark wizard!" Fides exclaimed.

Andy bounded toward the clear wall for a better look. "We've got to stop him before he destroys the ring again."

The sky grew dark as the company bolted from the security of their hideaway. A clap of thunder cracked and wind began to swirl, hurling dead grass and stray objects at them. The heaving ground made Andy feel like he was in a bounce house.

Andy drew an arm up to shield his eyes. The phoenix was no longer constructing her masterpiece. Only her head with its long slender beak was visible above the edge of her fortress.

A bolt of lightning streaked across the sky followed immediately by a pair of thunderclaps directly above. The grating sounds of shifting lintels accompanied two more streaks of lightning. Energy lit up the dim sky and a peal of thunder barked. Sergeant Fulk charged headlong toward the dark wizard with outstretched sword. The rest of the company stumbled after him as the ground continued seizing.

Two jagged streams of light flew low over Andy's head, distracting him. He looked back through squinted eyes and saw Fides had stopped running and now directed energy toward the dark figure.

Fides's bolts struck the wizard and it let loose a shrill, ear-splitting squeal. Everyone stopped and covered their ears. The villain returned a volley and the company found themselves caught in the crossfire.

"Crawl!" Captain Baldric shouted, heading toward a stone sentry.

Another thunder peal roared overhead and lightning danced across the sky as the group retreated toward safety. Crawling in a dress proved impossible, so Yara sprang up, hoisted her skirt, and ran. She barely avoided zaps from two streaks of white light before finally plunging behind a stone column. The rest of the company piled into her in their haste. A duet of lightning and thunder protested the company's safe retreat.

Fides and the dark wizard locked in combat and lit up the ring as if it were midday. Andy peered out and gasped as he saw the red dragon emerge from behind the dark wizard. Abaddon, hunched over, fought to remain upright as he navigated the undulating ground. Six of his seven heads sagged as he dragged his wings and tail, adding eerie scraping sounds to the cacophony of discordant notes.

What is that? Melodic notes rose above the din, and Hannah's mouth gaped as she stared wide-eyed at the phoenix's nest. Andy followed her gaze.

Aray held her head back and opened her beak wide to the skies as she sang slow, ponderous notes.

It sounds like death. A shiver scurried up his spine.

Scrape. Scrape. Scratch. Scrape. Abaddon's form continued its slow march toward the bird. When the dragon got within ten yards, three sharp cracks of lightning snapped the sky above, followed by a chorus of claps.

The two wizards seemed oblivious to the tumult. The conjoined arc of their powers swayed and pivoted near the ground, making movement about the area perilous at best and deadly at worst. Fides's face strained with the effort.

If Abaddon gets phoenix tears...

"Andy, don't do something rash," his inneru prompted.

Throwing caution to the wind, he bolted from safety.

"Andy!" Captain Baldric and Sergeant Terric cried, grabbing for him but missing. As he dashed into the fray, Andy overheard the captain bellow, "Alden!"

The arc of energy pitched violently and Fides shouted, "Nooo!"

Andy longed to stop and see what was happening. *No. Stay focused. I'm the only one who can intercept Abaddon!*

Methuselah led him along a zigzag path that narrowly escaped the wizards' game of jump rope. A bolt of lightning cascaded from the sky and struck the ground two feet ahead of him. He sidestepped and continued forward, closing on the dragon, which was now just three feet from the woodpile.

Where to strike… Andy quickly scanned the myriad of scales. He decided a direct hit to the bandage around one of the beast's lethargic heads would produce the desired result and raised his blade. Abaddon turned one of his heads toward Andy and held up a hand.

An eerie piercing wail tore through the ring. *What was THAT?* The thought scurried through Andy's brain just before an explosion rocked the woodpile, catapulting him backward. He landed hard on his back, still clutching his sword. The dragon, being heavier, did not falter. Rather, it held its ground at the edge of what was now an inferno.

"Aray!" Andy shouted.

Abaddon smiled, turned, and stepped forward. His body danced like heat rising off a hot sidewalk, then his wings disappeared, and finally his tail slithered into the blaze.

Flames licked at Andy, sending him scuttling backward. A final melodic note rang out from inside the blaze, then everything went quiet: the ground stopped trembling, the swirling wind died, the thunder and lightning ceased, and the sky regained its morning hue.

"Aray…" Andy whispered.

Had the fire no longer burned, he would have thought this was all just a bad dream. But flames licked and crackled.

What just happened? Abaddon wasn't after phoenix tears? Then what? Andy stared at the now knee-high woodpile.

"Are you okay, Andy?" Alden questioned, stopping abruptly next to his friend. Yara and Hannah arrived seconds later, bookending the boys.

Andy retracted his blade and holstered it before replying, "I'm fine."

Maniacal laughter sounded from behind them, and the four whirled around to see the dark wizard dusting off his sleeves as he stood. A white-robed form lay unmoving halfway between. Evil raised its arms once more, and a bolt of jagged white light shot from each of its fingers, clawing at the lintels.

Andy drew Methuselah and dashed toward the adversary. From the corner of his eye he saw several zolt stream onto the field. The officers rallied from behind the stone columns to meet the enemy.

The dark wizard diverted a bolt at Andy. He instinctively brought Methuselah's blade up and directed the pulse toward the ground, infuriating the mage. It loosed its grasp from three of the listing lintels and redirected the energy no more than a foot over Andy's head, causing him to duck.

Shrieks and howls erupted behind him and he pivoted. His friends lay scattered like toys after an angry child's tantrum. Alden convulsed as a beam assaulted his chest. Hannah shook violently and yelped as another ray bit at her leg like a frenzied dog. Yara writhed, howling as a bolt zapped her shoulder.

"Stop!" Andy demanded. The officers continued the fight across the field as he rushed back for his friends. Reaching Alden's side, he intercepted the wizard's beam and Alden's body ceased its jerky movements. He grabbed one of Alden's feet as the girls continued to yelp and howl. Fumbling to keep his blade upright, he dragged Alden two yards to where Hannah thrashed. Once out of the bite of the beams, they both lay quietly.

Andy wiped away beads of sweat from his lip, trying to convince himself they were from exertion and not fear. *How to get Yara.* He knew the instant he left the pair to retrieve her, his friends would again feel the wrath of the dark wizard's energy, but there seemed to be no other solution.

Scratch. Scraaaape. The foreboding sounds coaxed Andy's gaze upward in time to see three crossbeams begin to teeter. They begged for intercession, but Andy refused.

He raced to where the princess flopped about and found her staring blankly with her mouth stretched in a silent scream. Andy deflected the bolt, stilling her form, and the features he found so captivating relaxed. For a moment he stopped and appreciated.

"No time, Andy!" his inneru shouted.

He grabbed an arm and dragged her to where the others were again shaking like marionettes in the hands of a cruel puppeteer.

Scratch. Scrape. Silence.

Andy glanced over to see two of the lintels dive from their pedestals, as if announcing their assessment that his priorities were skewed. The ground shook as the columns collapsed, and the dark wizard belted out another chilling laugh. The officers continued fighting not far from the impact zone.

On its own, each bolt of energy did not require significant effort to deflect, but concentrated, the three cords pressed hard on Methuselah and made

Andy's arm shake. Adding his other hand, he steadied his blade, then surveyed his friends. No one moved.

Scrape. Scrape. The wizard had directed his energy toward enticing three more lintels to leap.

"Andy?" Dad's voice in his head drew out the syllables.

Ping-ponging his head between his friends and the mage, Andy nodded in determination then took off running toward the agitator. Within seconds the cords that had impaled his friends morphed into a rope that whipped about, a serpent readying a strike. As Andy neared Fides's still form, the snake struck, launching the keeper ten feet into the air.

"No!"

The dark wizard greeted Andy's protest with more laughter as Fides's body thudded to the ground. The serpent of energy picked up its toy again and repeated the gesture.

Andy gritted his teeth as he charged past.

Seemingly disappointed that Andy refused to watch him play, the conjurer whipped the energy snake around and bit Andy's leg.

"Youch!" A wail escaped, and Andy took several run-hops before working through the pain. He was ten yards from his objective, however, when a black cat-man bolted from behind the wizard.

Mwahaha.

"Crap!"

Andy whirled around and headed toward the three precariously perched crossbeams. Running proved difficult while keeping Methuselah between himself and the energy cord, and Andy barely managed. The bellicose bounded after him, preparing to pounce.

Scrape...

Andy skidded to a stop at the base of a stone column and pivoted to face his nemesis. The mage's angry beam proved useful as Andy deflected it toward the cat-man, delaying its assault. But the bellicose was quick and nimbly avoided it.

Andy backed between the columns, using their bulk to shield him from the wizard's energy. He assumed a ready position and his pursuer did likewise.

Scratch...

Come on! Fall, would ya?

The cat-man lunged and Andy sidestepped, but the evasive maneuver took him from between the stone sentries and the energy beam stung him once more.

Scrape…

Biting back the pain, he thrust Methuselah up to block the dark wizard's energy, then snuck a glance upward. The lintels teetered, daring gravity to have its way with them, so he again backed between the stone blocks and forced them to take the punishment the evil sorcerer exacted. The move forced the bellicose from between the stone columns.

Scratch. Scrape. Silence.

Seconds later, Andy felt a thud as the ground hugged its stone prizes and his nemesis disappeared.

"You show much spirit, my plaything," a maniacal voice echoed.

Andy peeked out from safety and saw the officers continue cutting down zolt. The dark wizard launched Alden, Hannah, and Yara into the air.

"Oh. No. You. Don't!" Andy took off running for the mage. Brilliant bolts of energy instantly connected with his blade, stymieing his progress. His enemy now abandoned its quest to topple more crossbeams or toy further with his friends and directed the whole of its power against him.

"Uuhhh," Andy grunted. He pressed forward, taking one labored step after another, as if slogging through quicksand. His arms shook with the effort.

I. Must. Win. The words circled through his brain, strengthening his resolve as he drew nearer.

Coming to within five feet of his adversary, Andy planted himself. A thread of energy leapt from the cord and found the back of Andy's leg once more. He winced and bit down on his lip, but quickly refocused. Andy tried a fake to his right, but an energy tongue licked his other leg. He yipped, hopping. He attempted another fake, this time to his left, with the same result. Fury bore fruit and Andy's surroundings slowed.

Brilliant, slow-moving threads of energy glided from the dark wizard in graceful arcs. Andy ducked a tentacle that wafted toward him as he bounded forward. Another appendage nearly kissed his arm as he drew Methuselah back, but the blade quickly dispensed with the threat. He jumped, barely missing arms of energy that attempted to snag his foot. The wizard took a step back, but Andy matched. The mage's chest loomed within reach and Andy thrust his sword, plunging it into his heart. The blade met no resistance as he slashed downward.

The wizard fell backward in slow motion but called nature to his defense as he did. Angry thunderclaps hurtled sympathetic lightning at Andy. In his warp state, he easily sidestepped the attack, but dark forces refused to be bested and split the ground beneath his feet.

Andy jumped to solid footing, but the ground split again in a fast-paced game of hopscotch. A whirlwind formed and quickly descended on the body of his adversary. Andy hopped and barely found a foothold as it shredded the corpse and scattered the fragments like dandelion seeds.

Gross! He ducked to avoid contact.

A final crack sounded as the last vestige of his enemy took flight and the ground abandoned its game. The warm, late-morning sun celebrated the victory as Andy's world slowed. A white silhouette bleached the ground, marking where his adversary had fallen. He exhaled.

Thud. Scratch. Scrape. Thud. Scratch. Scrape.

Andy ducked even as he glanced up to see the two fallen lintels soar back onto their platforms. *The ring's repairing itself!*

"Ohh!" A chorus echoed across the plain as company members paused to marvel and catch their breath amidst a sea of zolt carcasses. Andy hobbled toward where Hannah, Yara, and Alden lay.

Please be okay. Please be okay.

As he reached the trio, Alden stretched, then sat up. Hannah yawned and did likewise.

"I feel like I just woke from a wonderful dream," Yara said, rubbing her eyes.

"What?" Andy questioned.

"Yeah, I haven't felt this rested in…I can't remember when," the princess confirmed.

"Me too," Alden added. He stood, then helped Hannah up.

"Really?"

The three nodded.

"Do you have any idea what just happened?"

Alden glanced between the girls and furrowed his brow. "What do you mean?"

Hannah bit her lip and Yara frowned.

Andy shifted and realized the backs of his legs no longer hurt. "Wow! I think the ring healed my legs."

Andy saw Hans emerge from between stone sentries. *Hooh-hrooo. Hooh-hrooo,* Calum cooed from atop his shoulder. As soon as the healer reached the group, the bird started bouncing.

"Whoa, Calum, you'll fall off," Alden laughed, reaching for his charge. Alden stroked the dove, holding it close.

"Hey, see if his wing is healed," Andy encouraged.

Alden set the bird on the ground and carefully removed the bandages.

Hooh-hrooo. Hooh-hrooo, Calum chirped, then extended both wings and flapped them briskly, testing their reliability. Seconds later he took flight.

"All right!" Captain Baldric congratulated.

"Looks like your patient has fully recovered," Hans complimented, receiving a broad smile from his apprentice.

Calum made several passes overhead, cooing each time he approached the company. At last he fluttered to a stop on Alden's shoulder.

"So, what did we miss while we were sleeping?" Alden queried.

Andy reiterated the events and was met with incredulous looks.

"The ring must have healed our bodies and wiped our memories of the events," Hannah deduced.

"What, so we're not emotionally scarred?" Yara teased.

"Yes," Hannah replied shortly.

"Where's Fides?" Yara queried.

Andy turned and nodded toward the still form.

"Oh no," Hannah whispered as her eyes welled with tears.

Yara covered her mouth as the group walked slowly toward the white-robed keeper.

CHAPTER SEVENTEEN

Fusion

Andy knelt, holding his breath. The keeper lay on his side with eyes closed, his legs and arms at odd angles. Had Andy not witnessed the battle Fides waged against the dark wizard, he would have prayed the man was just unconscious. But even as he gently cajoled the upturned shoulder, his gut confirmed his fears.

Andy looked hopefully to Hans. The healer approached and felt for a pulse, then shook his head, drawing gasps from several as they formed a circle. There would be no healing. Fides had made the ultimate sacrifice. Captain Baldric knelt on one knee and his men followed, bowing their heads.

"I heard a banshee wail, but I still hoped," Hans murmured.

Andy looked over. "A what?"

"A banshee. They're spirits from the underworld. Somehow they know when someone is going to die, and they let out an eerie, piercing wail."

"That's what that was," Andy replied softly. "From the underworld?" A chill rippled through his body as Hans nodded.

"He saved our lives. We should give him a befitting send-off," Yara intoned, receiving several nods in reply.

"He loved the phoenix. I think we should help him join her," Andy suggested.

"That would make him happy," Yara agreed.

Sergeant Terric approached and gently lifted the body, then processed toward the pyre that had burned down to shin height.

"Lay him on the ground here," Hans instructed, pointing to a spot a couple yards from the edge. "I need someone's canteen."

Alden offered his and the healer knelt, sprinkling the white robes and chanting: "Into the presence of the Ancient One I commend his spirit."

At length he rose and asked the captain and Sergeant Terric to place the body on the glowing embers, which they did. The company stepped back, distancing themselves from the heat. *Earth, air, fire, and water. The Elementals for eternal life.* Andy's chest ached and he sniffled.

The hot coals licked at the form, seeming to taste it before deciding to engulf it. Andy couldn't divert his eyes from the transformation, and his thoughts whirled. *Fides died protecting us. And Spark...oh, that pixie.* He smiled before his thoughts continued. *She died because of Alden and me. I vowed no one else would die on my account...* Andy clenched his jaw, then ran the back of his wrist across his eyes.

Several minutes passed and a booming voice interrupted the solemn silence, "What is the meaning of this, Imogenia?"

All eyes searched the sky for the source.

"Father?"

Imogenia's silvery form floated not far behind the company.

"The Afterlife of Cromlech is in an uproar. Crossover collectors came demanding answers."

"What are you talking about?"

"This letter! Moments ago a dark spirit from Hadession forced its way into their Terminal and assaulted a wizard before he had chosen his eternal destination. It overwhelmed his inneru."

Imogenia drew a translucent hand to her mouth. "That's possible?"

"They said they had never seen it before, but that doesn't excuse it. They know you were present, and they want answers."

"I didn't do anything, Father! I've just been watching the whole time, I swear."

"Then how do you explain it?"

"How should I know? I didn't even know it was possible. Did they say how it happened?"

"They've launched an investigation, but initial speculation is that evil of Hadessic origin somehow mingled with the wizard's body shortly after he crossed over. It's the only way the dark spirit could have breached Cromlech's terminal."

"I don't know what to say. What happened to the wizard?"

"It snatched him."

"How's that even possible?"

"No one knows, but I need you to come with me and tell the Committee on Afterlife Affairs what you just told me."

Silence returned and without thinking, Andy offered, "That was my grandfather and my aunt…from the Afterlife." A sick feeling thudded in his gut. He scanned the company and saw a look of astonishment on every face.

It was my suggestion!

"What have we done?" Andy squeaked.

"What's going to happen to Fides?" Yara stammered.

"What did he mean, 'It overwhelmed his inneru'?" Alden questioned.

Hans took a trembling step forward, then opted to sit. "I fear we may have given our enemy a powerful tool."

"How so?" Captain Baldric queried.

"I served as royal healer when Abaddon first started transforming people into vulture-folk. As you know, the queen of Cromlech was a sommeil. She often spoke about working with victims whose relatives had brought them seeking relief. She said their minds all felt 'dark,' as if evil festered in their thoughts and even in their innerus. They would grow hostile, especially when asked about the events that had caused their condition. It frustrated her to not be able to help them. I only ever heard of one case where the person's mind was restored. We speculated these folks formed the core of Abaddon's followers."

"But not all vulture-folk are hostile," Andy objected.

"Quite right, but that's a more recent development. It seems Abaddon changed his tactics. When he transformed people to draw energy to strengthen himself a year ago, it appears he did not infiltrate their minds quite so much. It's all I can figure since, as you point out, those newly transformed are not hostile. I don't know why. And because I don't know of any sommeils who treated these patients previously, we can't understand the differences.

"My worry with Fides's inneru being overwhelmed is that evil will use him. With the wizard's tremendous powers, the dark forces would have a significant advantage over us. We may have exchanged one set of problems for something greater."

Will I have two to battle in the end? Andy wondered.

"We should eat before we head out," Captain Baldric suggested.

"No! We can't leave yet," Andy objected. "I need to get a tail feather from the phoenix once it resurrects."

"There are feathers all over in the tunnel. Aray was molting badly," Hannah offered.

"Last night Fides told me I need a new feather."

Hannah raised her eyebrows and Alden questioned, "How would Fides even know about your quest?"

"I don't know, but he did. I'm just glad he told me last night."

"Do you suppose he knew what would happen today?" Hannah pondered.

Yara raised a hand. "Would someone mind explaining what you all are talking about?"

Realizing the princess had not been privy to the earlier conversation, Andy opened his mouth to recount the tale, but the captain interrupted, "How about you fill her in while we eat?"

No one dissented, so the company headed back toward their hideaway. "Wow!" and "Oooh!" echoed from those who entered the domed space first. Andy instantly understood the exclamations as he entered. The two tables overflowed with dried meats, cheese, fruit, and pitchers of water, but four more tables had been added and they too held a bounty.

"Fides!" Hans cried. "He knew we would need sustenance while we waited for Aray to emerge."

"When did he have time?" Yara questioned.

Silence overwhelmed the group until Alden's stomach grumbled loudly. "Excuse me," he apologized, breaking the spell.

Hans moved toward the closest table, coaxing the others on. After grabbing a handful of the provisions, Andy surveyed the chamber. Hannah and Yara had waged nonverbal combat since they had returned to the hideout, so Andy was not surprised to see the princess retreat to a spot on the floor well away from the others as she ate. Andy joined her, receiving a warm smile. Butterflies instantly took flight in his belly.

As he munched on a fresh roll and moonberries, Andy told Yara about his quest for the phoenix feather. Assessing she posed no danger, he divulged tales of claiming the previous three ingredients. When she probed further, he revealed how he had come to learn he was the chosen one. She marveled at this, but was even more surprised when he told her how he had discovered the King was his father.

"You're so easy to talk to," Andy concluded.

"Your story is interesting," Yara replied, looking into his eyes.

"I have to ask you something." Andy assumed a thoughtful expression and chose his words carefully.

"What is it?"

"Did you plant a suggestion in my mind to go after the dark wizard?"

Yara turned her eyes downward and slowly nodded. "I couldn't see any other way to defeat him. The ring would have been lost again. I couldn't let that happen. Cromlech's healing powers would have been destroyed. As queen—" Returning her gaze to Andy she added, "I'm sorry."

"Hans is right."

Yara furrowed her brow in a question mark.

"We have a lot in common. Ruling is not easy."

The princess nodded. "Captain Baldric said something else."

"What's that?"

"He said we should get to know each other." She added a smile.

Andy felt his cheeks warm, then offered his hand and helped the princess up.

Hans winked as Andy and Yara rejoined the rest of the group, then deflected, "We've been talking about what happened out there. What did you two see?"

Andy directed Yara toward an open spot on one of the benches surrounding the fire, then sat down beside her. Hannah raised an eyebrow.

Andy told of watching the weakened Abaddon navigate the field under cover of the dark wizard's strikes, and of the dragon's subsequent plunge into the fiery furnace.

"I don't understand. I thought he wanted phoenix tears to heal his wounds, not to incinerate himself. And the way he looked at me just before he did it. He smiled, like he had won some contest."

"Well, look on the bright side, you don't have to battle Abaddon anymore," Hannah rejoiced.

"Yeah! That bad dude is dead!" Alden quipped, pumping a fist.

"I'm not so sure," Andy cautioned.

"What do you mean? You just said he walked into the fire. Bye-bye, 'Baddon," Hannah waved her hand and laughed.

"That sounds good," Alden added.

"Yeah, after all he's done," Yara scowled.

Andy cocked his head in disagreement.

"Oh, come on, Andy. He's dead. Dead is dead," Alden countered.

Yara glanced over and caught his eye, then nodded her support.

"Well, at least we know for a fact the bellicose is gone," Hans encouraged. "That lintel smashed it into the ground not far from me."

"I'd like to see for myself," Andy declared.

"Looks like we've all got things to do," Captain Baldric asserted, rising. "We'd best move all those bodies before wild animals come scavenging and your phoenix is endangered."

Called into action, the company headed outside. The officers formed a work detail while Andy and the others headed for the pit punched in front of one of the golden stone sentries.

As the five passed the pyre with its glowing coals, Andy furrowed his brow. Yara reached over and took his hand. "We can't change the past. We can only make a better future for both our lands."

Andy smiled his appreciation, squeezed her hand, and nodded.

They approached a rectangular crater that would have measured five feet square had the crossbeam fallen evenly. The grass had been sheared off, leaving a clean delineation between the sod and the brown dirt beneath. The group stopped at the edge. Andy hesitated briefly, unsure what revolting sight might await. Mixed relief came when he did not see a mutilated body but the white-scorched shape of his adversary silhouetted in the dirt.

"It can come back," Andy murmured. "How do we kill it once and for all?"

No one hazarded a reply.

"Maybe with Abaddon gone it won't return," Hannah hoped.

Andy shook his head. "Like I said before, I'm not convinced he's gone."

Andy glanced about the group, but no one betrayed their thoughts on the subject.

The afternoon passed uneventfully as the five of them helped the officers dispose of the enemy carcasses, after which they retreated back into their hideaway. Andy and Yara paired off and continued their earlier conversation. They laughed as they talked about all manner of topics, from pets to favorite colors and foods. As the two grew more comfortable, they shared their dreams for the future, and at one point the princess confessed how unprepared she felt to rule the people whose welfare had been entrusted to her. Andy readily agreed.

So oblivious were they to the goings-on around them that when Hans announced dinner was ready, Andy felt as though he had been dragged back through a time warp.

"Hey, they're back!" Alden exclaimed, winking.

"Yes, thanks for joining us," Hans kidded.

Hannah held Alden's hand, but her expression extended no grace.

Dinner and laughter gave way to yawns, and all but Sergeant Fulk bedded down for the night. Despite the feeling of security in their cozy abode, Captain Baldric felt it important that they not grow lax, so the night watch resumed.

Dreams came quickly for Andy, but like the night before, they brought him back to the dunk tanks. Father, Mom, and Mermin sat bound and helpless on the three narrow beams. An armed zolt brandished a shiny blade next to each of them. A horn sounded and the enemy inched closer. Andy looked down, expecting to see spongs, but instead found marshmallows. He picked up a handful and began hurling them toward the enemy. The zolt crept closer. Andy screamed and grabbed more sugary ammunition, throwing as hard as he could. Still the adversary drew closer. The marshmallows morphed into chocolate chip cookies, but his attempts to defend yielded the same result. The first vulture-warrior reached Mermin, turned and smiled at Andy, then lopped off the wizard's head.

"No!"

"Andy!" Yara shook him to semiconsciousness as others scattered around the fire mumbled and rolled over.

Mercifully, Andy's mind ventured elsewhere when he returned. He stood before a roaring fire that illuminated a scene from a previous dream. A pair of couches stood perpendicular to the hearth. Two silent, silvery forms reclined opposite each other. The male spirit sipped a drink, then queried as he set it down, "Imogenia, what's troubling you?"

"You won, Father."

"What's that?"

"Abaddon was my only hope for killing the boy so the curse could not be broken. Everything I've tried has failed. The only saving grace is that the dragon stepped into that fire of his own accord. Your champion did not kill him, so you cannot remove the curse."

The king nodded, then added, "Have you considered that the Ancient One had his reasons for allowing things work out as they have?"

Imogenia looked at her father but remained silent.

"Your mother was concerned that when we removed our support of the curse for the sake of the people, it would splinter our family irreparably."

Imogenia stared into the flames.

"I believe the Ancient One desires the curse to end. That's why he has given the boy ingredients to collect."

"If what I want doesn't matter, why has he not lifted the curse himself? Why go through all this?"

The sovereign smiled. "How else could your heart be healed from its hate?"

Imogenia studied her hands. "But collecting ingredients seems so slow."

"My guess is that from the trials the boy must endure to gather them, he is being prepared to rule our people well."

Imogenia looked up. "You haven't called them 'our people' in years."

Her father nodded, then added, "Surely you're happy that they will have a wise sovereign."

"Yes, but I'm still not convinced Kaysan has repented for what he did to me." She fell silent for a minute before asking, "How will I know?"

"That's an excellent question, and the answer requires faith."

At this, the dream began breaking up into flinty shards, like glass. The images shimmered, then vanished.

Inspection of the cold coals the next morning revealed only that earthworms had begun work to reclaim the embers. The company spotted three of them wiggling about.

"That's strange. The worms here are different from any I've seen before," Andy commented at seeing a red one, a black one, and a variegated one crawl through the ashes.. "I've only ever seen brown worms."

That night dreams again terrified Andy's thoughts. He held a ready position in the ring as Abaddon, Fides, and the bellicose circled, stalking. Father, Mom, and Mermin sat gagged and bound together at Andy's feet, their arms behind their backs.

Abaddon taunted, "Thought I'd give myself up willingly without a reason?" The dragon laughed, then shot a burst of flame. Methuselah easily deflected the blast, but then Fides took a turn, upending the captives with a stream of energy.

Andy again screamed, disturbing his companions.

After that nightmare, Andy approached the ashes the next morning with a tempest raging in his stomach.

"Oh, look!" Hannah pointed at a baby bird shivering and struggling in the debris. It had no feathers, but from the variegated coloring of its skin it was easy to guess how bright its plumage would be.

"It's cold. Should we warm it up?" Alden queried.

"I don't think I'd touch it," Hans cautioned. "The sun will soon remedy its chill."

"It's ugly. Hard to believe something as beautiful as a phoenix starts out looking like *that*," Yara commented.

Andy laughed and, despite the bluntness of the comment, Alden directed a smile toward the princess. Hannah remained expressionless.

Andy studied the ashes for further signs of the black or red worms but did not see them.

That night, instead of returning him to the Land of Nightmares, Andy's dreams bought him a roundtrip ticket to La La Land. As he landed, welcoming singing filled his mind. Father, Mom, Mermin, and Dad threw open their arms at the first glimpse of him, then swallowed him in a long hug that calmed his frayed nerves. He sighed contentedly.

"I've missed you all so much."

"And we've missed you. More than you know."

Excitement filled the air as the company approached the extinct pyre the next morning. Sitting in the middle of the circle was a fledgling phoenix. Its pinfeathers poked out every which way, making it look fuzzy.

"It's so cute!" Hannah oozed.

Yara, who stood next to her, laughed in agreement.

The bird stood on shaky legs and wobbled a few steps before collapsing.

"When are you supposed to get a feather?" Alden queried.

"Fides said to wait for it to offer me one."

"At the rate its growing, that may be today," Hans speculated as the phoenix rose and took several wobbly steps.

The five watched with rapt attention all morning, marveling at how it grew before their eyes. Not wanting to miss any of the action, the group ate a quick lunch and resumed their vigil.

The phoenix had lost its pinfeathers in their absence and now wore a nearly full set of mature red, orange, and yellow plumage. It had also grown taller by at least a foot so that it was now at eye level with Andy.

"Is the pile of ashes getting smaller?" he wondered.

"Yeah, I think it is," Alden replied.

Several hours later, the bird stepped out of its nest and tested its wings. It repeated the exercise half a dozen times before lifting off three or four inches. Another half dozen tries and it could rise a couple feet before coming to rest again.

Apparently satisfied at its readiness, the phoenix sang the song the company had first heard as they approached the Giant's Ring. The tone and tempo created an upbeat mood this time.

"Thank you for all you've done. I can never thank you enough," Aray broadcast in their minds. "As a token of my appreciation, I want you each to have a feather." The phoenix plucked nine variegated plumes and distributed them amid exclamations.

"And for you, Andy, a special feather." Tears formed in Aray's eyes as she reached back. She used her tail to dab away the moisture, then plucked a deep red plume and offered it to Andy.

Thank you, Aray. It was all Andy could think as he studied the gift.

With that, Aray took flight. Everyone stood in awed silence as she circled a half dozen times and sang. At last she rose above the lintels and disappeared into the distance.

Andy had barely placed the feather in Methuselah's holster when the ground began to shake.

Not again!

The group pivoted toward the epicenter. Emerging from the remaining ashes were the forms of a seven-headed red dragon and a sinister being clad in black robes.

CHAPTER EIGHTEEN
Reciprocation

A host of zolt came into focus seconds later.

"Retreat!" yelled Captain Baldric. "They're too strong. We can't defeat them!"

Everyone bolted through the entrance to the hideaway, panting.

"Fides knows about this place! They'll follow!" Hannah choked out.

"Trust in the power of the ring," Hans encouraged. Several glanced questioningly, but the healer held a calm expression as he watched the enemy fan out across the field.

The tension was palpable. No one uttered a word.

Five zolt scoured around their hiding place but discovered nothing. Abaddon strutted several feet, flapping his wings. He paused, scanned the area, thrust his hands into the air, and roared, "I live forever!" He proceeded to transform into a thunderbird, drawing gasps from Andy's friends.

The creature flapped its enormous wings. In a rush of wind that downed several nearby zolt, it became a karkadann with a jet-black corkscrew horn. The beast pawed the ground and snorted, readying a charge.

Hooh-hrooo. Hooh-hrooo, Calum sounded at seeing this.

The white beast shifted into what looked like water in the form of a person. As the figure stood and wildly waved its arms, it morphed into a herewolf, complete with a smashed-in nose and huge paws. This in turn became the now-familiar monstrous blue serpent.

Out of the corner of his eye, Andy saw Alden rub his forearm.

In an instant, Abaddon shifted back into the seven-headed dragon and threw a blast of flame that incinerated several of his own warriors.

Fides stopped next to him, drew up his hands, and directed bolts of energy at the lintels.

ANDY SMITHSON: RESURRECTION OF THE PHOENIX'S GRACE

"The ring!" Yara shrieked.

"I believe it will be fine," Hans reassured. He seemed nonplussed and received more doubtful glances.

Andy rubbed the back of his neck. Hannah bit a fingernail. Alden crossed and uncrossed his arms. The officers held ready positions.

Though Fides's energy continued clawing at the stones, none so much as shivered.

Eventually Abaddon bellowed, "Follow!" and he and Fides vanished. The flock of zolt launched skyward.

"How did they not find us?" Hannah exhaled.

"The Fides we knew was aware of our hideaway. The dark Fides could not access his earlier memories." Hans shook his head, "This is bad."

Andy's stomach sank.

"As for the lintels, I think the dark wizard was able to upset them earlier because Aray was weak. I believe the ring manifests her condition. Because she is newly reborn, she is strong, making the ring strong."

"We need to move out quickly," Captain Baldric commanded. "No telling when they might return."

A few short minutes later, the company emerged from their hideaway. Thanks to the "good" Fides, their packs were heavy with provisions to last until they reached home.

"The most direct route back to Castle Avalon is a path skirting Mount Mur Eyah," Captain Baldric announced from up front as they ventured forth. "With any luck, we should be home in five days."

"But what about Calum?" Alden objected. "We need to make sure he gets home safely."

Hooh-hrooo. Hooh-hrooo!

"It'll add a full day," the captain cautioned. When no one objected, he relented and adjusted their course.

Andy scanned the skies for zolt. When his search turned up empty, he let out a sigh. Yara, who walked beside him, looked over quickly and returned her gaze to the ground.

"You're awfully quiet. What's wrong?"

The princess picked at her fingernails and shook her head.

"Come on, what is it?"

"I've never been to Oomaldee."

"Oh," Andy laughed. "Well, you're gonna love it." He proceeded to recount the tale of his arrival, including discovering a practical use for cow farts, which drew chuckles from the other three who walked in front of them. As Andy spoke, his longing to again see Father, Mermin, Marta, and the others grew.

The air was warm the following morning as they set out from their campsite. They had stopped short of karkadann territory the previous afternoon, hoping to avoid contact with any of the beasts as they returned Calum to his home.

Hooh-hrooo. Hooh-hrooo.

The dove bounced on Alden's shoulder and took flight several times as they drew near familiar landmarks.

"He's so excited." Hannah smiled at the dove's antics, which proved contagious until Sergeant Fulk, who led the group this morning, thrust his arm into the air and closed his hand quickly, stopping forward progress and silencing conversation.

Andy felt the ground rumble, and judging by their expressions, so did the others. Captain Baldric joined the sergeant at the front and motioned them to hurry into the shelter of a rock outcropping that jutted up not far to their left.

Hooh-hrooo. Hooh-hrooo.

"Shhh, Calum," Alden cautioned as they approached safety.

The ground shook more violently.

"He needs to go," Hannah squeaked.

Hooh-hrooo. Hooh-hrooo.

Ducking into the cave, Alden retrieved the dove from his shoulder and drew it close, whispering to it as he stroked its feathers. Then he placed Calum on the ground. The bird looked about before strutting over to Yara.

Hooh-hrooo. Hooh-hrooo.

The princess knelt and petted it, receiving several raised eyebrows. "That's right, Calum. We'll miss you, but you can serve here more effectively than at the castle. We'll let you know if we need your help."

Hooh-hrooo.

Yara laughed, "You too. Bye."

With that, Calum rose and fluttered out of the cave. Alden, Andy, Hannah, and Yara plugged the exit as they peered after the bird. A huge white beast with a jet-black corkscrew horn stood waiting.

Hooh-hrooo. Hooh-hrooo.

The dove circled three times before touching down on the mammoth head. With its passenger secure, the beast scanned its surroundings, stamped a foot, and snorted. Finally it turned around and meandered off the way it had come.

"What was that about, Yara?" Alden questioned.

"I was just firming up help. Never know when we might need a friend or two."

"Karkadann?" Hannah clarified, her eyes wide.

"Why not?" Yara smiled.

"You talked to Calum?" Andy questioned.

"Let's just say I gave him a few suggestions and he did the same."

"We've got company," Sergeant Ranulf interrupted. He had been keeping watch near the exit.

Captain Baldric hastened to join him, peeked out, then motioned everyone to huddle. In a whisper he informed, "A flock of twenty zolt just landed. Let's see what they do."

Everyone silently drew their weapons and assumed ready positions. A low, nasally voice announced, "She's here."

Andy quickly glanced to Yara who stiffened, then shook her head. After a long wait, Sergeant Ranulf informed, "They just left."

Sighs greeted the news.

"What do you suppose that was all about?" Alden questioned.

Andy shook his head.

After the close call, everyone studied the skies the rest of the morning. Only when the beginnings of tree cover appeared in the distance did the company relax as they neared gnome lands.

They stopped in a shaded place to eat a lunch of dried meat and moonberries. Alden started smiling and his eyes danced.

"What is it?" Hannah questioned.

"I've been thinking…" He flicked his eyebrows, capturing the others' attention. "Why don't we prepare a thank-you for the gnomes? Their welcome was so warm last time." He kneaded his hands, drawing laughter from Andy and the princess. "Yara, I'll need your help."

"What do you have in mind?" she replied with a grin.

"What most scares gnomes?"

"Dragons, most definitely," interjected Hans.

"Perfect. Dragons it is!" Alden raised his hands in answer to their questioning looks. "Hear me out. Yara, you can plant suggestions in people's minds, right?"

The princess nodded.

"We'll make camp and go about our business. We know the gnomes will notice."

"And probably set up some prank," Hannah added.

"But we don't have anything that looks like a dragon," objected Hans.

"Wait!" interrupted Andy. He removed the pouch from his neck and extracted a red ruby and a blue sapphire. "These could work as shiny eyes."

Alden beamed.

"Ooh! And Methuselah could shoot out fire!" Hannah innovated. "If I get on Andy's back, I can hold the stones and you can make Methuselah flame."

"Yara, can you make the gnomes believe the stones and flame are a dragon swooping in to attack them?" Alden probed.

"I've never implanted thoughts in more than two people at once, but I'll try."

"We'll see what you're capable of," Hans encouraged, at which Yara beamed.

"We'll need to let them think they're scaring us before we launch our counterstrike." Andy cracked up as he said it.

"Just remember, whatever they do, it isn't real," Hans intoned, receiving nods.

Andy waltzed over to the gathering of officers and filled them in on the plan, receiving hearty approval. They even offered to position themselves around the camp and quietly signal at the first sign of gnome engagement.

Excitement carried them over rolling hills and a steep mountain all that afternoon. As the sun began casting long shadows, Captain Baldric declared they should stop and set up camp. After canteens had been refilled from a nearby stream and wood was gathered to last the night, Andy lit the campfire with Methuselah and Hans began preparing a hearty stew from the dried meat they carried. Sergeant Fulk and Alden agreed on two coos, like Calum made, that would serve as the signal. With that the officers dispersed to blend into the forest.

Daylight had expired and the savory aroma of the stew announced supper was almost ready when *hooh-hrooo, hooh-hrooo* wafted across the still evening. The five exchanged glances and forced down smiles as they took their places around the fire, feigning conversation.

Skreek. Skreek.

Hannah made like a gopher and glanced about with wide eyes.

Skreek. Skreek.

The others scanned the forest. Nothing moved. The dense woods seemed to hold its breath.

Skreek. Skreek. Skreek.

Hannah grabbed Alden's arm and cowered. "Why'd they have to do bats this time? Why not butterflies or snakes?" she choked out.

"Don't give them any ideas," Andy whispered back.

Skreek. Skreek.

Andy spied movement over the treetops. Large wings flapping.

"Not yet," Alden instructed quietly. "Keep looking around, like you're scared."

Hannah whimpered.

"Almost there," Alden directed as the wing flaps drew near.

Skreek. Skreek.

"Now."

Andy raised Methuselah's hilt as Hannah climbed on his back. She lifted the two highly polished gems, positioning one over each of her steed's shoulders. They reflected the firelight, which made them look like angry eyes. Andy took slow steps toward the forest, then willed his blade to shoot flames. A ten-foot stream of fire lit up the campsite.

"Yipe!" "Yikes!" "Arrggghhh!" sounded from the dense woods.

Andy repeated the procedure, receiving more shrieks.

Alden gave them up as he convulsed with unrestrained laughter and fell to the ground, holding his stomach. Laughing became an epidemic rapidly spreading to Andy and the others.

Snickers and exclamations erupted from the surrounding foliage as Hans praised, "Well done, Yara!"

A minute later, the officers guided Gelon and fifteen other surprised but chortling gnomes into the firelight.

"Gelon!" Andy greeted with a broad smile.

The gnome dipped his head, appreciating the prank.

"I can't take credit. Alden came up with the idea."

Alden approached and the little man embraced him in a bear hug, then winked. "It's been a mighty long time since we've been had." Wagging his finger, he added, "We'll be watching out for you."

"Andy," Hans interrupted from behind.

He turned to find the healer sitting next to Yara on one of the logs that surrounded the fire. The princess stared down and held her hands to her temples.

Andy rushed to her side and Hans speculated, "I think she overexerted herself."

"Yara," Andy drew close and placed his hand on her back. "How are you feeling?"

The princess barely nodded.

The gnomes had quieted and Gelon offered, "We have a poultice we use for headaches. We can get some if you'd like."

"Thank you," Hans replied. "I didn't bring my full complement of remedies."

"Bilnus," Gelon called. A portly gnome with an abundant black beard broke ranks and approached, dipping his head as he stopped before his leader. "Please retrieve the herbs we use to cure the mind."

The gnome nodded, then hastened toward the woods, opened a door in the trunk of a tree, and quickly disappeared.

No sooner had he vanished than a six zolt swooped down and landed in the clearing.

"There she is! Grab her!" The command shattered the jovial mood, and sounds of combat quickly filled the air.

"Ahhh!" Yara shrieked as a burly vulture-warrior snatched her from the log before Andy could react. The zolt bolted toward the forest and transformed. Andy grabbed Methuselah and pursued.

Andy drew to within ten steps when the vulture-man flapped its wings and went airborne, eliciting more shrieks from Yara.

Five steps.

Her feet dangled. *If I can just…*

Two steps.

Andy leapt as the zolt thrust upward, and his hands missed Yara's foot by less than an inch.

"No!" Andy protested, planting his face in the ground. He sprang to his feet and watched as her silhouette rose up and over the treetops. Had she been closer to the ground, Andy would have thrown his blade, but he feared a fall from that height would injure her.

Sergeant Hammond halted next to him and together they stared helplessly. "We have to save her," Andy begged as the officer drew an arm around him and led him back to the campsite.

Alden, Hannah, and Hans stepped forward and enveloped him in a hug. Their guests stood quietly on the perimeter of the clearing.

A minute later, Gelon roused the four-member scrum from their embrace as he intoned, "If you'll excuse me."

Andy glanced toward the gnome leader who stood pointing. He followed the extended arm and strained in disbelief.

"That's right, you can set me down nice and easy."

How?

The zolt who had abducted Yara moments before spread its wings wide, gliding in for a landing. The gnomes cleared a path and the creature touched down softly, extending a wing to help her up.

Andy rushed forward and threw his arms around Yara. "I was so worried."

The vulture-warrior dipped its head and stepped away. "I apologize for the disturbance. Now if you'll excuse me, I'll take my leave." With that, it extended its wings and retreated. Woots and cheers engulfed the campsite.

Andy took Yara's hand and led her to the log from which she had been snatched. "My head feels like it's going to explode," she complained, drawing her hands back to her temples before Andy could ask what miracle she had performed.

Bilnus emerged from the woods and ambled into the firelight. "What'd I miss?" Another round of celebration ignited.

The gnome handed the herbs to Hans and joined his companions.

The healer grabbed a spare cookpot and water that had been heating on the fire and went to work. In no time he had concocted a paste. Andy helped Yara to her bedroll and Hans applied it to her brow. "She'll need sleep."

Andy sat down next to her to keep vigil.

Taking the hint, Gelon quietly gathered his associates and they disappeared into the trees, promising to return in the morning to check on the company.

CHAPTER NINETEEN
Paradigm Shift

The sun had nearly reached its peak when Yara awakened the following day. She rubbed her eyes and looked about, trying to assemble the pieces.

Andy sat on a log near the campfire with his back to the recovering maiden. When she stirred, Hannah nodded, directing his attention.

"How are you feeling?" Andy questioned when he reached her.

She paused to consider before replying, "Good. My head feels much better. Is there anything to eat?"

Andy laughed and helped her up.

After a hearty brunch, Andy helped Yara remove the fashionable poultice smeared on her forehead. Then she sat next to him and told the tale everyone was dying to hear.

"The zolt who grabbed me was one who used to guard me. Somehow he knew I was around, like he always did. Anyway, he snatched me and took off. My head felt like it was going to explode, so it took awhile before it dawned on me to suggest he bring me back. Once I managed to implant that thought in his mind, he turned around."

"What about the other zolt?" Hannah questioned.

"It hurt a lot, but I managed to plant a suggestion that they should land and wait patiently for their buddy to return. Oh, and I also suggested that they had seen nothing of me or anyone else."

Hans grinned. "Well done, Princess."

"How do you think they knew I was here?" Yara questioned.

Captain Baldric rubbed his chin and glanced among his soldiers.

Andy offered, "I overheard one zolt say 'She's here' as they walked past the cave yesterday, so they knew you were around then too."

The words lingered but no one offered any speculation.

"Well, one thing I know, you need to strengthen your sommeil skills before you try suggesting something to so many at once," Hans interrupted the silence. "You must possess quite a gift. Only the most skillful sommeils have reactions like yours if they've tried something too advanced before they're ready. You can do serious damage to your mind if we don't help you strengthen your skills."

Yara nodded.

Andy saw movement in the trees, and seconds later Gelon led a contingent of familiar but quiet gnomes into camp. Exclamations of joy erupted as they set eyes on the princess.

Bilnus stepped forward and held out a small package. "A few more herbs should you encounter further difficulties."

Hans accepted with a nod, which Yara repeated.

Gelon took several steps toward Andy. "Our dwarf friends share with us news of all that is happening in and around these parts. We know about more people being turned into vulture-folk. They tell us their prisons are overflowing with zolt. Perilous times are in store until the evil is purged from our lands."

Andy swallowed and nodded slowly.

"Know that we stand united with the kingdoms of Oomaldee and Cromlech, and we will lend whatever help we can. Please do not hesitate to call on us." The round gnome's full beard brushed the dirt as he bowed to Andy and then to Yara.

"Thank you, Gelon. Merk has been helping build weapons, but hearing your commitment to defeat the enemy means a lot. I'll be sure to pass this on to my father." Andy stepped forward and embraced him.

"Aw...well...you're welcome," the gnome replied, his balding head taking on a deeper shade of red.

The gnomes surrounded Andy and his group, and the solemn melody of their blessing ballad, which had so moved him the first time, again filled the air with its themes of sincerity, fidelity, warmth, and brotherhood.

"These are good folks," Andy's inneru put words to what his emotions felt.

When the song ended several minutes later, joking and jesting ushered the gnomes back from whence they came.

They broke camp to skinny fingers of sunlight probing through the dense tree cover. The air smelled of fir, and fallen evergreen needles crunched beneath their feet as the group made its way down a sloping hill. Andy walked next to Alden. Yara had pulled Hannah in front of them as they set out, and Hans brought up the rear. The boys could overhear only bits and pieces of the girls' conversation, but from what he picked up, Andy knew it was serious.

"I'm sorry… Didn't mean… Want to be… I thought…" Andy overheard Yara.

Hannah nodded.

"When you… You're… You make me feel… You were being…" Yara continued.

Hannah scowled at the princess.

"Oh, come on… Either we can…"

At last Hannah laughed. "I guess you're right."

Andy and Alden shared raised eyebrows as the girls continued their tête-à-tête.

Several minutes later, Alden drew Andy's attention. "I heard you yell in your sleep."

"I've been having nightmares. First it was reliving that test—"

"I haven't been able to forget either."

"But on top of that, I'm worried about what Abaddon will do now that it appears he will live forever. And has Fides helping him."

Alden nodded.

Andy confided, "I keep seeing Abaddon torturing my father and mom. It's awful! It scares me. I can control my fear during the day, but at night… I've got to do something, but what?"

"Never forget, you're not waging this battle by yourself, Andy," Hans chimed in, moving forward to join them. "You may be the chosen one to break the curse, but defeating that fiend will require everyone's help, not the least of which is that of your father and the military. The King brags about what you so boldly declared at the tavern: 'We are as strong as the love we choose to share.' Those aren't just words."

Andy nodded.

Hans added, "And it appears we'll have Cromlech's help."

Andy felt his cheeks warm as the healer gave him a playful wink.

Laughter from the girls interrupted their conversation, but when Hannah placed an arm around Yara, curiosity compelled them forward.

"What's going on?" Alden questioned.

"We've decided—" Yara began, glancing at Hannah. Receiving a nod, the princess continued, "—that since I'm going to be staying in Oomaldee for a while, we should be friends."

Hannah smiled.

"About time!" Hans joked.

About midafternoon they passed through a curtain of thick fog, which drew exclamations from Yara. The others explained that they had entered Oomaldee.

The princess wrinkled her nose and assessed, "Smells damp."

"It makes me feel claustrophobic," Andy confessed.

"I understand why you want to get rid of it."

"That's not the half of it."

For the next few days, as they navigated the moist and mountainous terrain of the ogres' territory, Andy shared stories about getting stuck in quicksand. His experiences being manhandled by giant plants in the Forest of Giants. Marta and her chocolate chip cookies. Ox, Emmadank, Merk, and the rest of his Oscray team. Sir Gawain and Sir Kay and all the stone statues that came to life. Adventures with Glaucin and his family. As he recounted each adventure, Andy's excitement grew at the thought of seeing everyone again.

They halted their journey that day after descending a hill that marked the end of ogre territory. They had encountered only a handful of the hulking green creatures, and a rousing game of freeze tag with hand signals had kept their presence a secret. Except for a thick layer of drying, odiferous mud that caked everyone's feet, they had emerged unscathed.

Captain Baldric permitted a campfire tonight, a treat after going without one the last two nights. Sergeants Ranulf, Fulk, and Hammond had bagged no less than thirty squirrels as they traversed the rolling hills today. The dinner of savory fresh meat filled their empty stomachs, and a satisfied calm overcame the group.

"Unless I'm mistaken, we should reach Castle Avalon tomorrow," the captain announced after dinner, sparking a chorus of excitement.

Home! It'll be so good to see everyone again.

Andy was not surprised when sleep played games with him that night, and only after considerable effort did he succeed in nabbing the slippery imp. As he floated into dreamland, a familiar fireside scene greeted him. The silvery figure of Imogenia was seated on one sofa. Across from her sat her parents.

"I'm surprised you're not gloating, Imogenia," her father intoned.

"Why would I?"

"We figured with Abaddon reappearing you would—"

"Be excited? Celebrate?"

"Well, yes," the queen confirmed.

"He has regained eternal life. That does not make me happy. I only wanted to use him to—"

"Kill the boy."

"Keep the curse in place," Imogenia corrected.

"Well, it looks like the boy can still pursue him to fulfill the curse. That, or continue collecting ingredients for that curse-breaking recipe," the king observed.

The princess shook her head. "Abaddon has overcome the sting of Methuselah once and for all."

The king nodded thoughtfully. "Yes. Yes, I suppose he has."

What's that supposed to mean? Andy's thoughts interrupted.

"The only option for removing the curse is for me to request it be lifted or for the boy to successfully gather the remaining ingredients," Imogenia summarized.

"And you don't plan to manipulate that dragon to thwart the boy?" her father questioned.

She shook her head once more. "Even if I wanted to, I no longer have anything of value to offer in exchange."

The king and queen traded glances.

"*If* you wanted to?" the queen probed, receiving a nod from the princess.

"Why the change of heart?" her father asked.

"Now that Abaddon will live forever, he will focus his efforts on conquering Oomaldee. What's to stop him?"

"Then why not lift the curse so our people have a better chance at defending themselves?" her father suggested.

Imogenia sat quietly for more than a minute before replying, "I'm still not sure if Kaysan has repented for what he did to me. Look, I know the timing is bad, but I need to see this through."

Her father thought for a second before trying again. "The boy said something very profound on his last visit."

"What's that?"

"We are as strong as the love we choose to share."

As the princess pondered this, the queen raised a translucent hand. "If I may make a suggestion. Emmalee has returned. Why don't you ask her what she thinks?"

"Why would I do that?"

"Because she is more detached from the situation than any of us, yet she knows Kaysan. Perhaps she can offer you some insight that we can't."

"And perhaps wisdom from her five hundred years among the living," the king added.

As this scene faded, Andy found himself standing in foggy sunlight that streamed through a window into the sitting area of King Hercalon's chambers.

Father! Mom? Andy dreamed.

The two sat and talked in overstuffed chairs.

"I'm so happy you've returned."

"I was so surprised. I never expected to see my homeland again," Emmalee smiled.

The King reached over, picked up her hand, and patted it.

Mom scanned the room. "I remember the day they completed this castle and we moved in. Newlyweds."

Father grinned broadly. "We were so in love."

"I never forgot you," Mom offered. "How could I, especially when you and Andy look so alike?"

"Yes, there's a portrait of me at the Library of Oomaldee that was painted when I was only a bit older than he is. It had been years since I'd seen it. Imagine my surprise," he chuckled.

"I remember rumors and lies spreading." Mom's visage flashed to a coldness Andy had rarely seen.

Father held up a hand. "Emmalee, there's something I need to tell you. I deceived you."

Mom's eyes instantly connected with Father's.

He recounted the story that was now familiar to Andy, leaving out no detail.

Mom's expression journeyed from joy to horror to disbelief, finally turning to sadness as she listened, spellbound. When the King finally finished speaking, she remained silent, wiping tears from her eyes as she tried to digest all he had shared. For his part, Father's moist eyes pleaded for understanding and mercy, but he remained silent.

Before Mom could fully compose herself, the shimmering form of a young lady in a royal gown materialized and startled her.

"Imogenia!" the King exclaimed.

Mom's eyes grew wide as she searched for an explanation.

"I'm sorry, Emmalee. This is my sister, from the Afterlife."

The silvery princess curtsied, ignoring her brother.

"I'm sorry, I didn't recognize you," Mom acknowledged. She then turned questioning eyes on the King. "Your sister visits often?"

"No. This is the first time in quite a while. To what do we owe the pleasure of your visit, sister?"

"May I call you Queen Emmalee?" Imogenia asked.

Mom nodded slowly.

"What did you see in Kaysan? Why did you marry him? How can you still love him after what he did to me? Do you believe he's sorry for killing me?" The questions spilled out, and Imogenia drew a hand over her mouth to staunch the flow.

"Imogenia!" the King protested.

"I'm sorry. I didn't mean to be so direct. It's just that I'm trying to understand—"

"It's okay," Mom countered, holding up a hand. "My daughter does the same thing when she has something on her mind."

The spirit's stiff posture relaxed. "Thank you."

"Let's answer your questions one at a time. First, you want to know what I saw in your brother?"

Imogenia nodded.

"I come from humble beginnings. I was a servant in the royal household, so you'll understand that more than a few eyebrows raised when Kaysan began flirting with me and finding excuses to visit me as I was helping with the laundry or cooking."

The ghost smiled, and the King added a chuckle.

"At first I didn't know how to interpret his advances. Why would he be interested in me? I had nothing to offer him, or so I thought. But as we spent time together, I began to understand I gave him a respite from the stifling demands of royalty. He didn't care about my station in life. He looked past that and loved me for who I am, just the way I am."

Emmalee directed a smile toward the King, who reciprocated.

"That is a precious gift. How could I not marry him?"

I wish Dad would love me like that, Andy dreamed.

"As to your next question, Imogenia, you question my judgment when you ask how I can still love Kaysan knowing what he did to you."

"Oh no, I didn't mean…" Imogenia drew her silvery hands to her mouth.

Mom dismissed the slight with a nod, while the King frowned.

"Since I returned, we've been practically inseparable. As you might imagine, it takes a while to work through five hundred years of history. He is not the same man I married. I didn't expect him to be. And while I'm shocked at what he did…I'm so sorry, Imogenia…"

The spirit sniffled.

"I will not condemn. He has been punished by living with the guilt of his actions. And while that may not be sufficient to satisfy you, it has spurred him to reflect, learn, and become wise. So you question how I could still love him after what he did? How could I not?"

Mom winked at Father before proceeding.

"Now then, you also want to know if I think Kaysan is sorry he killed you? Imogenia nodded.

"As I think about what he has shared, I sense his passion to undo the curse. I believe he told me in order to ask forgiveness for his deception."

The King nodded.

"He risked my rejection, but he took responsibility for his actions. Why would he do that unless he was truly sorry?"

"He's sorry for deceiving you, but is he sorry for killing me?"

"Imogenia, you're splitting hairs. He would not have confessed if he were not sorry for both deceiving me as well as harming you."

The King nodded again.

"So just because someone takes responsibility, you believe that means they're sorry?" Imogenia questioned.

"Yes. I do."

As the ghost considered this, Emmalee posed, "What would you have him do? What would convince you he's sorry?"

The King's expression took on a scowl. Mom reached over and placed a hand on his arm.

After a lengthy pause, Imogenia replied, "He will never understand how deeply he hurt me, and I don't just mean physically."

"What do you want me to do?" the King's voice rose. "I've tried apologizing, but you refuse to accept."

Mom held up a hand.

"Words are easy," the spirit added. "I need to *see* that you're truly sorry."

"What do you mean?" Emmalee requested.

Imogenia thought for a second. "I can't explain it. I'll just know when I see it."

The dream faded as the King rolled his eyes in frustration, and Andy drifted into peaceful slumber.

True to the captain's prediction, by late morning they had crossed two bridges, one of which Hans informed Andy was the rebuilt Entente Bridge. Recognition sparked, and Andy told Yara the tale of his being impaled in the shoulder by a projectile when the span had collapsed. Everyone laughed as he shared about the young dwarf girl calling him a weenie as her mom extracted the fragment.

Around lunchtime they passed through the city of Oops. Seductive smells wafted from several buildings and enticed them to stop. Being so close to their destination, however, the company opted to polish off their remaining provisions as they walked.

The path curved to the left, and Andy saw the turrets of Castle Avalon in the distance.

"Look!" he announced, hastening their pace.

Several minutes later, with the drawbridge only five hundred yards away, Hannah suddenly cried, "Andy! The bellicose!"

CHAPTER TWENTY

Razen

The drawbridge had scarcely been lowered when the company sprinted across its span, their adversary in pursuit. Andy chanced a backward glance as he reached the portcullis. The beast halted upon reaching the wooden bridge and released a snarl as it began pacing.

"Why doesn't it come any farther?" Yara wondered, drawing furrowed brows from all within hearing.

The princess held her hands up in surrender. "No, don't get me wrong. I'm glad it's not."

"Unless I'm mistaken, I think it remembers its run-in with the King. Beware his majesty's wrath when it comes to his son," Hans offered, placing a hand on Andy's shoulder. Yara's eyes grew large.

"I'll tell you about it later," Andy whispered.

Their not-so-subtle arrival had launched a host of soldiers into action. As they ascended the grand staircase to a bevy of cheers and boisterous celebration, Andy spied the King, Mermin, and Marta amongst the crowd gathered at the top. The throng parted and Andy dashed up the final steps into Father's outstretched arms.

After a protracted embrace, Andy stepped back. "It's so good to see you again!"

"I've missed you, son." The King's smile underscored his affection.

Mermin grabbed hold and engulfed him in an embrace before Andy could say more. "It's good to see you again, my pwince."

The arms of a purple-haired woman snatched him from the wizard and surrounded him in a bear hug. "What a surprise!"

Alden stood not far away. He cleared his throat animatedly, then with a grin added, "What am I, leftovers?"

"Oh, Alden!" Marta grabbed her son and gave him a welcoming hug.

Nearby, Cadfael and Lucee embraced Hannah. Yara shrank back in the jostling until Andy motioned for her to join him. She rewarded him with a relieved smile. As she mounted the final two steps, the King and Mermin parted and drew a familiar figure to the forefront.

"Mom!" Andy exclaimed. "You're really here!" He wrapped his arms around her as Yara reached them. "I had a dream. You and Father were talking in his chambers—"

Mom's breath caught in her throat.

"How?" Andy struggled to put the pieces together.

The King laughed. "Been spying on us have you?"

"We'll have to sort this all out, but in the meantime, who's your friend?" Mom questioned.

"Sorry! This is Princess Yara of Cromlech."

The King, Mom, Marta, and Mermin all tipped their heads and directed their gazes to Hans who now joined them.

The healer placed his hand on Yara's shoulder before confirming, "It's true. Our quest proved successful. This is the only remaining member of the royal family of my homeland."

"My deepest sympathies." The King bowed his head low and the others did too.

"Thank you for your kind words," Yara replied, closing her eyes.

Andy reached over and took her hand. Mom tried to hide her surprise, but Andy caught it, launching a flight of butterflies in his belly.

"Well, I think you all might do well with baths and a change of clothes before dinner," Marta intoned, breaking the discomforting silence. "The princess needs a room. Where's Razen?" she continued rapid-fire.

A cry went up for the castle's operations manager, and the vulture-man waddled his way through the throng. While it had been quite some time since Andy had seen the man, his appearance sparked unpleasant memories and a decidedly deleterious distrust.

Andy's inneru cautioned, "Let it go."

Upon seeing Andy, Razen kept his expression even and slowly nodded.

Andy caught Yara wrinkling her forehead in response.

The bird-man turned his attention to the princess and welcomed her with a charming smile. "So glad to make your acquaintance. If you'll follow me, I'll show you to a private bath while we prepare your chambers and find more suitable clothes for you." As he said it, his eyes darted from her matted, disheveled hair to her filthy tattered dress to her mud-crusted shoes.

Yara blushed and Andy's temper began to simmer. He gave the princess a reassuring nod.

As the welcoming congregation turned to head into the dining hall, a flock of at least fifteen zolt materialized in their path, drawing a chorus of shrieks from the celebrants. "She's here!" boomed a nasally declaration.

Captain Baldric and the four officers who accompanied them on the journey had been enjoying the greetings and celebration, but seeing the foe, they dashed up the stairs to join a handful of comrades. Methuselah instantly appeared in Andy's hand, and he saw Mom draw a knife. Father, Alden, Yara, Hannah, and Cadfael drew weapons and together they bounded after the officers.

The hall erupted in terrorized cries harmonizing with clanging and clashing metal. Andy engaged a burly zolt whose size gave him pause. He moved to block a downward strike, but the force made his arms buckle and he barely escaped as the enemy brushed Methuselah's blade aside and him with it. The brute proved more nimble than Andy expected as it thrust a leg in his path, bringing him down. He scrambled to put his feet beneath him again, then popped up, slicing at his foe's legs as he rose. Methuselah found flesh and the zolt belted out its rage. His adversary hobbled as it turned to face off once more, then quickly raised its blade and brought it down. Andy side-stepped the blow, but as the zolt passed, its elbow connected with his temple. Andy saw stars, staggered, then wilted to the floor.

I'm gonna die...

"No, you're not! Get up, Andy!" Dad's voice in his head demanded.

As Andy struggled to sit up, the brute turned, took three lumbering steps toward him, and raised its blade.

"Don't kill him, you oaf! He's worth more alive than dead," Razen berated as he hurriedly waddled past.

The butt of the zolt's sword rang Andy's bell, and everything went dark.

A sudden and violent jolt of the wooden door propping Andy up awakened him.

"Huh?" Andy mumbled, then reached up to rub the tender lump on the side of his head.

Clang. Crash. Ahhh!

Darkness surrounded Andy, but the distinct sounds of battle quickly roused him to full consciousness. He struggled against inhuman foes before locating the handle, wrenched it open, and bolted out.

Methuselah!

He froze and scanned the hall when his sword did not materialize in his hand. A host of zolt corpses and a few soldiers of Oomaldee lay scattered, covered in blood. Father stood nearby with Mermin, his sword at his side. All across the hall, blue-uniformed warriors bowed to their queen as she stood over Andy's adversary, Methuselah protruding from its chest.

Mom righted herself and surveyed the room. Her gaze stopped at Andy. "Mom!"

A smile crept across her bloodied face and she exhaled, "You're okay."

Andy hastily made his way toward her, and Father joined. Instantly they formed an Andy sandwich, setting off sighs throughout the hall.

Father broke away and shouted, "How about Queen Emmalee!" drawing a cacophony of cheers.

"Andy!" Yara bounded toward him and was quickly joined by Alden and Hannah.

"What happened to you?" Alden queried.

"I got knocked out."

"Razen dragged you into that closet," Hannah informed.

"What?"

"Yeah, after that brute knocked you silly, he grabbed you and pulled you through all the fighting."

Andy stood speechless, exchanging looks.

"For what it's worth," Yara intoned, "I scanned Razen's mind just before the zolt arrived." The princess shook her head.

"And?" Andy asked.

"I've only rummaged through a few zolt minds, but his was different."

"How so?" Hannah inquired.

"First, it didn't feel as dark as usual."

"Hannah says the same when she's near him," Alden offered.

"Yeah, it's like he's a combination of warm fuzzies and cold pricklies."

Yara nodded and continued, "But it's beyond that. The zolt I've looked into, their thoughts flow smoothly. Razen's thoughts go in spurts. It's hard to explain. It's just different than anything I've sensed before."

The conversation Andy had with his inneru several days before jogged through his mind: *"Some innerus are paralyzed, then used as channels through which their human's thoughts are broadcast over the whisper stream. They can't control what they share."* Unsure of any connection to this earlier discussion, Andy chose not to share, tucking the thoughts away for further consideration.

Suddenly, Andy broke their contemplations, "Wait a minute! Yara, you said you looked into Razen's mind just before the zolt arrived?"

The princess nodded.

"You also spoke to Calum right before they appeared, right?"

"Oh! Wait! And they showed up when I used my power to make the gnomes believe there was a dragon."

Andy nodded and grinned.

"But they didn't show up when you made me act like a chicken," Hannah frowned.

Andy rescued the penitent princess by countering, "Yeah, but we were still in the ring. There's no telling what all it did for us."

"I have to agree with Andy. It seems like every time you use your power, the zolt know," Alden summarized.

"Well, we'll certainly know when you do," Hannah joked, receiving a smirk from the princess.

Mom and Father approached, beaming as they held hands.

"Youch!" Andy's inneru yipped. "Don't take your confusion out on me!"

Oh. Sorry. I just...

Mom sent him a reassuring smile.

"What a grand welcome home," Father joked. "I'm glad you returned when you did though, because tomorrow evening we're having a celebration in honor of Queen Emmalee. It will rival the party we held in your honor last year, son." The King sent him a wink as he placed a hand on Mom's arm.

"Easy…" Dad's voice cautioned.

Andy weakly pushed the corners of his mouth upward as he caught a glance from Yara.

Razen joined the group. "Princess Yara, if you'll follow me I'll show you where you can get cleaned up."

Yara looked to Andy for reassurance. Receiving a hesitant nod, she excused herself.

"Well, I better go get a bath and then help my mom," Hannah begged leave.

"Yeah, me too," Alden added.

Mermin joined the trio, announcing, "Looks like things are well in hand." Andy looked about. The zolt carcasses had been removed and a host of servants were restoring order, scrubbing the floor and furnishings. Across the hall, Hans knelt and dressed a soldier's wounds.

"What say we get cleaned up and rendezvous in my chambers," Father suggested.

"Sounds good. We'll join you in a bit," Mom agreed, giving a reassuring nod.

Father and Mermin disappeared up the stairway and Mom turned. "I guess you'd like your sword back?" she laughed, handing Methuselah's hilt to Andy.

"Thanks," he replied, adding it back to the makeshift holster. "Mom?"

She nodded toward two chairs and they sat. Leaning forward, she met his eyes. "Andy, I know this must seem strange to you. You've only ever seen me with Dad."

Andy nodded.

"I love Dad very much, but I also love the King. He was the husband of my youth. While we were parted after such a short time, I never stopped loving him even though I never thought I'd see him again. When Dad and I met…what can I say? He swept me off my feet. The King and Dad are alike in many ways but also different. I love them both for who they are."

Mom brushed a stray lock of Andy's hair aside.

"I never imagined having two husbands. It's certainly not something I set out to do." Mom smiled then continued, "I haven't quite reconciled it all. I'm not sure it can be."

"I love Father. I feel like he's okay with who I am, like I can just be myself."

"And you don't always with Dad, huh?"

Andy nodded.

"Dad loves you more than you'll ever know, honey. It hasn't been easy on him. He just wants the very best for you."

"I know."

"It'll take some time for you to get used to the King and I. Just know that my love for your father does not mean I don't also love Dad."

Andy laughed. "It's just weird seeing you hold Father's hand. And here I was just getting used to you being the queen."

Mom reached over and roughed up his already unruly hair. "Come on, let's both get cleaned up and meet the others. I'm sure you've got lots of stories to tell."

An hour later found Andy, Mom, the King, and Mermin comfortably seated in Father's chambers. They all looked and smelled considerably better.

Andy recounted the highlights of the past several days, receiving a satisfying mixture of laughter and alarm as he spoke. When he finished, he extracted the deep red phoenix feather from his makeshift holster. The trio looked on in silence as he held it up.

"You said Aray offered this to you?" Father asked.

"She dabbed her eyes with it, then plucked it."

"Phoenix tears, whether moist or dwy, are a powerful healing agent," Mermin intoned, smoothing his beard.

"Do you suppose she knew about your quest?" Mom speculated.

"I know she did."

Silence filled the room as everyone considered this.

At length, the King suggested, "Best add that to your invisible book before anything happens to it. Come on, I'll walk with you." Father winked at Mom and Mermin, halting their movement to follow.

They headed downstairs to Mermin's library. As they entered, Andy inhaled the familiar musty scent of old texts.

"Ahh, I love that smell."

Father chuckled but then turned the conversation as Andy extracted the book only he could see. "It's good to see you again, son. I've missed you."

Andy looked up from the gold book.

"I missed you too. Although I have to say I was frustrated at not hearing anything from Oomaldee for a year. I didn't know if something had happened to everyone. Alden and Hannah said you ordered them not to contact me."

The King opened his mouth to respond, but Andy continued, "I understand why. I really do. But it was hard not knowing if you all were okay." The words drew moisture to Father's eyes.

"It was not an easy decision to make," he confessed, bowing his head. "It was not my intention to hurt you. But given the circumstances, I would do the same again." Catching Andy's eye, he added, "Your safety was far more important than my indulgence."

Andy nodded. "How did the zolt get through the barrier from Oomaldee anyway?"

Father shook his head. "It's hard to say. Dark magic doesn't play by rules."

Andy cleared a spot on Mermin's table and opened the book. The first page was blank, so he moved it aside and opened the compartment. The prized unicorn horn, the vial of venom, and Abaddon's red scale lay untouched. Andy gently placed the crimson phoenix feather atop these prizes and glanced back at the first page, which now revealed a note:

"Knowledge and growth you did not scorn.
The reward: these ingredients you have borne.
Responsibility, diligence, and dignity,
Cause hope to be reborn."

Andy drew in a sharp breath.

"What is it, son?"

Andy beamed as he looked up. "This note says I'm acting with responsibility, diligence, and dignity."

"Never been accused of that before?" Father laughed.

Andy shook his head.

Father wrapped his arm around Andy's shoulder and squeezed.

"I'm kind of surprised, actually."

"Why's that?"

"On our trip, I messed up. I led Alden on a mission to free Hannah and Captain Baldric when they got captured by the zolt. Sergeant Fulk said we'd go after them later that night under cover of darkness. But I didn't know what the vulture-guys might do to them, and I wasn't taking any chances."

The King nodded.

"Once we rescued them, the captain was unhappy with me because I hadn't followed orders. He said I need to respect the chain of command in order for his officers to trust me."

"And why is that important, Andy?"

"Because their job is to protect me and you and Mom, and if they don't respect me, how could they be willing to sacrifice their lives for me if it ever came to that."

Father smiled. "Learning to build trust is a big lesson. People want to know we mean what we say, that we know what we're doing, and that they can count on us. Sounds like you were off with your sincerity and reliability."

"Well, I didn't really know what I was doing either," Andy confessed.

"I shall give Captain Baldric my thanks for teaching you this valuable lesson. He didn't have to."

"He said he did it to help me rule well, when the time comes."

"He's a good man."

Andy nodded, then closed the gold book and reshelved it.

CHAPTER TWENTY-ONE

The Queen

T he sounds of stringed instruments floated up the circular stairway as Andy made his way down to join the festivities the following evening. He wore new black dress robes since his first set remained at home where he had last worn them.

The hall was adorned with new banners tonight. The King's royal blue crest hung against a white field rather than the traditional black background. The abundance of streamers betrayed the enthusiasm of the decorators at the news of their queen's return.

"Prince Andrew," came a commanding, nasally voice. Razen's expression remained impassive as he informed, "Your parents request that you join them at the top of the grand staircase to welcome our guests."

As he made his way to the requested destination, Yara caught up with him. While he had seen her cleaned and scrubbed yesterday, the flowing white gown she now wore, combined with the golden locks that fell loosely over her shoulders, made Andy's jaw drop.

Words escaped him and the princess giggled. "I guess I look okay then, huh?" she teased.

All manner of flying creatures took flight in Andy's belly. He adjusted his robe collar and wondered why it suddenly felt so constricting, then shook his head, trying to clear his stupor. "You...you...you look...beautiful."

"Thank you." Yara dipped her head and curtsied.

Alden and Hannah, who had also dressed for the occasion, rescued Andy as they approached hand in hand.

"I'm not on duty tonight, so I'll get to dance with my lady." Alden winked at Hannah and received a warm smile in return. "Oh, Andy, Queen Emmalee asked us to go find you and have you join her and the King as soon possible. Dignitaries are beginning to arrive," Hannah informed.

"Duty calls," Yara intoned, grabbing Andy's hand and excusing them.

"I'd rather stay with you. The last time I greeted guests my feet ached and my face hurt from smiling," Andy confided as they strolled across the hall.

"Your people need you," the princess encouraged. "Besides, we can dance the night away once you're done."

"I'm not a very good dancer."

"Don't worry, I'll make you look good. My parents made my brother and me dance first at every celebration. And we had to do it well. 'We represented the monarchy, after all,'" she recited, then laughed.

Andy smiled. "That sounds like something my dad would say."

Hans, Cadfael, and Lucee, all cleaned up and well attired for the occasion, stood chatting. Andy waved as they passed. Marta scurried about putting last-minute touches on decorations and table settings. Ox lugged a heavy barrel toward its stand.

As they reached their destination, Andy spotted Regent Bellum's wife hugging Mom. The officer gushed with praise at meeting the King's beloved who had been lost for so long.

Scanning the length of the staircase, all manner of public officials with their elegantly clad spouses crowded the span, and more flowed through the front door.

"Prince Andrew! So good to see you again," the regent exclaimed, wrenching Andy's hand from Yara and shaking it vigorously.

The princess winked then turned, and as she did an eerie, piercing wail wafted through the open door, stopping all conversation.

Banshee!

Yara pivoted back, her eyes like saucers. Andy sidestepped the regent and wrapped his arms around her.

"Emily? Andy?" The fear-filled whisper echoed about the stone chamber, causing everyone to look up and search for the source as everything went dark for Andy.

The thick sod of Dad's formerly pristine lawn cushioned Andy's landing, but the thud still rattled his bones. A cursory glance was all he had time for, however, as a zolt charged out the open front door, swinging.

Methuselah!

The hilt materialized in his hand but did not extend. Panic threatened to devour him before a fleeting thought raced through his brain: *You don't have to be afraid. You have a choice!*

The enemy reached him a second later. Andy blocked the downward strike with the hilt as Cadfael had taught him during dagger training. The foul adversary quickly brought its weapon up to try again, and as before, Andy deflected the downward thrust. The parry served to slow the pace of the contest, and Andy now assumed his ready position, looking for a vulnerability. The villain quickly grew impatient as they circled, and it lunged for Andy's chest. Andy sidestepped, but as the zolt rushed past it was at the mercy of momentum and Methuselah's hilt connected with the back of its skull. The bird-man crumpled to the ground.

Andy wiped his brow and scanned the area as he caught his breath. He chanced a look at the neighbor's house, and through a downstairs window he could see Mrs. Nosey Neighbor talking on her cell phone and gesturing wildly. Andy headed for his front door.

Where's Mom?

"Dad? Madison?" he called as he stepped inside. Blood splatters across the living and family rooms bore evidence to the struggle that had raged.

No bodies? Andy pondered, but the thought fled as he saw the hall closet door peek open.

"Dad?"

"Andy? Oh, Andy!" Dad emerged from hiding with Madison clinging to his shirt. "It's okay, honey. They're gone."

As Dad engulfed her in a hug, Madison wiped her eyes.

"Where's Mom?" she asked quietly.

As if on command, Mom, still wearing the gown she had on at the celebration, dropped onto the sofa and startled the three of them.

"Is everyone okay?" Mom worried, bounding up.

"Our nerves are a bit worse for wear, but otherwise we're unscathed," Dad assured.

Mom embraced Dad in a hug that lasted a full minute. Seeing Mom in Dad's arms restored normalcy for Andy. That, combined with the calm, made him feel wrapped in a comforting embrace. A glance at Madison told him she felt it too.

"How come I never manage a soft landing?" Andy joked when Mom and Dad finally separated.

"This place is a mess," Mom assessed.

"Where'd all the bodies go?" Andy wondered, drawing wide eyes from his sister.

"They disappeared as they died," Mom informed. She gave him a knowing look and he deduced her meaning: *back to Oomaldee.*

Dad ricocheted a look between Mom and Andy before suggesting, "Madison, why don't you and I go attack the upstairs?" Andy's sister shot him a look of horror. "Okay, poor choice of words," Dad grimaced.

Receiving no further resistance, Dad wrapped an arm around Madison's shoulders and the pair headed upward.

"I came as soon as I could," Mom explained. "I didn't want to leave the King without his queen at the celebration."

"You had the ability to decide when you returned?"

"The King and I saw you disappear. Before anything happened to me, he pleaded, 'Please don't go yet.' And I didn't. I disappeared after the celebration concluded."

"What happened to Yara?" Andy demanded.

"As you might imagine, the princess was more than a little upset."

Andy's shoulders sagged and he looked down.

"You really like her, huh?"

Andy managed a nod.

"Well, I'm certain you'll see her again."

"Yeah, but it'll be a long time."

When Mom didn't respond, Andy looked up.

"You begin to understand." She smiled and ruffled his hair.

"Oh. Right."

"What say we start with the kitchen," Mom suggested.

As they scoured the counters, Mom asked, "Have you seen my carving knife and meat cleaver?"

"Umm…I may have dropped them in the Oozy bog where I landed."

Mom could not hold back a much-needed laugh, then added, "Do you know how strange that would sound under any other circumstance?"

The comment made Andy reciprocate with a deep, tension-releasing laugh.

"Did you hear that banshee wail just before I left?" Andy managed, composing himself.

"It would've been hard not to."

"What do you suppose it meant?"

"I hope it was nothing." Mom's expression betrayed her fears, and Andy's stomach rolled.

Sounds of scrubbing were all that broke the silence for several minutes.

"I dreamed you and Imogenia talked."

Mom turned. "So you mentioned. Oh thou seer, pray tell what we said," she kidded.

Andy proceeded to summarize the conversation, ending with, "She sure can be frustrating: 'I'll just know he's sorry when I know.' Good grief. So what are you going to do?"

Mom put her sponge down. After a long pause she explained, "Since Methuselah appeared, I've known there is a task I must fulfill in my homeland. I just didn't know what it was until now."

Andy tilted his head.

"I believe I must help defeat Abaddon. I'm still not sure in what capacity, but he is the greatest threat to the land, especially now that he's regained eternal life. I can't sit around here in comfort and let that devil rain down death and destruction. It was no mistake that I returned when I did."

"What about Dad and Madison?"

"I don't know yet. What I do know is that everything will work itself out. It always does."

"Father says that."

"Maybe that's where I got it from."

Andy Smithson Trivia

Did you know L. R. W. Lee leverages symbolism extensively?

- The fog of the curse symbolizes blindness and oppression.
- The magic key unlocks doors, brings stone statues to life, as well as revives. Put another way, it symbolizes bringing forth, opening up, and revealing (aka taking responsibility).
- Methuselah is not only a weapon and helper, but also represents justice as it divides good and evil. Consistent with life, justice requires diligence to uphold.
- Spheres have no beginning nor end. They also represent wholeness or dignity.
- Blue is the color of freedom, strength and new beginnings. The color of the household of King Hercalon V is royal blue for this reason.
- Purple is the color of royalty.
- The purple message spheres trumpet and then broadcast words from the king's father in the Afterlife.
- Because of its resistance to heat and acid, gold is a symbol of immutability, eternity and perfection. The gold envelopes contain messages from the Ancient One who knows the end from the beginning, and orchestrates events.
- Rubies with their deep red beauty, represent dignity, passion, and fierce love. They are believed to dispel discord.
- Saphires with their stunning blue, represent calmness, constancy, purity, truth, and virtue. They are believed to bring the wearer courage and strength while pacifying anger and subduing hatred.
- The fact that King Abaddon is a shape shifter is consistent with how evil shifts its form, but at its heart retains the same nature.

- The name Mount Mur Eyah is a phonetic spelling of the biblical Mount Moriah, the location where Abraham was tasked with slaying his son Isaac. A ram was provided as a substitute in that account and shows provision will be made.

Did you know that in keeping with traditional fantasy narratives, L. R. W. Lee uses the numbers three, seven and twelve for a reason?

- Three is considered the number of perfection.
- Seven means security, safety and rest.
- Twelve is the number of completion or a whole and harmonious unit.

Did you know names are also important in this series?

- Andy means brave or courageous.
- Alden means helper.
- Hannah means favor or grace.
- Imogenia means blameless.
- Kaysan, the king, means administrator.
- Hercalon is a derivation of Hercules.
- Mermin is a parody on Merlin.
- Methuselah was a priest whose origins were unknown. He appears suddenly in the historical biblical record and has therefore, become equated with having no beginning.
- Stone of Athanasia – The term athanasia mean deathless or immortal.
- Bellicose – The term bellicose means displaying eagerness to fight.
- Fides means evidence that serves to guarantee a person's good faith, standing, and reputation.
- Sommeil – The name for these gifted healers of the mind is a French word meaning sleep.

Have you noticed Alchemy used throughout the series?

- Alchemy played a significant role in the development of modern science. Alchemists sought to transform base metals into the gold or silver and/or develop an elixir of life which would confer youth and longevity and even immortality.
- In the series, the first instance of alchemy begins with the gold weavers, Max, Oscar, and Henry, spinning straw into gold to manufacture the wealth of the kingdom.
- The four elementals: air, earth, fire, and water are then seen on Methuselah's hilt.
- Jada and Naria, the unicorns, employ the elementals in sending their father to his eternal life.
- The power and circular structure of the Giant's Ring is restored when the elementals are refreshed.

Did you know the titles of the books manifest yet another layer of meaning? The titles reveal Imogenia's evolution.

- Beginning with Blast of the Dragon's Fury, Imogenia is furious at what has happened to her and she fuels her emotional hurt.
- In Venom of the Serpent's Cunning, Imogenia turns venomous (or spiteful) and cunning in seeking ways to continually punish her brother.
- Disgrace of the Unicorn's Honor has Imogenia act in a manner disgraceful to the honor of royalty.
- In Resurrection of the Phoenix's Grace we see Imogenia's grace reborn as she begins to reflect.

The Andy Smithson series continues with more adventures to break the long-standing curse plaguing the land of Oomaldee in Books 5-7 of the series. Book 5, Vision of the Griffin's Heart is coming Winter 2015.

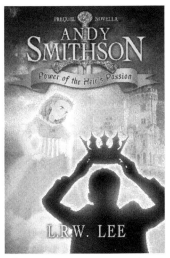

In the meantime, learn how the curse came to be, in the Prequel Novella. Available at Amazon

Reviews
Be sure to let others know what you thought about Book 4 in the series. Please submit a review at Amazon.com. It would mean a lot to the author.

Sign up to receive notifications of new releases at:
http://www.lrwlee.com
http://www.twitter.com/lrwlee
http://www.facebook.com/lrwlee

56441360R00116

Made in the USA
Lexington, KY
21 October 2016